STONEWALL INN EDITIONS
Michael Denneny, General Editor

By Lev Raphael

Fiction

Dancing on Tisha B'Av
Winter Eyes

Non-fiction

Edith Wharton's Prisoners of Shame

A Novel about Secrets

Winter Eyes

Lev Raphael

St. Martin's Press
New York

Design by Tanya M. Pérez

Library of Congress Cataloging-in-Publication Data
Raphael, Lev.
    Winter eyes / Lev Raphael.
        p.   cm.
    ISBN 0-312-08338-6 (hc.)
    ISBN 0-312-10576-2 (pbk.)
    I. Title.
PS3568.A5988W5   1992
813'.54—dc20   92-25163
                                                                    CIP

First Paperback Edition: February 1994

10 9 8 7 6 5 4 3 2 1

For Kris and Gersh

"There are some people, they are *like* countries. When you are with them, that is your country and you speak its language. And then it does not matter where you are together, you are at home."

Christopher Isherwood
The World in the Evening

Acknowledgments

Michael Denneny has been just the editor I needed: sensitive, encouraging, patient, good-humored, thoughtful, in tune, and his ideas about this book were very stimulating. Keith Kahla and Ray De Luca have made publishing with St. Martin's even more enjoyable.

Kristin Lauer nursed and nurtured *Winter Eyes* from the very beginning, and over many rocky years. She always believed it would be published even when I didn't, and consistently encouraged me not to give up. And here we are, almost twenty years after she started making her colorful predictions. . . .

This book would have been impossible without the love and support of my partner, Gersh Kaufman. It was as alive for him as for me, and besides offering many invaluable suggestions, he was always willing to help me talk out difficulties in the novel. He also gave important technical advice, proofread the manuscript, helped me over the rough spots, and was cool and resourceful in emergencies. Sharing the book with him was a great joy.

Contents

Part One
Lessons

1

As soon as Stefan woke up he went straight to the kitchen without a bathroom stop. His mother turned from the sink where she scoured a pan. "You're up early." She smiled. "I just made juice." And then she said good morning in Polish: *"Dzień dobry."*

Stefan opened the humming fridge, enjoying his mother's smile, the rushing water, the familiar way she leaned against the sink, the large glass pitcher of juice which was always so heavy and wonderful and looked so round when he carried it with both hands to the table. His mother went on washing; he got his Peter Pan tumbler.

"Put your slippers on before Daddy comes back with the papers." She dried the pan and stacked it away under the sink as quietly as usual; Stefan loved crashing pans a little and did so whenever his mother asked him to get one out.

"Remember your slippers," she told him. His father got very

angry when Stefan went around barefoot: "The floors are dirty."

"Mommy *washed* them," Stefan would protest but it was no use; his father had a great many rules Stefan knew he had to obey. Stefan's father rarely yelled, instead his father got all tight when he was angry, like a squeezed balloon.

"I had a bad dream."

"You did?"

"I did. I was lost—I couldn't find you—or Daddy."

"Did you wake up?"

"No. Maybe."

His mother left the kitchen now and Stefan clutched his glass, wanting to run after her. Instead, he drained his juice, slipped off the chair to go to his room—and to see where she was. The bathroom door was closed.

"Mommy?" He pulled the slippers out from under his bed.

"A minute," she called.

Stefan walked around the room trying to forget how much he needed the bathroom.

When his father came back bearing the newspapers and fresh bread and onion rolls, Stefan sat in the kitchen with his feet out so there would be no mistake about the slippers.

"Why are you up so early?" his father asked, depositing the pile on the table.

Stefan didn't know why, and didn't know what to say—his father liked answers, and the right ones.

"Well, we'll all eat together." Usually on Sunday his mother and father had an early breakfast and sometimes his father ate alone. Stefan leafed through a magazine, looking for pictures, and for words he didn't know. There were a lot of those, but also a lot he'd just learned, like "choir" which he'd first thought was said "choyer." Really, though, he had his eyes on the frying bacon, the eggs as his mother plopped them from their white shells into the big white bowl. The sizzling was a more important sound than his parents' conversation which moved in and out of English, Polish, and Russian, so that even if he listened carefully he'd lose the thread of what they were saying. He felt very safe and happy at

4

the table, surrounded by smells and Sunday. He glanced at his mother often enough to realize he was doing so more than usual, and that made him restless a little, but with both of them in the room it wasn't as bad as his dream.

"You're quiet today," his father said, putting on a pot of coffee to brew. "What are you up to?"

Stefan shrugged.

Later Stefan left the table because his father was reading. His father always cracked the large wide pages and slapped them down as if he was angry at the news. The crack-slam made Stefan wince, and it seemed to cut through doors and walls. In his room, lying on the floor, Stefan tried again and again to draw an eagle as good as the one he drew Friday morning in art hour, but no matter what he used, what kind of crayon or colored pencil, and no matter what kind of paper, he couldn't do it. Stefan always had trouble drawing something he wanted to—the only time he did well was by accident, when he doodled in class, or changed his mind and began drawing without plan. There was magic in lines, only he didn't know it so they wouldn't listen to him. He tore up all the sheets now and threw them away.

His mother came in before lunch.

"We're going to see Uncle Sasha in a while."

Something in her voice, or the way she held the ends of her open white sweater kept him from saying anything, even though he liked his uncle very much.

Stefan watched his parents during lunch and on the short car ride to Sasha's because they didn't say anything in English except when they spoke to him to point out a tree or some funny dog. He felt left out and didn't answer much. When his mother and father became Russian he didn't really know them; they were meaner somehow. Polish and English were the same to him, even though it was only English at school, but Russian was strange and pushed him away.

"Well, you look sulky," Sasha grinned a while later, ruffling his hair.

"I'm not," Stefan said, edging off into the living room, which

5

always delighted him because of the three stairs down and the curving iron railing on each side. He hovered on the steps while coats were hung away in the hall closet. The room looked very big to Stefan because there wasn't too much more than the fat black piano and places to sit, and the floor was bare and so pretty, all made of squares of wood, with a dark thin border around the edges of the room.

"Do you want me to play for you?" Sasha asked behind him. Stefan hesitated; he couldn't decide if he wanted to be happy or not. Sasha passed him to sit at the broad baby grand piano that was like a tame bear: obedient and waiting. Sasha played a few notes and Stefan, forgetting his parents who were still in the foyer, still talking Russian, was drawn down the stairs across to where his uncle sat.

Sasha smiled and played something very loud and fast, his big hands as quick as squirrels. Stefan leaned on the vibrating piano, staring down at the keys and up at Sasha who always played with closed eyes. This amazed Stefan—it seemed more wonderful than drawing, to make a piano do what you wanted and not have to look. He hardly noticed his mother and father settle onto the couch nearby. Sasha's face, wide and pale, expressionless, awed Stefan, and sometimes made him want to laugh too, though he didn't know why. His uncle was a big broad floppy-haired man, like a clown almost, but not a clown. He liked coming to Sasha's bare apartment because he liked this man who was so different from his father, but he was also afraid of Sasha—he was a kind of wizard. When Stefan had once read a big King Arthur book, the picture of Merlin made him think of Sasha, even though Merlin had a beard and different clothes. Sasha was special in a way his mother and father were not.

"How about tea?" Sasha moved off from the piano, smiling down at Stefan. "Tea?" Sasha repeated, and Stefan's parents stopped talking. His mother looked very tired and his father had that squeezed face. They nodded. Stefan drifted into the small, bright kitchen. He didn't usually like tea because it made him think of the time he was sick with chicken pox, and even smelled a little of the pink lotion his father had smeared on him every night he was still bumpy, and made him think of sticky pajamas—but with Sasha's tea he thought of Sasha and it smelled like the sunshine in his kitchen.

"What do you want?" Sasha asked, reaching into tins and finding cups.

"I don't know." He could say that to his uncle without being embarrassed.

Sasha looked at him very slowly. "You like when I play for you?"

He nodded happily. Steam from the kettle clouded behind Sasha.

"Shall I teach you?" Sasha took out a large silver tray and arranged things on it.

"Me?" He could almost not say it.

Sasha picked him up and hugged him.

"I wish you were my daddy."

Sasha flushed and put him down, shook his head, looked like he wanted to laugh, or was afraid.

"Are you growing the tea?" Stefan's father called, and Sasha bore out the heavy tray.

"Stefan?" That was his mother but he didn't want to go to them; he liked this small private room and didn't care about the tea cakes and whatever else was on the tray.

"But can I learn?" he said as soon as he seated himself on the couch.

"Learn what?" His mother took a sip of the strong-smelling tea.

"I offered to teach him to play," Sasha murmured through a cookie, looking very big in the little chair he'd pulled up across the low table. Sasha *was* big, while his father only looked it.

"So that's what was going on in the kitchen." His father grimaced. "It's a waste of time."

"It's my *life*," Sasha put down his cup very hard. Stefan edged down the couch.

"A waste for him to learn," his father explained. "And it's too hard."

7

Stefan shrunk; he agreed with that—it couldn't be easy. It *was* hard, it sounded hard, he could never do it.

"I want to!" he burst out, full of tears.

"Stefan—" His mother frowned.

"I want to."

"See?" Sasha popped a tea cake into his mouth and crunched it very calmly. "Nothing is hard if you want it enough."

His father said something very low in Polish—words Stefan had never heard. He still wanted to cry; he didn't know if they'd let him or not, and he didn't know why everyone was so strange today, and he felt like a baby. He wanted to break something; sitting on the couch made him feel sick. The tea was not hot anymore and smelled of measles.

He went to the bathroom, and ran the water a lot when he was done.

His parents didn't say anything all the way home. His first lesson was to be next Sunday and Stefan hid in the back seat under a small blanket, pretending to sleep. The picture of himself sitting at the piano and commanding the keys like Sasha thrilled and scared him. What if he couldn't do it? What if his father was right?

At night he heard his parents yelling—it was almost always in Russian and he never really knew why. Once he'd seen them—all red and ugly—and he'd cried, unable to run back to his room, but they didn't even notice: his father paced in and out of the kitchen, loud, fists thumping the air near where his mother sat at the kitchen table answering him.

Their voices were as heavy as when a building was being made; he couldn't get away, he heard them now even in his room with the pillow over his head. He didn't know why they shouted at each other and he was much too afraid to ask.

It was the worst thing they did.

The next Sunday his father drove him to Sasha's; they didn't say much in the car. His father mostly cursed at other drivers and Stefan sat as firmly planted in his seat as he could—in case something happened. He had never seen an accident except on TV, but the way his father gripped the wheel and criticized every other driver made Stefan keep silent. He didn't want his father to be mean to him. The quiet in the car was even worse than usual because his father had broken the radio jabbing at a button. Stefan wished his father would drive straight up Broadway instead of taking the highway—everything went by too fast and there was always a big truck shadowing them, making Stefan clutch his seat. His father would shake his head then and Stefan blushed; he knew he wasn't supposed to be scared—like of the dark or bad dogs—but it was very hard. His father didn't ever call him a baby, but Stefan could tell that he sometimes thought it.

Sasha did not scare him as much, hardly at all. Sitting on the piano bench next to his uncle he felt very safe and warm. Sasha was so big and the open piano very tall and wonderful—shining, streaked and carved, mysterious. He was almost unwilling to put his hands on the keys the way Sasha showed him after he started learning their names. He listened very hard and became almost dizzy with not understanding. Sasha rested an arm on his shoulder and helped him push down the keys of his first chord and then a scale. It was new, all new, more exciting than anything at school except maybe reading—but even that wasn't much unless you read out loud.

"Let's take a break." Sasha went to get lemonade. Stefan sat at the keyboard running a finger down the white and black lengths; the keys were so hard and all alike and they led inside to the secret. He stood, looked down at the strings, depressed a key, saw the little hammer, watched and heard the dull buzz. It was a marvel to him.

"You really like that?" his father asked, staring from where he sat with a pile of magazines.

He knew the answer. "I do."

"It's hard work, you don't know how hard. You won't be playing like Sasha for years. Maybe never."

And Stefan's purpose blurred; his father was so *sure*. Sasha emerged from the kitchen with two full glasses. "If he wants to learn, let him." Sasha stood over his father's chair. His father shrugged.

"I don't see the point," his father said.

"The point is music. That's enough."

"For you perhaps."

"*Proszę*," Sasha said heavily. Stefan knew that was Polish. It meant please. He wanted to say it too in case they started to yell.

His father shrugged again, plucked a magazine from the pile.

"Here." Sasha joined him at the piano. "To your lessons," he toasted.

"I wish we could get you a piano," his mother said one afternoon, sitting by his bed. Stefan had stayed home from school with a cold, drinking tea and listening to the radio, falling in and out of a light sleep. Even though he was tired, the steady stream of music cheered him, especially when there was a piano in it; he listened as hard as he could then. They weren't just sounds anymore but pieces—sonatas and capriccios—the names and directions were in a beautiful language, and the way you wrote music was also beautiful. Not like arithmetic—there was art in it *and* numbers. Somehow he understood everything Sasha said now, or knew he was almost ready to understand.

"Sasha says you learn very well. You can even play." Stefan's father was impressed too, she said. "But I'm not surprised. You read so well for your age."

Stefan grinned. He knew he was an "advanced" reader at school, but this was even better. And it made him feel like his parents did about how good their English was; his mother and father often joked about other Poles and Europeans who couldn't pronounce the English "th" sound.

"It's *wonderful* in just a few months." His mother stroked his cheek, felt his forehead; that was the best part of being sick: his parents touched him, were in and out of the room, talked to him and listened.

"I wish we could get you a piano," his mother said again, not looking at him even though her hand still lay on his forehead. He

10

wanted to touch her hand or for her to take it away, he didn't know which. When his mother stopped looking at him while she spoke it was as strange as his father's anger that simmered like bad soup with pieces in it (Stefan liked his food as smooth as possible).

"But we can't. . . ." His mother drew her hands together in her lap.

"Are we poor?" Stefan had a flash of his mother in rags, like in a book, but poor people didn't have apartments, did they? And poor children never played the piano.

His mother laughed. "No, darling, no we're not poor! It's just that your father—" but she didn't finish what she was saying, left him to make more tea.

He thought of having his own piano; it seemed like something that would only happen when he grew up. Where would they put it? There wasn't any room at home for even one of those little squashed ones unless they took something out, and that didn't make any sense. The living room was very crowded with his father's desk and file cabinets and bookcase taking up half the room, even though he had an office at school. And he thought his father wouldn't like the practicing anyway, because he always wanted it quiet in the house at night, so he could "grade papers."

Stefan didn't really want more tea but drank it anyway when his mother returned.

"Why doesn't Uncle Sasha have a family?"

His mother moved to the window, stood there with her hands on the sill. For a terrifying moment in which he thought her hands were shaking, Stefan wondered if his mother weren't about to cry. He knew women cried—but not his mother.

"He can't," she said.

"Why?"

"He just can't. Drink your tea." On the way out she turned off the radio.

Later, when his father came in to say good night Stefan asked again.

His father stared at him as if he'd said a terrible word, the kind you couldn't even write down.

"Why can't he have a family?" his father echoed. "He has us."

Stefan had never exactly thought of himself as belonging to Sasha; the idea was a pleasing one. Still, though, he wanted a real answer, the kind his father liked to hear from *him*.

His father stood at the foot of the bed, hands in his pockets, eyes very small and sharp.

"He can't, there was . . . an accident."

That Stefan could understand, accidents were bad and you died or went to the hospital. There was a big one with lots of dark dirty buildings near Sasha's house. It looked like the castle of witches, and it had a long funny name that was almost like where his father was a teacher—Columbia Presbyterian—and Stefan was always a little scared when they walked or drove by it.

"There was an accident," his father repeated.

Stefan nodded and his father said good night.

So Sasha *was* his daddy, then—in a way.

His father stopped sitting through the lessons, would go drive somewhere or take a walk in Riverside Park across the street from Sasha's building, and so Stefan stayed at the piano with Sasha longer and longer. Sunday grew to be all he really thought about, in school, on the school bus; he would look down sometimes to find his fingers moving slowly as if they were on keys. The feelings of warmth that came from Sasha's large comforting bulk at his side and from the uncluttered apartment stayed with him week after week, like a secret. It was like the time when he was very little and found a small chunk of glass near a tree in front of their building. He scooped it up, washed it later, dazzled by the glittering edges. Stefan kept it for days behind some books until his father found it.

"What are you doing with this?" his father demanded.

Stefan didn't explain how he'd found his diamond.

"You could hurt yourself." His father bore it away. Stefan hadn't protested; it seemed natural that his father would throw out his treasure. He didn't cry, not right then or when his father came back.

"What did you need it for?"

"I just wanted it."

12

His father had frowned.

Stefan liked it that Sasha's small apartment wasn't crowded or as neat as his, where everything shone and smelled of polish. His mother was always tugging at the corner of something, scrubbing the sink, spraying, vacuuming. His greatest fear at home was to knock a vase over or drop a glass or even spill something; no one scolded him but there was so much cleaning afterwards that every movement seemed directed at him.

At Sasha's there wasn't very much outside of the kitchen to break, and he could put his feet up on the couch, sit on the steps into the living room. That was his favorite place to be, after sitting at the piano, because if he sat to the left he could see the keyboard and Sasha's hands while he played. Sasha even let him put his glass on the floor, which didn't look less clean than at home—but floors were "dirty" and it was kind of exciting.

"Am I your best student?" he asked one day, many months after the first lesson.

"You're my favorite," Sasha beamed from the bench, smoothing his hair back and leafing through a music book on the piano. "And you learn well."

"Mommy said she wished I had my own piano." Stefan didn't mention his parents to Sasha much, only when he asked; for the few hours there every week it was almost as if he didn't have parents—or those parents.

"Hmm?"

"Why don't they take lessons too?" he wondered.

Sasha closed the book, set it aside.

"Not everyone wants to play." Sasha faced him. "Besides, your mother used to."

"When?"

Sasha rose. "Are you hungry?" He moved from the piano. Stefan wasn't, but he liked Sasha to make things for him so he said yes.

"Your father will be back soon. How about eggs? Did you have eggs today?"

They were in the kitchen. Stefan shook his head but Sasha's grin made him admit the truth.

13

"Well—a little French toast? Yes?" Sasha busied himself with the ingredients. Sitting at the table, Stefan was not as intent on the milk and eggs, cinnamon and vanilla as usual; the whirring toaster and the oil in the pan almost annoyed him.

"When did Mommy play piano?"

"Before— When we were all young."

"Before what?"

Sasha stirred the batter and dipped a slice of lightly toasted bread, laid it in the pan; his movements were very big in the kitchen and something usually got knocked over or almost. Sasha laughed when he broke glasses or dishes.

Sasha turned, leaned against the sink, eyed him in the same unseeing way his mother sometimes did.

"The two of them used to fight to practice. . . ."

"Who?"

"Your mother and Eva."

"Who was that?"

Sasha flipped the toast over, dipped another piece and set it to fry.

"She would've been your aunt," Sasha said quietly.

His father came back before Stefan could find out more than that Eva had been Sasha's and his mother's younger sister and had disappeared in Poland, which was also called *Polska*. He knew his parents' families came from Poland, a place he'd seen in lots of picture books, a place he thought of as full of castles, statues, churches, and soldiers. He liked castles; there weren't any here and they were so big and neat looking, with flags and little windows, dark and pointy at the top. Not everyone over there lived in castles, his mother had told him once, not even small ones, but he bet they wanted to. When Stefan played with cutouts the best ones were the castles; he could even make castles on his own, stand books together on their ends. It took a lot of them to make a really good castle, and he needed pencils for flagpoles and paper cups for towers and all the little men—animals and soldiers from different games and sets—marched along the top and in and out the doors. He hadn't done that in a while, though—since he'd begun playing the piano; that was more important, and more fun than anything else.

"Why don't I have a sister?" he asked on the way home; it was an old question that got the old answer.

"Because we wanted just you," his father said, honking at a man who crossed the street in front of them too slowly. The man didn't jump or even look up, just kept going and Stefan admired that— car horns frightened him.

"Did *you* have a sister?" he asked, clutching his seat as they roared through the intersection. This question was new.

"No."

"Did Mommy?"

"Why?"

Stefan was silent; being questioned in reply to a question unsettled him, made him unsure; it was worse than when his father came into his room and said: "Why is there such a mess here?" Stefan would look up from his book or drawing and glance around a bit wildly. He didn't know, it just got like that. "Why is that shirt on the floor?" His father would point and Stefan would stare at the shirt as if hoping *it* would explain. Stefan had a vague sense that you couldn't really control a lot of things; they fell or crept behind bookcases, rolled under beds or ripped because they wanted to. To be in charge you had to straighten and dust the way his mother did: without stopping. "Are you going to pick it up?" his father would continue.

"Why do you ask?" his father said now as they stopped at a red light.

Stefan squirmed.

"I don't know."

His father disliked that answer—you *had* to know. "If you don't know, then don't ask."

They said nothing more.

After he'd done his homework Stefan lay on the floor picking at the blue rug, listening to the radio which was playing a piano concerto he had heard a few times already. It was written by a deaf

15

man, Sasha had told him, or a man who went deaf, Stefan couldn't remember which—but either way it was magic. He listened to the long proud melodies that were so big compared to the tiny things he was beginning to play. He wondered what the man at the piano looked like, and how many scales a day he practiced. Sasha had promised to take him to a concert some day; that seemed as much a dream as having his own piano.

"Stefan?" His mother knocked and entered.

He sat up to protest when she turned the radio down—she was always doing that.

"Did Sasha say anything to you today?" She sat on the edge of his bed and the careful way she did it was so unusual that Stefan understood there was trouble. "Did he say anything, anything about—"

Stefan glanced from her to the door; he felt very angry and didn't know why. He didn't want her in his room or on his bed.

"He said you had a dead sister." Stefan looked her right in the face. He felt very mean; it was scary and thrilling. He wasn't used to feeling like he'd swallowed a hot drink when he hadn't.

His mother nodded, crossed her arms, uncrossed them, smoothed her graying hair back the same way Sasha did, and with the movement he relaxed.

"I'm sorry."

"What? No, not you—" She looked behind him, or somewhere. The idea of a woman like his mother, but someone who was dead, a woman he'd never met, but was his aunt, took hold of him. It was like being hungry in a new way.

"Was Eva pretty like you?"

His mother's face went hard and white and she rushed from the room. Her bedroom door slammed and Stefan knew he was in trouble.

"Anya?" he heard his father call and then there were quick heavy steps down the hall. A door was wrenched open and Stefan listened, transfixed, to a sound he'd never heard before: it was thin and high and tired—crying that made him shiver. His father's thick fast words merged with it and Stefan heard nothing else. He felt

16

lost the way he once had at school when he'd passed a kindergarten class and said hello to a friend in another class also on the way to the bathroom. . . .

"Young man!" From behind, a dull ugly voice had stopped him in the hall. He was afraid to turn. "Come *here*." Reluctant, he had obeyed. "Come here and sit down." He entered the large kindergarten class of children doing fingerpaints. He sat on a chair too small for him at the front of the large-windowed room, still not looking at Mrs. Lewis, a thin old woman who read Bible at assembly (until someone told him, he'd thought *she'd* written those things about pastures because of the way she held the big black book).

"What class are you in? Mrs. Johnson's? And does she let you talk in the hall and disturb other classes? I didn't think so. And why did you?"

Stefan sat on the horrible chair, clutching the large wooden bathroom pass, dizzy, unable to answer. He could hear little children giggling at him.

"Why don't you answer? Are you a *stupid* little boy?" Stefan couldn't remember how he escaped or what he said.

He never went past Mrs. Lewis's class to the bathroom again, but took the long way around no matter how bad he had to go. . . .

His father stood in the doorway now, black with anger. "*Psia krew!*" he shouted in Polish. Stefan didn't know what that meant, but he knew it was something terrible. His mother had never said it, and his father, only a few times. "If you ever make your mother cry again I swear I'll—"

Stefan stumbled back to his bed. "I didn't do anything!"

"Max?" came his mother's thin call. His father disappeared. The murmuring radio suddenly seemed very loud to Stefan, who edged towards it, eyes on the door. He shut it off and closed the door very softly. "I didn't do it," he thought stubbornly, but he *had* done it somehow, and that was what he couldn't understand. And why his father had threatened him. Stefan winced at how his father had stood dark and terrible at the door.

17

"It wasn't my fault," he muttered, finding a bit of strength. Whose fault was it? What had even happened? "I made Mommy cry," he thought with sudden horror—how had he done such a bad thing? She would surely be mad at him.

When his mother woke him for school the next morning he jerked back from her hand.

"It's only me," she murmured, as if he'd been dreaming. She was so nice to him all morning and at the bus stop that he didn't know what to say. "I'm sorry" wouldn't be enough; he felt like a very bad boy all day, almost cried when Mrs. Johnson corrected an arithmetic mistake of his in front of everyone. His lunch tasted nasty.

Nobody said much at dinner; Stefan ate everything on his plate, slowly—what he wanted to do was run away or cry but he knew he wouldn't do either. His mother and father talked in English when they did say anything, mostly about the food. Stefan slipped away from the table with as little noise as possible when they began to wash up. He didn't turn on the radio in his room for fear someone would yell at him. Stefan sat at his desk fiddling with schoolbooks. Mrs. Johnson had asked him three times today before he answered the math problem—and wrong too. Later she called him over and asked him if he was all right; he loved Mrs. Johnson sometimes, when she smiled at him and smelled pretty, but not today.

"What'd you do?" someone asked as they'd clambered aboard the bus and Stefan shrugged. A fight broke out between two girls in the seat across from him when he was almost home and Stefan watched as if it was television. He didn't care that they were crying and screaming and the bus driver had to stop and that everyone was all excited. He didn't care.

Stefan went to the closet, half-guilty, to get Scotty. His father said he was too old for a doll, even a dog doll, so he couldn't decide whether to take Scotty or not. His dog looked so battered that finally he couldn't resist and dragged him out from some old shoes. Sasha had given him the white dog with a plaid hat and blanket around his middle a long time ago. One of Scotty's shiny black eyes was missing. Poor Scotty; he cradled the half-blind dog,

18

telling it everything would be all right, but Stefan knew that was a big lie and Scotty couldn't be fooled. He was glad Scotty wasn't a real dog—you couldn't hold a real dog that tight and it could bite you.

If he knew how to drive a car he would run away to Sasha. Sasha never made fun of him or was mean when he made mistakes at the piano. Stefan leaned back against the closet door, hugging Scotty, imagining how his mother and father would beg him to come back and how he would stand at the piano and shake his head and they would cry and promise never to be mean to him again or go away. Stefan felt his cheeks hot and wet before he realized he was crying. He clutched old Scotty and trembled, the tears coming without a sound. It scared him to cry and make no noise—it almost wasn't him. He stopped very suddenly, wiped his face with Scotty's bad ear and rose to turn on the music. The gentle glide of violins was the first thing he heard; he forgot to pay attention when it was over so he didn't find out what it was. It calmed him down though. Next was something he'd never heard before; very long and in a strange language. It was just a man and a piano—very sad songs even when they were fast or angry sounding. He fell asleep on his bed once or twice, but he heard all of the end; he thought the announcer called it *Winter Eyes*. The name was creepy; it made him think of ghosts and blind dogs in the snow.

At his next lesson Sasha acted very funny, didn't smile or make any jokes and even missed some mistakes he made. Sasha's face was paler than most times and Sasha and his father said nothing to each other before the lesson started. Stefan wanted to cry. His parents must've told Sasha how bad he was. At the break Stefan just wanted to go away from there and never come back. He and Scotty would leave and no one would ever find them.

"Your mother and father were very angry," Sasha said, stirring sugar into his tea. "They wanted to stop your lessons."

Stefan froze.

"But I said I was sorry and it wouldn't happen again." Stefan felt

19

sticky and hot, like he'd been running too much. "So you mustn't ask me about Eva or anything or they'll take you away."

He thought Sasha wanted to cry—this terrified him.

"Why were you sorry?" Stefan managed.

"Because I shouldn't have told you."

In a flash Stefan understood his parents had been angry at *Sasha.*

"Was Eva a bad lady?"

"No—she died. I can't tell you."

Stefan was sure then that he loved Sasha and Sasha loved him; he wanted to do something, say what he thought. He didn't know how; the words were too big. He wished he could give Sasha a present to make him feel better.

"Are you mad at me?" Stefan asked.

"You?" Sasha laughed. "Never—how could I be mad at you? Until you started lessons I didn't have anything to look forward to."

"Not all the other students?"

"No."

Stefan wanted to laugh he was so bursting with pride. Sasha was talking to him more adult than ever. That was why he liked being here; even with Mrs. Johnson at school he felt like a little kid no matter how nice she was. Sasha acted different, was nicer to him.

"Why can't you tell me about Eva?"

Sasha looked away. "Your parents won't let me. You're too young."

"When can you tell me?"

"Maybe some day."

"Promise?"

Sasha sighed. "Let's go back."

Stefan played that afternoon with new assurance; for the first time he felt something special at the piano—he didn't worry about fingering or counting in his head or the sharps. His hands moved on the keys without a break and he heard the little piece all the way through.

"That was *very* good. Very," Sasha told him again as Stefan was leaving with his father, who smiled at the compliment.

"So you're doing well," his father said in the elevator.

Stefan nodded, reluctant to let his father into the world he and Sasha shared. As his father preceded him out onto the street, Stefan had a sudden hot wish not to have to go home with this man, to stay always with his uncle who would play for him and cook and never leave, never yell.

And then the nastiness of his thoughts almost hurt him; it was very bad not to want to be with his father. But he couldn't make the wish go away; all during the drive home he tried thinking of everything but the dark open piano that was like a ship sailing on the sun-bright wood floor which complained when you crossed it.

Sasha came by one night a few days later; since the lessons began Sasha had visited less often.

"Why don't you come listen?" Stefan had asked his mother many Sundays but she was always busy or tired from being busy. He didn't think he would mind her sitting while he practiced: his mother would be quiet—even though his father didn't say anything the few times he stayed, just the way he sat there was noisy somehow, and Stefan made more mistakes than usual.

They all sat this evening in the dark thick-curtained living room that had come to look odd to Stefan because it didn't have a piano. Sasha and his parents spoke slowly, with lots of space between what they said; he didn't think they were having a very good time. His class was like that just after someone had been yelled at for not behaving.

Now and then Sasha would glance his way and smile, so Stefan didn't feel left out even though tonight no one spoke in English.

"Do you know *Winter Eyes?*" Stefan piped up after what sounded like a long silence to him.

Sasha frowned. "*Winter*—?"

"It's a man singing and a piano. It's songs. I heard it on the radio."

"*Winter Eyes?*" his mother repeated to herself.

"I didn't know the language," Stefan added.

21

"*Winter Eyes, Winter Eyes,*" Sasha was saying. He clapped his hands. "*Die Wintereise?* It must be."

They laughed and Stefan recognized the sound of the words.

"It's German, it means *winter journey,*" Sasha explained. "By Schubert. I played you something of his, remember? The *Impromptu?*" Sasha hummed and Stefan knew it.

"Can you play it?" he asked, eager, but embarrassed he'd called it the wrong name.

"I could get the music."

"And sing too?"

"Oh my voice. . . ." Sasha smiled.

"It's ugly," his father announced. "It's German, I hate German." His father shook his head.

Sasha and his mother were looking down.

"I don't want you to play it for him," his father warned, adding something in Russian that made Sasha go very pale.

"*Proszę,*" his mother said, and to him: "Shouldn't you—?"

It *was* time for bed. He said good night and left them. When he closed his door he kicked a book across the room. Why did they say things he didn't know? Why were they mean to Sasha? He hated them, especially his father, who never wanted him to have any fun *ever*.

In the bathroom washing his hands he said defiantly "It's not ugly, it isn't," though all he knew of German was the way it had sounded on the radio and how Sasha said *Winter Eyes.*

2

Stefan didn't like his second grade teacher very much; Miss Zimmer wasn't friendly and didn't let you even whisper when she was talking. Also her face was as hard looking as her desk. There was one boy in class—David—she was always punishing because he never listened, and he said things back. Stefan kept very quiet—he was afraid of what could happen to him. When David misbehaved Stefan watched, hoping somehow Miss Zimmer would lose, but she never did. She was so big, and the teacher besides. Stefan didn't volunteer for anything in her class and was glad because of the alphabet that he—Stefan Borowski—sat in the row with the other A's and B's that was furthest from her desk, and closest to the windows. He didn't look out at the park ever in case he'd get yelled at; he could smell the trees, though, and hear them, and he liked that. When he saw Mrs. Johnson from last year in the hall he always said he liked his new class a lot—Miss Zimmer might be listening.

"Your new teacher isn't as nice as Mrs. Johnson," his mother said when she and his father came back from parents' meeting night. He hoped no one had said anything bad about him.

"She says you're very well-behaved. And polite."

"Of course he is," his father said, wrenching open his paper. "What does she expect, an animal?"

"Max—" His mother put a hand on his father's arm, as if to keep him from hitting someone.

"That stupid woman." His father's voice was harsh and thick. "You're a teacher too, Stefan tells me," his father mimicked, and Stefan couldn't help giggling at the way he made his face stiff just like Miss Zimmer. His mother smiled too.

"What did you say?" Stefan asked with respect, delighted they didn't like his teacher much either.

"I am a *professor,* Miss Zimmer, there is no comparison."

Stefan gulped. "Why did you say that?" He felt sick—his father didn't have to sit in her class, but *he* did. He wanted to die.

"If she does anything. . . ." his father warned.

"It'll be all right," his mother assured him.

But they didn't know, and he had trouble falling asleep that night.

It was bad but not too bad. Miss Zimmer just kind of ignored him. He was confused until he understood she wanted as little to do with him as possible, and then he didn't care. He stopped being afraid of her because he knew she would leave him alone. When other kids complained about Miss Zimmer at lunch or on the bus Stefan didn't join in, even in his head.

"I wish I didn't have school," Stefan told Sasha. "I wish I could just come here and play whenever I wanted to."

"Even scales?" Sasha teased.

Stefan nodded.

"I didn't like school when I was young. Neither did your mother or— You're lucky you have something you do like."

He and Sasha didn't talk about school a lot when they were

together, though when Sasha asked him a question Sasha really wanted to know, not like his parents sometimes. Mostly they didn't talk; he had his lesson and then Sasha would play for him. That was beautiful; Stefan would sit on the steps, leaning against the curved iron rail, watching Sasha's long white hands.

"Did you always play piano?" he asked one fall afternoon. Sasha had just finished a very sweet *Canzonetta* by Dussek—Stefan liked to say the names to himself sometimes, thinking of how the music looked on the page, hearing the best parts.

Sasha closed the lid but stayed at the piano. He nodded, once to the piano, once to Stefan.

"But I didn't take it seriously when I played, not like you," he smiled and Stefan wriggled at the compliment.

"Then why did you keep playing?"

Sasha sighed. "Except for your mother and father I had nothing else. The War," Sasha said wearily, and in the silence that followed Stefan suddenly was afraid to ask any more questions. The way Sasha spoke was so heavy and he looked as sad as poor Scotty. He didn't like his uncle to be sad: it made Stefan feel lonely and far away, as if even English had become a language he didn't know. "We lost *everything.*"

"Do you ever cry?" he brought out so low Sasha didn't hear him.

"Hmm?"

"Do you cry?" Stefan asked.

Sasha shook his head. "I won't."

Stefan considered this. "Then what do you do when you're sad?" Sasha opened the lid and began to play. "I do this," he said, eyes closed, back very straight. What he played was as sad as *Winter Eyes* but worse because there were no words to it. Sometimes Stefan was just like this music—all hurt but unable to say anything. In the piece there was a melody that always sounded like it was going to finish but never did, struggled and faded like it wasn't strong enough to be complete. The iron railing was cold against Stefan's cheek as he clung to it. Sasha's solemn playing kept making Stefan feel he would cry, but each time he went tight inside, the piano led him away. He wondered what Sasha meant by "the War," if he had been a soldier. He heard different things about "the War"—on TV, on buses, even in the supermarket as he helped push the cart, but he didn't know if it was all the same war they meant. He knew war was very bad, and that was why his parents didn't want him to have gun toys. People got killed. It was hard for him to picture what war looked like; he wasn't allowed to see it on TV even when it was just Indians. He sort of thought it was like a big accident, bigger than the worst accident possible, and there would be hospitals in it too.

His father sometimes complained about his back and had to lie down with a heating pad and be very quiet. Stefan couldn't remember, maybe that was the War too. Sasha finished playing just as the telephone rang. Sasha didn't move, even though the phone was by the piano on a small table. Sasha met his glance with a grin; it seemed daring to Stefan not to answer the insistent cry, too daring. He half-rose and Sasha reached for the receiver.

"Hello?" Sasha smiled into the receiver and went quickly on in a language that didn't sound to Stefan like Russian or Polish or anything he'd ever heard. He didn't like being alone with Sasha and not understanding what his uncle was saying. Stefan stood and wandered down the little hall. The door to the bedroom was not closed as usual and he stood there, gazing in. There wasn't much to see but a bed and tall bureau, and curtains and a window that did not face the same way as the living room: towards Riverside Drive and the narrow park running along it, the Hudson River, and the Palisades. He was hardly ever in this room; and the sound of Sasha on the phone seemed to ease him through the doorway. The floor here was bare, too, and the dark clean-smelling room made him think of his mother even though there wasn't anything much here, except in the corner on a round table. He moved across to the table on which there were grouped several small gold-framed photos. He saw his mother in one—very pretty and very sad, from long ago, and his father and Sasha; they were all so young they looked funny to him. Sasha's hair was very black and there weren't any lines on his mother and his father seemed happy even though he wasn't smiling. Behind the three was one he'd never seen before;

it was very heavy. There were four small people on a street corner, walking, his mother and father, Sasha and someone else, a woman. He knew it was Eva. She looked like his mother.

She looked like *him.*

He crept to the door; Sasha was still on the phone. Stefan stole across to the bathroom and held the picture up by his face in the mirror. She looked like *him,* even though she wasn't a boy and he was. Stefan felt excited as if he'd found a huge treasure all alone and wouldn't have to share it with anyone. Reluctant, he returned the wonderful picture to the bedroom table and then slipped into the bathroom. He made a lot of noise there flushing and washing up. It was very strange to have this much of a secret from Sasha, but as he walked back to the steps and Sasha hung up, Stefan knew what he'd found was a secret from everyone.

"I have wonderful news." Sasha came to him, clamped his hands on his shoulders. "Would you like to go to Carnegie Hall tomorrow night?"

"A concert? Really?"

When his father came Stefan was still plaguing Sasha for details of what it would be like; the closest thing in Stefan's head was the circus but he knew it was different.

"How did you get the tickets?" his father was trying to move into the foyer—Stefan couldn't tear himself away. It was going to be a recital! And he even knew some of the music—well, he'd heard it.

His mother smiled when he burst into the kitchen with the news. All the next day Stefan wanted to tell everyone at school about the concert he was going to. And that he was even going to sleep away from home; hardly anyone's mother let them sleep over. Stefan felt proud and full and excited; on the way home in the bus he didn't mind not telling anyone. Sometimes kids laughed at things you said, even though you weren't being funny, and a lot of times they just didn't listen. Nobody bothered him because he kept quiet; the worst thing at school was to be made fun of. There was a boy in another second grade class who had bad teeth—they weren't a nice color, he didn't know why, it couldn't be not brushing, wouldn't the boy's mother make him brush?—and lots of kids called him "Yellowteeth" when they were mad or chasing him or something. It made Stefan squirm to hear that; it wasn't fair or polite to make fun of any kind of cripple, even if they bothered you.

He didn't think this kid bothered anyone. Stefan once found him crying in the first floor bathroom during recess and quickly backed out into the hall. Sometimes he thought he should talk to the boy, but he wasn't sure.

He almost could not eat dinner and his mother had to straighten out his clothes when he got dressed. He felt like a soldier in his suit and stiff shoes. His mother kept fixing his hair.

Sasha talked to him all the way to Carnegie Hall on the bus. Stefan didn't know how long a ride it was; he hardly heard anything, almost couldn't breathe the excitement made him so tight. It wasn't his tie, Sasha had fixed that. He'd never seen his uncle all dressed up before; the black suit made Sasha look more important than anyone, like a king. The street when they got off the bus was very crowded; Sasha took his hand and led him through the suits and fancy dresses. Everyone moved like they came to recitals all the time. Stefan saw gold flashes and jewelry and drowned in the perfume. He clutched Sasha's big hand. He'd never gotten lost before—even in the biggest department store—but here, where everything was blinding and big and crowded he was sure he could. Inside it was too much to see when he looked up from their seats to all the balconies that went to the top. Sasha explained things to him, opening the program, but Stefan's eyes swam. The noise was slow and shiny like ocean waves on TV. He stared everywhere, thrilled into silence, seeing a blue hat with funny feathers, a silver cane, a very white shirt, lots of different glasses, a fat lady in a tight and shiny dress, but there was too much for him to talk or even point. His neck got stiff and finally Stefan sank into the chair to peer at the stage and the long proud piano. They wouldn't be able to see the keyboard from where they sat; that didn't seem so bad, though—he was here, at a recital, in Carnegie Hall with Sasha.

"Ahh." Sasha nodded and a man in a suit with a long jacket in the back strode out. The applause was so loud Stefan didn't know right away it was applause until he saw Sasha's hands clapping different from the way he did. Stefan tried copying it, but people were stopping.

He didn't say a word all evening except when Sasha bought him an orange drink at the intermission and he sipped it standing at the wall, watching everyone. "Thank you," he managed, the straw giving him a little trouble. Sasha grinned down at him. In the thick exciting crowd swarming for drinks Stefan felt strangely at home because there were languages he recognized. The beginning of the recital was nothing compared to the second half; from the opening notes of the Liszt Stefan sat bolt upright in his seat, transfixed by the sweep and power. There was one place that pounded and pounded like drums—it was so strong it brought Stefan near tears. He had never heard music so large and stirring; that was why it was a grand piano, the dark wood and dark music were together. He couldn't applaud when it was over and people shouted, though not exactly like at a ball game, it wasn't as wild. He grabbed Sasha's arm.

"Yes?"

But he couldn't get any words out.

And then the pianist came back! Everyone sat down and there was more. Sasha explained the word "encore." Stefan couldn't take it all in; he was hot and very tired but also somehow more awake than ever.

"The Bach was beautiful, no?" Sasha said as they headed up the long aisle, an arm on his shoulder to keep him from being swept off by the streams of people; all around him he could feel a happiness like his own. Stefan wondered if going to pray was like this.

"I like *The Wanderer Fantasy*." Stefan pronounced it carefully.

"Yes? It was too—"

Stefan frowned.

"You're right, it was gorgeous," Sasha went on, and Stefan smiled.

Outside, the street and the air seemed very new to Stefan; he could've stood in front until it was time to sleep, but Sasha led him to the corner.

"Shall we have ice cream?"

This was too much for Stefan—he wanted to yell. He nodded and Sasha hailed a cab. The yellow screech was like everything tonight: big and fast and more real than he was used to. In the cab he kept thinking of a line someone had said in a movie: "This is the happiest time of my life." He wanted to say it and thank Sasha but the words got all tangled up and instead he mumbled "This is happy time."

Sasha didn't seem to notice he'd said it wrong. "Yes, this is happy time." Only when Sasha spoke, it didn't sound as happy and Stefan wondered why.

They had ice cream in a restaurant near Sasha's building; well, *he* had a giant sundae and Sasha just had coffee. Lines of music kept going through Stefan's head so he ate in time with them, sometimes fast, sometimes slow, waving his spoon a little. Sasha talked to him about what they'd heard, explaining things, but Stefan could only listen a bit with the music in his head and the ice cream and everything.

"Did you ever teach Eva to play?" he suddenly asked.

Sasha made a noise, looked at him very hard, started to speak.

Stefan didn't think Sasha would get mad at him; the evening was too much like a story with happy endings.

"How did you know?" Sasha finally asked, smoothing his hair.

"I didn't."

Sasha shook his head, and then his eyes went funny the way Stefan's mother's did when she wasn't really paying attention.

"She was such a good pupil—like you. Your mother had lessons from a teacher, but Eva wanted me. . . ." Sasha laughed a little strangely.

"How come I don't have grandparents? Everyone at school has some."

Sasha shook himself like a dog getting up from a nap. "They died."

30

"Were they sick?"

"No."

"Was it an accident?"

"No, not an accident. You shouldn't ask." Sasha's eyes were very big and sad. It was "the War" Stefan felt sure, he didn't know why. He wanted Sasha to say it, to explain what was so bad, to tell him the truth. He began to feel tired and like sleeping.

"We'll go now," Sasha said, beckoning over the waiter.

Stefan was soon washing up in Sasha's bathroom. He changed into his pajamas and slippers.

Sasha had made up the couch for himself.

"I never was in a big bed," Stefan yawned.

"Do you want a glass of milk?" Sasha was still dressed. What Stefan wanted was Scotty but he'd only brought clothes for tomorrow and his book bag. Sasha would take him to school.

"Yuck," Stefan muttered.

"Yuck?" Sasha ruffled his hair.

"School."

Sasha shrugged. "But tonight was nice?"

Stefan lit up. "Yes." He searched for words.

"Why not sleep now, it's late."

Stefan wanted to kiss Sasha good night but was too embarrassed. He went in and slipped under the covers. Sasha closed the door for him. Pulling one of the pillows into his arms, Stefan thought he heard Sasha at the piano. Maybe it was just the music in his head, though.

Playing punchball wasn't any fun for Stefan because he didn't hit well; as soon as he got up at home everyone moved infield, sure he wouldn't get further than first. He felt awkward. Nobody laughed at him, though, because he could catch so good. Stefan usually sat out games at recess when the weather was nice; no one called him a sissy or anything, which was what he most feared. He didn't sit too far from the game for that reason.

That morning a few days after the recital, there'd been a book fair and cake sale and with his dollar Stefan had bought a copy of

31

The Three Musketeers with pictures—there was a sword fight on the front—and some cookies he'd already eaten. This was the first book he'd ever bought for himself and he held it and studied the way it was made before he even read the first page. He sat in the sun by himself near the wall while kids shouted and screamed, ran around, called each other bad names, jumped rope. It was like being in the kitchen when different things were cooking, first you'd smell one pot, then another and the smells would get all mixed up. Now he heard different voices and words blowing around him. He sat with his eyes closed sometimes, remembering the noise and shine of Carnegie Hall. The next day after the concert when Miss Zimmer was mean to a girl in class, Stefan thought, "Well, nobody took *you* to a recital," but instead of laughing inside, he began to feel sorry for his teacher. What if she really wanted to go and didn't have anyone to take her? This sudden change in what he thought of Miss Zimmer was very disturbing and he wished he could ask somebody about it. Maybe Miss Zimmer wasn't very nice because she was lonely?

"Tell me please," he heard a girl saying. He looked up. Two older girls sat down the wall from him. Both had very shiny black shoes, pink dresses and white hair ribbons. Could they be sisters?

"Tell me," one begged.

"You're too little."

Stefan thought they looked the same age.

"Tell me, what were they saying?"

Someone hit a home run and all the jumping and *yays* covered what the girls said next.

"Go Evan!" guys yelled and then Stefan heard: "*Go*, Yellow-teeth!" The boy running bases stopped and walked away from the game back into school. "Evan! I'm sorry!" "He's sorry!" There was lots of confusion; kids buzzed around the boy who had shouted the ugly word. Someone threatened to punch him but the two boys just stood and called each other things for a while and then stopped. Stefan felt very bad for Evan, and he was impressed; he could never have walked away from a game no matter what anyone said to him. Stefan looked down at his book—it was crumpled, he must've been holding it too tight.

"—and they put them in camps," one of the girls was saying.

"What's wrong with that?"

"Not summer camps, dummy!"

"What kind?"

"The other kind, where they hurt you."

"Why?"

Stefan sat with his eyes closed; the game had broken up and there was less noise in the yard. He'd never heard of any camp but the summer kind.

"Because Germans are nasty."

Stefan felt confused. Camps? Germans? Wasn't Schubert and *Winter Eyes* German? But his father hated Germans, and Stefan suddenly remembered that Sasha had promised to play *Winter Eyes* for him, but hadn't. Because of camps? What kind of camp did they hurt you in?

The two girls began skipping rope. "*A* my name is Annie . . ." but one stopped.

"Will they put us in camps?" she asked, her voice shaky.

The other girl went on skipping and spoke in time as she jumped:

"No—cause—we're—not—Jews."

The bell rang and Stefan headed to line up with everyone else to go inside. He was wondering about camps and had trouble working on his art project that afternoon—the trees he'd cut out looked stupid to him and he kept using too much glue to put the leaves on; his hands stuck to the desk and each other. Why couldn't he just go outside and look at the real ones?

On the bus the person next to him usually talked to someone across the aisle, or in front, in back, so Stefan could look out the window at all the different stores and buildings without being bothered. There was always so much noise after school that not talking was like being wrapped in a warm blanket on a cold night. Today, Evan sat next to him for the first time; Stefan thought someone usually got Evan by car.

"That was a good hit," Stefan said. What he wanted to say was how he liked it when Evan left the game, that it was brave, but Stefan didn't know how to start.

"Thanks," Evan said, and Stefan turned to the window.

"How come you almost never play?"

Stefan shrugged.

"It's easy."

Stefan was embarrassed because he had never been this close to Evan's teeth and he wanted to know why they were that yellow-white color. It was hard not to stare; at least blind people couldn't tell when you looked at them.

"Hey Stefan," someone a few seats back called. "What color are your teeth now?"

Evan stared straight ahead, biting his lip.

Stefan felt terrible. "George is stupid," he tried.

Evan didn't say anything, not even when he got off in a few stops.

The bus stop was only one block from their building, so he had been able to convince his parents he could come home alone now. Stefan wasn't really alone, though: a few other kids always came the same way. Sometimes he talked and sometimes not. Mostly now Stefan had enough music in his head for when he didn't have to think about something or listen. This was what he called his "secret singing" that was just there without trying—but as he swung his book bag, waiting for the light, Stefan heard those two girls talking about camps and Germans, and also Evan being called Yellowteeth. It was all mixed together somehow. When the light changed Stefan not only looked both ways but also behind him.

He liked being in the lobby of his building alone; once he was past the buzz-door it was like a castle to him—big and dark and gold. There were two giant old mirrors and deep window sills, a long table big enough for King Arthur and his knights, and alone, Stefan could imagine he had just crossed the moat and that there were towers above him.

Waiting for the elevator he wondered what kind of music they listened to in castles.

"There's this kid at school Evan who has funny teeth," he said at the kitchen table while his mother heated the milk for his cocoa. He bit a cookie and tapped the remaining piece the way his father did, like it was a cigarette.

"Funny?"

"They're like yellow. And white too." Stefan squirmed. "How come?"

"I don't know. Maybe his parents have it too. Or one of them."

"Like mumps?"

"No, you catch mumps, but some diseases you're born with. Those are genetic."

Stefan gazed down at the cloudy cocoa. His mother brought out things for dinner from the fridge but he didn't ask what they were having. He didn't know you could be born sick from your parents: he thought you were only sick from the air, from germs.

"Kids call him Yellowteeth."

His mother turned. "You don't."

"No, that's mean. But how come they do it if it's mean?"

"People don't always think." She was running something under water.

Stefan sipped his drink and started another cookie. "Do they do it on purpose?"

"Sometimes."

Stefan was trying to see if he ever did mean things on purpose, said bad names to anyone. He wanted to sometimes, but it made him scared to feel that mean.

"Like Germans?"

"What?" Something fell into the sink. "What?" She turned and he watched the water drip off her hand onto her dress and shoes. "What are you asking?"

Her eyes were scary and Stefan wanted to leave.

"I just heard something about camps," he said.

"Where?" His mother almost whimpered. "Who said this to you?"

"A girl in the yard after the book fair." He'd forgotten to tell her about his book.

"What did she say?"

"That people went to the other kind of camp, where they hurt you." Then he remembered. "Jews. What's Jews?"

His mother smoothed her hair back, looked around the room. "Go play, Stefan."

"Mommy, I'm sor—" He got up and tried to hug her.

"Please." She backed away from him.

He went to his room and sat on his bed unable to do anything. What did he say that was so bad? He wished Sasha lived right nearby, then he could have someplace to go, not run away to, just go when he didn't want to be home, someplace that wasn't the park. Stefan didn't really have friends in the building—most of the kids were older—and when anyone asked if he did, he got embarrassed. He had books, and the radio, and lessons, but he knew that wasn't friends. Once in class they'd pretended they were on a desert island and had to say who they wished would be with them from that class and why. Lots of kids said Billy, the class president, because he was smart and class president. Stefan was glad Miss Zimmer didn't get to him because there wasn't really anyone in class he liked enough to be alone with for lots of summers and birthdays. He thought most of the girls and the guys were snobby; someone was always getting the silent treatment or not being invited to someone's house for lunch or to play after school. Kids were always talking about new toys and Debby's mother had a fur coat and all sorts of stuff that was dumb. Someone once said he didn't live in a good street (because his was too close to Harlem, whatever that was), but his was just as clean as other streets and had trees too. Mostly no one bothered him; they said he was quiet, which wasn't as bad as being called stupid or sissy or cheat or worse.

Nobody at school knew about Sasha. A couple of kids took music lessons and one girl danced but they were always complaining they didn't like it, so Stefan decided not to tell how much fun he had at the piano. It wasn't even fun, fun was watching *Dumbo*; his playing was sort of work, but it made him happy.

Maybe Evan wanted to be his friend. . . . ?

"Wake up," someone was saying.

Stefan rolled over. His father stood over him.

"What did Sasha tell you?"

Stefan said, "Nothing," and thought of Eva's picture.

"Tell me."

"Sasha didn't say anything," Stefan was shocked by his lie. He edged back to the wall away from his father.

His father reached for his arm.

"He didn't, he didn't! It was a girl who said it!" He knew now what his father meant. His father took him by the arm and swatted his behind.

"You're a liar."

"He didn't!" Stefan screamed, hearing the next slap without feeling it.

"Stop it," his mother ordered from the door. "How can you hit him? Stefan, it's true? Sasha didn't tell you about the camps?"

"It's true." He shook, feeling his father's grip loosen. "He didn't."

His father let him go and tramped out of the room. "Max—?" His mother followed, leaving Stefan stunned and bewildered. He couldn't understand what it all meant, why they were just by themselves or locked up. From his parents' room he heard horrible yelling in Russian. He went to the door but didn't close it, didn't hide from the noise. If he listened hard enough maybe he'd understand or maybe they'd stop.

"You're not concentrating, I think," Sasha said at his next lesson. Stefan had been doing scales with both hands going in opposite directions, or they were supposed to be. His mother and father had hardly talked to each other all week. Usually after dinner his father went through the papers—he bought three—and read aloud terrible things that Stefan couldn't stand. But for days his father had read nothing and Stefan almost missed hearing about dead girls and cars crashed up.

Stefan stopped playing.

"What's wrong?" Sasha asked, touching his shoulder. Stefan flung his arms around Sasha and burst into tears; the tighter he held Sasha the more he cried. Each time he tried to stop it got worse. Sasha held him, one hand on the back of his neck, the other stroking his hair. Sasha smelled like polished wood, or maybe that was the piano. Stefan never cried with anyone but Scotty.

"You know," Sasha said softly, "when you were very small and just beginning to talk I used to beg you to say my name but you wouldn't. You said Ma-Ma and Da-Da but not Sa-Sa."

"Why not?" Stefan could feel his tears going away.

"I don't know—you just wouldn't."

Stefan giggled; it was funny to think of himself as a baby. "I thought you didn't like me," Sasha went on.

"I *love* you."

"Yes, I know."

Stefan felt very safe resting against his uncle.

"How about something bad to eat? I've got some fresh lady-fingers."

They had milk and ladyfingers crusty with sugar and cinnamon, and more ladyfingers.

"Do you want me to play for you?" Sasha asked when they were done. They sat on the couch.

"Was Schubert bad? Did he hurt people?"

"What?"

"This girl said there were camps where people got hurt by Germans, and Mommy got upset when I told her about the girl saying camps and stuff."

Sasha nodded. "Because you're too young to hear about all that."

"The Germans hurt people?"

"Yes, lots."

"Why?"

"You're young, you wouldn't understand. Nobody understands."

"We're Polish. Did the Germans hurt us too?"

Sasha didn't look at him. "The Germans were terrible, beyond terrible."

Sasha looked at him and around the room as if he was scared someone would get them.

"Why do Mommy and Daddy yell?"

"Things happened to them. To us. It's very hard."

"But you don't yell."

"Who would I yell at?"

"Is what happened to them like being sick?"

"Yes," Sasha agreed quickly as the doorbell rang. "Very sick."

Sasha let his father in. Stefan hardly said good-bye or talked about the lesson. At home he thought maybe he knew something more now: his mother and father were sick, like the mumps only you couldn't see it. His parents yelled, that's how they were sick, and his mother acted funny sometimes, and his father got mad. And if they were sick, so was he, but he didn't know how. He didn't yell at anyone, not even Scotty. Maybe Sasha would tell him.

"Your father says he's very sorry he hit you," his mother said to him at night. His father was in the shower and Stefan was about to go off to bed. He didn't know what to say; his mother looked like he had to answer.

Stefan pouted. "He said I was a liar."

"I explained—"

"He said it. I'm not any liar."

His mother fussed with her hair in a way he knew meant she was annoyed, first with one hand and then with the other; usually it was both together.

"You're being unreasonable."

"*You* are," Stefan challenged, though he didn't know just what the word meant. He had a sudden urge to tell her she was sick—it made him feel so nasty he fled the room.

Evan walked over to him in the yard one afternoon during lunch period. Stefan sat in his favorite spot opposite the side doors, reading *The Three Musketeers* (he hadn't asked anyone yet why there was a candy bar called that). There was a wild game of touch football going on behind Evan, boys whirling and ducking, and the girls who watched shrieked now and then whether they knew what was happening or not.

"How come you're not playing?" Evan asked him.

"How come you're not?" Stefan countered, annoyed—nobody asked him that.

"I have some candy. You want any?"

Stefan's mother didn't like him to eat candy on his own, but he nodded and stuffed his book into his back pocket. Evan brought out two kinds of bars and gumdrops; it was a lot of candy, Stefan thought. He just had a pack of mint chews which he didn't really think were that great.

"My mom says candy isn't good for you."

"So does mine," Evan mumbled through some gumdrops. They stood at the gray metal fence, watching the games.

Evan suddenly launched on a long story about his teeth, and about dentists, and about his mother. There were lots of long words in it, like the one his mother had said in the kitchen about diseases. Stefan didn't get much of what Evan said except that his kind of teeth were "in the family." Evan acted like they were special; maybe that was so, Stefan thought—he'd never seen teeth like them before.

"How do you spell your name?" he asked when Evan stopped.

"Why?"

"Why not?"

"E-V-A-N."

Stefan said, "My aunt's name is Eva," feeling strangely excited.

"Is she nice?"

"She's dead."

"Old people are dead a lot."

Stefan thought this was very smart.

The bell rang; Evan threw off a "seeya" and headed back to his class.

"Hey—" Stefan ran after him. "Want my mint chews?"

"Sure." Evan held out his hands and caught the tossed package. "Thanks."

"Hurry up, children," Miss Zimmer was saying in the yard. He didn't not like her as much as he used to, but still it was good she didn't always do yard patrol. Upstairs Stefan looked at the now-battered cover of his *The Three Musketeers;* Evan was like the middle one, with the same messed-up black hair.

It wasn't until a week later that he had the courage to ask Evan to come over after school with him. There was a lot of telephoning: his mother called Evan's mother and Evan's mother called twice and the day had to be changed. Stefan had a sense of a lot more being involved in Evan coming over than he could figure out.

His mother asked Evan a lot of questions about school, and his parents—too many questions—and Stefan felt embarrassed, wriggled in his chair, anxious to get his friend away from her.

"You have a radio?" Evan switched it on and they settled down for a good look at Stefan's books and anything else there was in the room worth pawing. He dragged things out of drawers and the closet, they played and talked about school. Evan didn't like his teacher either.

"You have neat stuff," Evan announced, surveying the disordered room, and Stefan was proud, but he had hardly anything left to show except Scotty and he'd never show Scotty to a stranger.

Evan asked him, "What church do you go to?"

Stefan shrugged.

"You don't know?" Evan seemed scornful, amazed.

"I guess we don't go to church."

"Why not? Are you a Communist?"

"I am not!" Stefan knew the word was a terrible thing, but he didn't want to say anything else, because he didn't understand about churches. On Sunday mornings you could hear the bells ringing from the church a few blocks up Broadway, and Stefan loved the sound. But his mother and father didn't. It even seemed to make them upset. And when he asked them why they weren't getting dressed up like all the people he had often seen going to church, his mother said, "That's not for us."

"There is no God," his father had said, his face red. "It's all lies."

"Then why do people go to church?" Stefan asked.

41

His father sneered. "They're idiots, that's why."

Stefan couldn't tell any of this to Evan.

"Can I see your thing?" Evan was now pointing to his pants.

Stefan looked down and blushed. He almost felt his father was asking a question he couldn't answer.

"Let's compare," Evan said.

"Okay."

They went to the bathroom to look at each other. Stefan felt he was doing something nasty, but he didn't want to stop, so he kept looking.

When they pulled their pants up, Evan said, "My brother told me that when you get older, snot comes out of them."

They both squirmed and said, "Yuck!"

"And my brother told me that Jew-boys get the ends of theirs cut off or something."

"Why?"

Evan snorted. "Dummy! How should I know?"

Evan's mother came to get him soon after; she was prettier than most mothers, and younger. Also she smelled like a few ladies put together.

"Did you have fun?" his mother asked as the door closed.

Stefan nodded, but he wasn't at all sure. He wanted Evan to like him and wanted to like Evan; they hadn't had fun, though, or not a lot of it.

Alone, he thought about his thing, and Evan's. It felt like a secret, looking at somebody else's.

Lying now on his bed, listening to the radio play quiet slow harpsichord music, Stefan remembered once when he'd take a bath with his father a long time ago. Stefan had stared; his father's thing was big and nasty, floating up in the soapy water. He hadn't asked why his was so little because he was scared and a little sick about it. He didn't like seeing his father without all his clothes on—his father was so dark and shiny, hairy in front and with bulging arms. Once when his daddy was fixing a chair, barefoot, in short pants only—it was a very hot day—his mother had come up behind in the living room to slap the back of his father's neck and she laughed real low and said something about "Gypsies." It made Stefan go all hot in the face. He wondered why now, and what everything meant; maybe he could ask Sasha.

At school the next few days there was a lot of whispering like when someone knew a bad word and no one else did and went around telling some kids and not telling some. Usually Stefan didn't ask; he didn't like spreading words you got in trouble for. Once he'd said a very bad one at home and his mother dragged him to the bathroom and made him wash his mouth out with soap. He'd been so scared, and he didn't know how to do it; he choked and spit and cried with soap water dribbling down his chin.

Only this didn't seem like it was a word somebody had just learned because no one stood around looking all smiley and secret. He finally asked Evan one recess; they hadn't talked too much since Evan's visit because Stefan decided he didn't like the way Evan had said he wanted to see his thing. He hadn't told his parents any of that; it might make his mother cry or his father might hit him and he never wanted to be hit again.

"Did they tell you?" he asked Evan in the yard.

Evan kept his hands in his jacket pockets, not accepting the stick of gum Stefan offered him.

"Who wants to know?" Evan challenged.

"I heard it already," Stefan said, amazed at his lie; he looked down at his book.

"Who told you?"

Stefan turned a page. "Nobody."

"Was it Billy?"

"Maybe."

Evan stamped his foot. "He's a cheat, he said he was gonna wait until he told anybody else."

"I don't care."

Evan ran off.

Stefan found out from Debby, who was not asked to join, but knew anyway, that the whispering was about "The No-Jew Club." In a few days everyone knew including the teachers and parents.

43

Stefan didn't mention it to his mother and father but they found out anyway. His father yelled and swore and wanted to take him out of school. His mother just looked disgusted. The principal had a special assembly and the little twisty-faced man had never scared Stefan more than on the warm afternoon he addressed the whole second grade about how all men were brothers. Stefan didn't listen because no matter what anyone said Evan was not his brother; Evan and the club people were mean. On purpose, too. He didn't want to be anybody's brother who was in a club like that.

Billy and the other two club members in class got the silent treatment for a whole day, which made Stefan very nervous and feel sorry for the three boys, but he was too angry to talk to them. Also, if he did everyone would get annoyed at him. Lots of kids in that class, he found out, were Jewish.

"So *this* is the land of freedom," his father went around saying for days.

"Please," his mother asked weakly. "Don't get so upset."

"They're all the same, Nazis, Poles, Americans. Full of hate and murder! We came here to be free of all that!"

Stefan was stunned by the things his father said after the No-Jew Club was stopped. They didn't make sense. How could his father say Poles were so bad when they were Polish? It all scared him. He didn't understand who it was besides the nasty kids who didn't like Jews. Debby was a Jew. He liked her.

Sasha was over at their house a few times that week; mostly he talked to Stefan's father in Russian, trying to make his father feel better, Stefan guessed. He thought it was his mother who needed to be helped, though he didn't know what there was to do. He heard her sniffling in the bathroom once as she was washing the sink. He wanted to go to her but he didn't: he remembered how she had backed away from him that time. The way she walked around the house was like someone was sick.

Because Sasha came by all that week Stefan was not surprised that Sasha opened the door for him Friday afternoon.

"Where's Mommy?"

Sasha hesitated and the look on his face was so weird Stefan

44

knew there was trouble. He dropped his book bag and rushed to the kitchen, but it was empty. "Mommy?" He went down the hall to their bedroom, Sasha following. Not there—he tried the bathroom. That was empty too. He stood in the middle of his room, glaring at Sasha, who hovered in the doorway.

"Where is she?"

"Stefan—"

"Where is she?" he screamed.

Sasha didn't move. "She had to go away for a while."

It wasn't a dream—his mother had left him. She was gone—she was gone. Stefan gasped and gasped, wanting to cry for her. Sasha crouched down next to him.

"She didn't leave you. She was upset. She had to go away." Stefan watched Sasha's wide mouth open and close, and he heard words, but all he understood was that she had left him. And when Sasha held out his arms Stefan couldn't move. He didn't want to; he wanted to be dead. He wondered at the strange chokey sound he heard—was it coming from him?

"It's best you stay with me for now, your father—" Sasha didn't finish and Stefan didn't care. He watched Sasha find a bag and begin to pack his clothes in it.

"Do you want this? This?" Sasha pointed and Stefan nodded or shook his head. When Sasha finished Stefan rose and silently added *The Three Musketeers* and Scotty, whose other eye was gone now.

They rode in a cab to Sasha's. Stefan didn't answer anything Sasha said to him. Inside him was a blare of word-music: She's gone, she's gone. He couldn't make the ugly sounds go away.

Sasha made him eat something, but Stefan threw up in the bathroom a few minutes later. He clutched the toilet with his hands, wanting to lose in the putrid water what he kept hearing in his head. Sasha held him and cleaned him up, put him to bed with a hot-water bottle and tea.

"Scotty. . . ."

Sasha went to the bag and brought Scotty in. Stefan tucked the blind dog under his arm.

Scotty can't see anymore, he said to himself.

Sasha sat on a chair right near the bed. Stefan fell asleep and woke and fell asleep while Sasha talked to him. Stefan could hardly hear it was so loud in his head. Sasha took his temperature once, or maybe twice.

"You're not sick, that's good. . . . you have to understand. . . . they try to forget everything that happened, but. . . ."

Stefan looked at Sasha's downturned face a long time. "Where did she go?" he whispered.

"I don't know. Maybe to stay with a friend?"

She was gone, she wouldn't come back, Sasha didn't know. "I don't want to go home."

"It'll be all right."

"No. I want to stay with you."

"Don't strain, of course you can stay."

"I hate them."

"Stefan, no. . . ."

"I do, I hate them."

"It's not their fault. We're all scarred."

"Scarred?"

"Inside, it's inside."

Was it like his music?

The phone rang and Stefan leapt up. "It's Mommy!" He tumbled out of bed.

"Stefan."

"It's her—I know it's her!" He raced out and down the hall. As he rushed across the living room he slid not far from the phone table and slammed right into the piano. The noise in his head went away.

When he woke up there was something funny in his head; like a lot of warm blankets, too many. It felt hot inside and he wanted to take some of them off but he didn't know how. Something was on his head too; he felt with one hand.

"No, leave the bandage."

He couldn't see well but it sounded like Sasha from far away. "You hit your head, Stefan, but it's all right."

46

He held out his hands and Scotty was put into them. "I can't see right," he whimpered.

"It's just for now, you'll be fine soon, except for your eyebrow." Stefan was drifting off.

"It'll be a little crooked," he heard Sasha say.

"Mom—"

"They're outside."

"Will I have a scar?" Stefan managed, unable to open his eyes.

"Yes."

Stefan smiled and hugged Scotty. He would be like them now that he had a scar. His mommy would always stay and his daddy would never hit him again or be angry.

"A little scar," Sasha added.

3

"But when is *Daddy* coming back?"

Stefan asked his mother again this time very low: maybe he'd asked too loud was why she didn't answer the first time. He fiddled with the bandage on his eyebrow, wondering what it looked like under. His mother had said very little to him when Sasha brought him back from the cold white hospital he never wanted to be in again. He held on to Sasha's hand all the way home, but it wasn't home anymore; he didn't know where home was. The big shiny halls of the hospital had taken him away and he didn't know how to get back.

Sasha shifted in his chair and said a few Russian words, but his mother still didn't answer. The meal went on in silence. Stefan looked sometimes at the fourth chair; he didn't say anything though—if he kept quiet maybe it would all be the same again. On the way here Sasha had told him something about his mother and

48

father but it was like a hard book that he would understand only when he grew up. He couldn't believe his mother was there.

"She didn't have anywhere to go," Sasha said now as Stefan's mother excused herself.

"She went away," Stefan insisted.

Sasha cleaned up, washed the dishes. Stefan sat watching his uncle, afraid to leave the safety of this room.

His mother was strange. She scared him the way she'd said hello before, her face looking all rubbed and white.

"Are you going too?" Stefan asked.

Sasha smiled. "No, I'll stay tonight."

"You can stay in my room," Stefan ventured.

"I can sleep on the couch." Sasha dried his large hands.

But Stefan was afraid to sleep all alone—no one might be there in the morning when he got out of bed.

"What do you want to do?" Sasha asked with a slow clap of his hands.

Stefan couldn't even shrug; he just wanted to stay near Sasha, that was all.

"Is Daddy coming back?" he asked; the question had stuck itself in his head like music.

Sasha sighed and sat down like he'd been standing somewhere too long.

"Why did he go? Why did Mommy?"

"People have to go away sometimes, when they're unhappy."

Stefan didn't understand how going away made you happier.

Where did people go? How come his father had a place to go and his mother didn't? What did that mean?

Sasha stroked his forehead, rose.

"How about some TV?" Sasha asked him.

They watched in the darkened living room for a long time, but Stefan couldn't see the screen; he was trying to know what "away" was, how you got there. He sat close to Sasha, feeling secure.

Sometimes he looked up to see the lights move across Sasha's face, but mostly he didn't really look at anything. The bandage on his eyebrow itched a little, and Stefan rubbed there trying not to let Sasha notice he did it.

The hospital wasn't away, or a visit; you came back from those. Away was when you never came back, Stefan decided, but not as bad as dying. If his daddy never came back, though, wasn't that kind of being dead?

He heard something funny—it was Sasha snoring. Stefan didn't move; he was anxious not to wake Sasha up.

Sleeping was going away, sort of.

And his mother too; she was home, but she was away. And even if he ate everything on his plate and tried real hard not to mess up his room too much and didn't say anything that made her cry, she might never come back. She would be there—all quiet and washed-out, not really hearing, not really talking, in Polish, or any language—but she would be away.

He didn't know which was worse—his daddy or his mommy. Sasha muttered something in his sleep Stefan couldn't understand, and then woke up like he'd been hit, eyes wide.

"It's me," Stefan assured him.

"It's late."

Passing his parents' room, Stefan called good night, but he didn't know if his mother heard. Sasha knocked on the door and Stefan moved down the hall, into the bathroom to wash. He brushed too hard that night, because when he spit out the white foam it had red in it. In the mirror he pulled open his lips to see where he was bleeding; he couldn't find a place, and nothing hurt. He wished he could be sick and have to go away. He didn't like the hospital, but Sasha would sit near his bed and talk, and pretty nurses would call him "cutey" and ask how Scotty felt and the doctor would make jokes. And his mother wouldn't have to be there—or not a lot.

He didn't turn on the radio in his room, looked around a long time like he might have to leave it some day, to go away too. He pulled back the covers and changed into his pajamas. Stefan folded all his clothes very neat so his mother wouldn't say anything and brought Scotty over from the desk.

Sasha came in and Stefan got into bed.

"Will you sleep here?"

"I'll sit up with you until you fall asleep. Okay?"

That was better than if he had to be alone, so Stefan nodded.

Sasha slipped off his shoes and sat on the outside of the bed, switched off the lamp.

"Is Scotty comfortable?" Sasha asked.

Stefan smiled.

"Shall I tell you a story?"

"Not a book story."

"Well. . . ." Sasha leaned against the wall, an arm around Stefan's shoulder. "When we were little, even younger than you are, I thought I was brave, and once someone dared me to put a pea in my ear because I said that if you did, you would swallow it."

"Did you put the pea in?"

"All the way."

"Then what happened?"

"I forgot it was there."

"You forgot?"

"It wasn't a very big pea, and maybe I thought I would swallow it someday."

"What happened?"

"Some time later I began to have a terrible pain in my ear."

"The pea was *growing?*"

"Right. It's nice and warm in there. But I didn't remember about the pea. When we went to the doctor and he found what was wrong he laughed, but my father thought it was a terrible waste of food."

"One pea?"

"That's what *I* said. Mother laughed, though—she said pea soup wouldn't have been so much trouble."

"What was your mommy like?"

Sasha didn't say anything for a while. "Aren't you sleepy?" he asked, yawning.

The War, Stefan thought, it was always coming in to mess things up; couldn't they ever forget it?

51

"Your mother's tired out," Sasha said, and the room seemed suddenly very dark and quiet to Stefan.

"Where did she go?"

"I don't know, Stefan. She wouldn't tell me."

It must be real bad to go away if she couldn't tell anyone, and looked so weird; maybe his father wasn't happy either wherever he was. Somehow that was all right, if everyone was unhappy. But then why didn't he come back?

Sasha had fallen asleep leaning against the wall; his mouth was open and he didn't look too comfortable. Stefan settled down to sleep but Sasha moaned and started shaking his head, talking and moaning, like he was being hurt. Stefan could feel the skin at the back of his neck all tight and tingly. Sasha was moaning worse and was all stiff like someone tied down who couldn't move. Stefan didn't wake him; a kid told him once that you died if anybody woke you in the middle of a dream even if it was horrible not to wake up.

Sasha's face was all wet when Stefan turned on the bed lamp; he was afraid to be there in the dark with Sasha's bad dream. Sasha began to whimper, his face drenched, twisted. Stefan had never heard anything so awful—people didn't sound like that. He edged out from under the sheets and down the bed away from the white wet face that was torn apart by something Stefan couldn't see. He crept off the bed and stood at the foot, then backed away slowly, quietly, barely able to breathe, while Sasha began to cry—a thin strange sound.

His mother opened the door, glided to the bed, sat and took Sasha up in her thin arms, like a child holding a huge teddy bear.

Sasha mumbled something, awake now, Stefan thought, trans-fixed by the scene on the bed.

"What was it?" his mother asked, soft and warm like she'd never been with *him*—the words were like a blanket.

Sasha shook against her. Stefan wondered how his mother was strong enough to hold Sasha up.

"It was her?" His mother asked in that same witch-like voice.

He thought Sasha whispered "*Tak*"—yes, in Polish—but he couldn't be sure; he felt cold and sweaty.

"Stefan, take linen and go sleep on the couch," his mother ordered without turning, and he was so scared, and so grateful she talked to him that he padded quickly to his closet, took up a blanket and pillow and went off in the dark.

He left Scotty on the bed in case Sasha needed him.

He woke up thinking about school. He sat up sharply, heard his mother in the kitchen and went to her.

"I called your principal and said that you were still not well," she explained, and Stefan was almost sorry he had to stay home. His mother set down his cereal and orange juice; she'd even poured the milk into his bowl—he eyed her, sat at the table.

"Did Sasha go home?"

"No, he's not well, either, he's still here."

"Sleeping?"

"Finish your cereal and you can see him."

He ate, watching her putter around the kitchen, scrubbing the sink and then the oven top. She didn't look so weird today, even hummed a little while she worked. It was scary because she acted all right, like nothing had ever happened, last night or any night.

But she went away, he told himself fiercely, finishing his cereal. "I'm done," he said, as if she might not believe him.

"Fine." She smiled, wringing out a dishcloth.

He stepped along to his room. Sasha lay in his bed, the covers high up, a glass of tea in reach on a chair.

"Morning."

"Are you real sick?" Stefan moved to the bed, overwhelmed by how helpless and sad Sasha looked. He wanted to cry, but you were never supposed to cry near sick people his father told him once, because they might think "it was bad."

"Real sick? Is that the opposite of fake sick?"

Stefan grimaced, sat on the bed and took his uncle's hand. "You feel hot."

"I am a little, but it's nothing." Sasha winked: "I just like to make a fuss."

Stefan laughed.

Sasha squeezed his hand and nodded as if he'd done a very good thing.

Then Stefan noticed Sasha was wearing one of his father's pajamas; he drew his hand away and wanted to break something or cry out. He grabbed Scotty.

"He's been very nice to me," Sasha observed, voice low, tired.

"Scotty likes you."

"Maybe I'll give him lessons too," Sasha joked. Stefan realized he hadn't played in a long time. He felt very lost to be sitting here on a school day with Sasha sick in bed, his father somewhere he didn't know. He tried to remember, but it was all funny to him— he'd think something and it'd get snowy like a bad TV picture. He was stuck right here in this room; other rooms and days were gone.

"How's the patient?" His mother called at the door.

"The patient what?" Sasha grinned. Stefan didn't get it.

She advanced to the bed, leaned down to feel Sasha's forehead, picked up his glass. "I'll get more. And some toast?" Sasha nodded and she left.

"Our grandmother always said tea and toast were the best things for a cold."

"Is that true?"

"Well they taste good."

"Scotty doesn't like tea," Stefan said, gazing down at the battered old dog which he held by its front paws.

"I know, I offered him some."

Stefan wanted to ask about last night, what had scared Sasha— he didn't know anyone could be that scared—and ask about his father and ask and ask. But the answers were so strange when he did get them, that maybe he should just give up.

"What do you want to do?" his mother asked, back with a plate and steaming glass. Stefan sniffed at the tea, not sure if he liked the smell or not. "What do you want to do today?" his mother asked him, helping Sasha sit up.

"Stay with Sasha."

"That's nice."

So Stefan sat in his room, talking to his uncle, reading to him from *The Three Musketeers*, not just straight through, but different parts he liked best, and Sasha fell asleep a few times. All day Stefan heard his mother move from room to room, cleaning. The washing machine sent out a steady rumble from its corner of the kitchen that the vacuum cleaner now and then drowned out. Smells of polish drifted his way. He didn't think Sasha liked all the noise and commotion either, but they didn't mention it, as if his mother wasn't really there, or was only a cleaning lady. She came in with his lunch not looking tired or any different than she used to—her hair was a little damp and maybe some dirt had got on her face. Around dinner time, when Sasha slept again, Stefan found food in the kitchen and his mother wasn't there. He hadn't heard her go out. The bedroom door wasn't open; he stood outside it trying to hear if she was inside, but there wasn't any sound and he couldn't be sure.

Was she really gone now?

Stefan checked on Sasha: he was still asleep, so Stefan sat alone in the kitchen, trying to make himself eat enough to be a dinner. He couldn't look at or taste the food, just forked and chewed and swallowed, and then tried to wash the plates, afraid he might break one, but more afraid to just leave them on the table. When he finished he gulped down some milk; it didn't taste good and he almost wanted to spit. The kitchen seemed very big to him by himself—all the cabinet doors, the humming fridge that leaned back a little like it was showing off, the glitter of pots on the wall over the stove. . . . What if he never came back, he wondered, what if this was the last time he ever walked out of the kitchen through the dining room, the foyer, down the hall to his bedroom. He didn't know—he couldn't think right.

Sasha was well enough to get up and make tea for himself. The pajamas were too short at their ends and tight too; Sasha laughed at himself in the closet mirror, but Stefan couldn't: even if they didn't fit, they were his daddy's.

55

Sasha went back to bed to drink his tea, sitting up now and not looking as white as before. Stefan didn't mention his mother once; he noticed how Sasha's glance kept flying to the door, expecting her. He didn't ask Stefan anything and Stefan kept quiet. If his mother was really gone then she was gone—he was tired trying to understand. At least Sasha wasn't gone, and Stefan knew without asking that Sasha would never leave him because Sasha felt bad too, left behind. They would stay together, Stefan was sure.

"Where will you sleep tonight?"

Stefan looked out at the dark sky; somehow night surprised him today. He counted the lit windows in the building across theirs.

"On the couch."

"Will you be all right?"

Stefan blinked—it was a funny kind of question, or maybe the way Sasha asked it.

He nodded.

"Shall I make you cocoa?"

"Ooh—" Stefan leapt up to follow Sasha into the kitchen, passing his parents' door as if there wasn't a room there, just a wall.

He had homework to catch up with, but the assignments he got the next day in class from Miss Zimmer were almost a relief. He would have something to do that wasn't watching television or talking or eating—what he really did when he did those things was worry and feel bad. Sasha took him to school because he was too late to get the school bus. Stefan wished Sasha could always take him places, but the wish wasn't too big: what he most wanted was for the bad things to not keep happening so fast.

The day went okay until at the end when they had free period for the first time in days. Kids flocked to the long low supply cupboards for paints and paper, clay, wire, crayons, tape, and glue, but Stefan stayed near his desk watching the jostling girls and boys at the back of the room.

Miss Zimmer came over. "Stefan, don't you want to make something pretty today?"

"No."

Miss Zimmer shook her head. "You have to make something

pretty." She moved on to direct her class and Stefan followed; if he had to do it, that was different. There wasn't too much left to choose from—everyone was settling down to their work—and Stefan surveyed the littered shelves dimly. How would he make something pretty of this stuff?

He got the bathroom pass so he could put off the decision. In the big white-smelling toilet (it was rude to call it a toilet even in your head, but he didn't feel too polite) he washed and washed his face with cold water and then hot, and sat up on a sink to look out the high deep-grated window at the park, wishing he could get sick. He knew if you stuck a finger down your throat you threw up, but he didn't know which finger, and how you did it exactly, and it was nasty. Still, he didn't want to go back to class.

Where was his daddy? Was he driving somewhere? Would he come back? Stefan began to feel his eyes wet and he got off the sink to hurry back to class; he didn't want to cry by himself in that place—someone might find him—and crying didn't help anything, Stefan was beginning to decide. So he raced back to class; it was okay, though, because Miss Zimmer had gone out and Sophie, her monitor, was too busy at Miss Zimmer's desk mangling bits of clay to care who came in or out. Stefan found some paper for drawing and colored pencils that were too sharp: they scratched on the paper. He was doing a project, though. He tried a house, and then a walk in the park, and finally a piano, but nothing looked close to what it was supposed to be. All around him flowers grew and blossomed, figures took shape—pretty things—and Stefan couldn't make anything at all, pretty or not.

When school ended Stefan tore up his drawings and threw them away. He didn't want to go home, he felt that like a heat inside him; he would go anywhere but home: it was so awful there with his daddy gone, his mother strange. He felt all alone as he left school in a sudden fog—everything looked unfamiliar: the yard, the metal fence, the kids and cars, like he'd been gone for years and years, or was from a different place now. He didn't want to go home; he didn't want to come back to this school either.

He would go to Sasha. Stefan almost trembled with the terror and demand of his thought, but suddenly he was not afraid. It was very simple—he knew he just had to skip the school bus and take the Broadway bus instead, and get off blocks before where his regular stop would be. Sasha was so unlike his parents that Stefan had always thought of the two apartments as very far apart, but it wasn't that many blocks when he counted them up; he even sometimes walked there on Sundays, with his parents.

He would probably never go anywhere again with his parents, even if he wanted to, which he didn't, not today. Stefan shrunk back to the entrance and inside, heard the school bus finally drive off. If anyone asked why he was in the lobby he would say he was waiting for his ride. He stayed there a few minutes and then hurried out to the city bus stop across the street. His mother always made sure in the morning that he had change with him "in case"; his father called it "silver" and Stefan liked the way that sounded. He stood now fingering his change, trying to look like he belonged there; he was afraid someone might find him, maybe Miss Zimmer, and make him go home, but no one did and he almost tripped up the stairs when the crowded bus roared up, huge front window like an eye. The bus driver stared at him, he thought, so after he dropped in the coins he squeezed as far back as he could, hiding in the forest of bigger school kids who were all laughing at something. Stefan clutched a pole, waiting to get off at Sasha's block.

The bus thinned out and he was nervous in case someone might know him and ask where he was going, but no one did and he got off on Broadway at Sasha's street feeling dizzy like the time in first grade he played a toy soldier in the Christmas play and had to march around and around when the long clock bonged—which was too many times, so that he almost got sick before the last time he had to march and when he bowed at the end and his big hat came off, his head was so funny he couldn't pick it up.

He was hungry; he hoped Sasha had cookies or something good. And cocoa. Stefan didn't look at anyone as he cut down to Fort Washington Avenue and turned the corner. Inside, though, he kept pressing Sasha's button and there was no answer. He stayed there real long, pushing in all sorts of different ways but no one buzzed back, Sasha was gone too.

Stefan turned and trailed out of the lobby. He sat down outside on the wide front stoop, holding his book bag tight so he wouldn't cry.

"Aren't you Mr. Borowski's nephew?"

Stefan looked up through blurred eyes at the tiny white-haired woman he thought he knew.

"I'm Mrs. Mendelsohn, dear. Do you remember me? I live on the same floor as your uncle."

He thought so—he nodded.

"Are you waiting for him?"

He nodded and she eyed him for a very long time, making him feel like she knew he wasn't supposed to be there.

"I'll wait with you," she announced, her voice thin and squeezy. She began to tell him all about her grandson without asking him to say anything, which was good. He kept wondering where Sasha was, beginning to feel really hungry; he almost asked Mrs. Mendelsohn if she would give him something to eat but he was afraid to—it wasn't nice, but also, worse, she might ask him questions and he didn't want to tell her anything. When he saw Sasha strolling up the block he was so upset he didn't even wave, just stared.

"Look who is here, Mr. Borowski," Mrs. Mendelsohn pointed. Sasha strode up to them. "Stefan?"

Mrs. Mendelsohn began a long shrill speech in Russian that followed them all the way upstairs; she was mad at Sasha but Stefan couldn't tell why. Upstairs, she patted Stefan's shoulder and murmured, "Poor child."

Sasha led him inside and sat him down. "She thought I kept you waiting," he explained flatly. "Now what is this?"

"I wanted to see you."

"You're too young to wander around the city." Sasha sat absolutely still, eyes hard.

"I didn't wander, I came here from school. I'm smart—I know how."

59

"What about your mother?" Sasha reached past him for the phone. "You should never do this," he said. Stefan had never seen him so far away and cold.

Sasha sat with the phone and it rang for a long time until he hung up.

"See? She's not home—she doesn't care."

"You have to go home. I have a set of keys."

Stefan jumped up. "No, don't make me!"

Sasha looked away. "You have to."

"Please?"

"You're not my son."

"I want to be!" He tried to hug Sasha but his uncle held him back. "Why can't I be? They hate me!"

"No, it's not true." The buzzer rang and Sasha broke away to answer. Stefan crumpled on the couch, wanting to die. If Sasha didn't like him then no one did.

He soon heard his mother's voice at the door and sat up. She saw him and smiled and she and his uncle were soon chatting as if she'd just come over for a visit, not to find him. Stefan watched her as she sat with hands folded, face attentive, interested; it was like being with someone who was pretending to be his mother. Sasha seemed angry at him still, so when his mother suggested a walk because the early evening air was "so fresh" he stood and headed for the door, not sorry to leave. If no one wanted him it didn't matter where he went, who he stayed with. The three of them strolled down the low hill and along the tree-lined length of the avenue as if it were a Sunday afternoon, but it was almost night. Usually Stefan liked the way the trees on both sides of the street reached up and touched the middle to make the street like a tunnel. Now, though, he felt confused and angry, answered when his mother and Sasha spoke to him but volunteered nothing; their interlocked voices—now English, now Polish or Russian—were no more to him than the whoosh of bicycles or the harsh-edged talk of strolling couples. It wasn't home he walked to, just a place he lived.

He would never play the piano again, he almost said out loud when they finally entered his building's elevator. His mother had dinner ready and they ate in the same way they'd walked. Stefan left the kitchen when he was done and left them to talk; he didn't care what they said, didn't care if he never saw both of them again.

Why didn't they all go away and stop being so mean to him? His parents' door was wide open and Stefan entered the dark musky room that used to scare him when he was little—thick curtains to beat back the light and the heavy black furniture looked like it wanted to be alive and do something nasty—but now he wasn't afraid. He entered the silent room where he'd sometimes fled at night when he woke from a nightmare or couldn't sleep because of a noise he heard in the hallway like something coming to get him. Always he'd have to go back, could stay under the covers just a little before they sent him away.

"I heard something," he would say, or "I was scared." Now he was in the room to find something. He stood looking at the bed, at the shelf of books behind it, the night tables, the dresser, the table with the mirror, looking for something more than the smell of his father's after-shave. He opened the closet where his father's clothes hung, large and silent, shirts and suits, and pants upside down, the tie rack inside the door dripped cloth icicles: red-and-blue stripes, and blue-and-red, gray, black, layers and rows of ties. He fingered them, wanted to pull one down and wrap it around his neck even though he didn't know how to make it fit. He peered up at the top shelf lined with hatboxes. He stroked the empty suit sleeves, soft or grainy, one was even rough, reaching into the pockets. At last, after all the empty ones, he found a hard bit of silver; it was one of his daddy's cuff links: round and flat with a fancy "M" on it. He wanted to close the door, crawl in among the shoes all lined up, each with its shoe tree holding it tight and stretched, and sit in the darkness that smelled like his father.

He bore the cuff link like a treasure to his room and closed the door while he decided where to hide it; he didn't trust his mother or Sasha. But there wasn't any place he could put it his mother couldn't find. Then he saw Scotty, and knew: a hole had grown under Scotty's blanket. He stepped to the desk, hesitated, and then picked up his dog. Wincing, he shoved the bit of silver as deep inside as he could, apologizing under his breath. He rooted in the bottom desk drawer, found a needle and dark thread. He sat on the floor, bent over, fixing the hole to make it secret. He kept sticking his fingers and the needle and thread were always separating, but he finally did it—no one would really notice since Scotty was so scruffy anyway. Even though he wasn't sleepy, Stefan washed up, changed and slid into bed so he wouldn't have to say good-bye to Sasha. He lay in the dark on his side, facing the wall, trying to pretend himself asleep but it didn't work; he felt all tight and squeezed and even breathing real deep like his mother once said would work only made him more awake.

"Stefan?" Sasha knocked on the half-open door.

He didn't move.

"Are you asleep?" Sasha stood there a minute and then left, closing the door.

Good, Stefan thought rolling onto his back to glare at the ceiling.

He woke feeling very hot and sick, but he knew it wasn't really being sick, just how you sometimes were when you slept funny, too long, or when you didn't think you would. In the cool bathroom he drank three cups of water, but then he didn't know what to do. He was too tired to go back to bed, or to eat anything, besides, it wasn't good to eat late at night—it was probably real late, he guessed. He switched off the bathroom light; out in the hall, though, he heard a funny noise. It came from the living room, maybe, a soft hissing noise like the flames that had once burst from a frying pan his mother held on the stove, sending Stefan under the kitchen table where he stayed, his mother said, until they gave him ice cream to come out.

Stefan was scared, pressed now against the wall, like something might be passing him he didn't want to get near. He edged down the hall, his bare feet sticking to the linoleum. At the end of the hall he heard it again; someone was in the living room, talking, whispering. Was Sasha still there? But there wasn't any light on. Then Stefan recognized his mother's voice. He stood in the dark hallway that stretched back to his room, his bed, unable to move from listening to his mother whisper to herself in a language that he didn't know, but it sounded like German a little. There was no one else in the room—Stefan was sure of it. She was in the living room all alone at night, talking to herself. She couldn't be reading aloud if there was no light. It made him afraid.

He didn't know how long he listened, how long he breathed as quietly as possible so she wouldn't know he was there, how long he did not move or think. Somehow, he made his way back down the hall, away from what he did not understand. He closed his door, wishing there was a lock on it.

At dinner the next evening, he and Sasha did most of the talking while his mother just ate quietly, slowly. Stefan told Sasha all sorts of things about what happened at school that day even though he didn't really care and could see that Sasha only half-listened. Sasha looked right at him, nodded a lot, asked questions in that funny sort of cheerful voice Stefan knew adults used when they were thinking of something else.

But someone had to talk—they couldn't just sit there at the huge dining room table and say nothing. When the doorbell rang his mother didn't look up; Sasha smiled across at him strangely and rose to get the door.

His father walked in, set down a small suitcase, ruffled Stefan's hair, kissed his mother's cheek and sat at the fourth place, opposite his mother.

"I'll get you something," his mother said, going out to the kitchen.

"Fine," his father nodded.

Stefan just stared and stared—his father was so beautiful he wanted to cry. But he couldn't even talk.

His mother returned balancing full plates and silver like a waitress and they went on with dinner.

"Your eyebrow will be all right, Sasha tells me."

Stefan couldn't stop gaping.

"Your food's getting cold," his father smiled, but it wasn't a real smile. Stefan looked from face to face, stunned, trying to find the answer. His mother's eyes didn't meet his; Sasha kind of shushed him with a raised finger, and his father didn't seem like he'd been away even a minute—but it wasn't real, it couldn't be: Friday no one was home and now everyone was.

"Where did you go?"

Hands stopped.

"Not far."

"How far?"

Sasha was trying to get his attention but Stefan wouldn't stop. "Why'd you go away?" Stefan slammed down his knife and fork.

"You're too little to understand—"

"Everyone says that!" Stefan stood so fast his chair fell behind him. He wanted to hurl his plates across the table.

"Take him to his room," his father told Sasha.

"So you can go away again!" Stefan cried. "So Mommy can too!"

Sasha took him by the shoulders, but he struggled and Sasha had to pick him up and carry him out. Stefan felt all white like he could kill somebody. Sasha took him down to his room the way *he* carried Scotty.

Sasha closed the door and moved to the desk, sat down, and Stefan followed, sat on his bed arms crossed tight, still wanting to break something, anything.

"You're making it very hard," Sasha began so gently it surprised Stefan, but that only made him feel worse now that Sasha wasn't going to yell at him, and he felt more like yelling himself.

"Where did he go?" Stefan demanded.

"To stay with a friend, another teacher."

"In the city?"

Sasha nodded.

"Why didn't you make him come home?"

Sasha sighed. "I couldn't. He had to come back when he wanted."

So his father had left first?

64

"Your mother couldn't stand it—she went to get him." Sasha rubbed his forehead. "It was very bad."

She went to get him? Like he'd looked for Sasha. Suddenly Stefan felt very sorry for his mother. She hadn't left him; she went away to look for his father. He wanted to laugh or run or something. She didn't leave him, not really.

"What—?" Sasha wondered when Stefan jumped off the bed.

"I want to see her."

"No—let them talk." Sasha came to him, held his shoulders.

"She didn't leave me," Stefan moaned, beginning to cry.

Sasha held him close and Stefan clutched the large warm man who loved him. Stefan hugged Sasha and cried, happier than he knew he could be.

"No, she didn't leave you," Sasha agreed and Stefan knew Sasha wasn't lying. This time.

4

There was music again—Stefan could listen to the radio now that his mommy and daddy were back; he could sit in one spot again for a long time without wanting to jump up and go somewhere or cry or throw something. The music could come to him again, persuade and love him like it used to. It was like eating when you hadn't known you were hungry. He had trouble turning the radio off, liked it to play even when he wasn't right there so it could make his room friendly and comfortable.

And the next Sunday he had a piano lesson—it was so neat to sit at the familiar broad smile of keyboard, catch the gleam of his smaller fingers reflected alongside Sasha's when Sasha corrected him or played along. Stefan's hands were stiff, though, like they'd been sick.

"It's okay," Sasha kept telling him when he made mistakes, and Stefan didn't mind so much that his parents were right there. He didn't know why, but his mother had taken the bus up with him and his father for this lesson. She had on a soft yellow dress that made her look pretty and young, and his father wore a light summer suit and light shoes—it was almost a kind of holiday.

"That was very nice," his mother said quietly when the lesson finished, smoothing her hair. Stefan flushed with pride.

"He's good, Sasha," his father added. This was too much for Stefan, who wanted to hug everybody and laugh. Instead, he held a music book tightly, almost crushing the pages together, and moved to sit in Sasha's chair.

"Sasha?" his father asked, and Sasha began to play something Stefan didn't know—it was ugly, but not really, with a stubborn melody: nervous sort of music. Stefan watched Sasha's still, closed face, while he glowed with praise, with the joy of having played again. To have his parents both there with him when he thought he'd never see them again was—

He didn't know what it was, except big enough to keep him from thinking why really his father had disappeared those few days. It would be nasty to ask now that everything was good again, nasty even to think about it.

"I'll know when I grow up," Stefan promised himself, pushing the problem as far away as he could.

Sasha finished; the piece was by a Russian composer whose name Stefan couldn't say—it almost sounded made up.

"Let's go have lunch," Sasha suggested, and they were soon out in the sun, strolling along to a nearby Italian restaurant. Stefan walked ahead; he kept turning to see where they were, usually not far. His mother walked in the middle.

At the dark crowded place—it was too dark for Stefan—Sasha told a long funny story about a pupil's mother who wanted the girl to play harder pieces than she ever could. Sasha had tried explaining to the woman who kept saying, "But she's very myoosical."

His father talked a lot about problems in his department at school. Stefan didn't get most of that, so he just ate his salad and soup and looked around at other families, other kids, and then dug into the main course, which looked a little wet, but Stefan wasn't going to complain. His mother hardly said anything, a little like she was giving all of them the silent treatment. She didn't look mean, though, just quiet.

Stefan didn't like it that after dinner Sasha didn't come home with them—he wished Sasha could always be at their house. They walked home since it was a nice night, cool, and lots of people were out. His mother was between him and his father and Stefan kind of thought they were taking care of her, but he didn't know how or if it was true. His father said things to her in different languages; she just brought out yes's and no's and not much more.

"She talked so much last week, at night," Stefan couldn't help thinking, looking up at her still, even face; he wondered why she didn't say anything. Once, when they crossed a street, she took his hand—he was so surprised he pulled it away, and then felt bad, and let her take it. And he walked a little closer to his mother.

When he was getting ready for bed, his father came in, turning down the radio.

His father took the desk chair and sat on it, looking as big as a judge.

Stefan sat on the bed, clutching his pajamas—he was embarrassed to change in front of his father, whose eyes were now squinty, like that nasty Mrs. Lewis who'd stopped him on the way to the bathroom last year in first grade.

"Why do you think I went away?" his father asked suddenly. Stefan caught sight of Scotty on the desk behind his father and thought of the cuff link inside. He shrugged.

"No, really," his father said, leaning forward.

Stefan couldn't help shrinking back.

"What did your mother tell you?"

"Nothing."

That seemed to surprise his father, who gazed off into a corner of the room. When their eyes met it almost hurt Stefan.

"You don't know what it's like."

Stefan gulped, afraid of what was coming.

"Before you were born I almost thought. . . ." His father shook himself, said good night and left without asking what Sasha had told him, which was a lot—it would've been hard to lie without getting caught. His father had a way of just staring if he didn't believe what you said, just staring until you told the truth. But his father didn't scare him tonight the way he used to before he went away—Stefan didn't know why that was; his mother did scare him, though, because she was different.

Stefan went to bed after he turned off the radio, wondering if his mother was still talking to herself at night, and what she said.

Dinner Monday night was pretty quiet until his mother announced: "I want to go to school."

Stefan looked up. His school was closed now; he didn't understand.

"School?" his father asked, eyeing her.

"I don't do anything—I want to do something."

Stefan thought of how she was always straightening and dusting and washing.

There was a silence and then his father said, with a funny smile: "But you have a degree from— From back home."

"I'll get another," she shot back, chin up. "Well . . . what do you think, Stefan?"

He didn't know what to think, and almost said that to test how much courage he had.

"See?" Stefan's father said. "Your son is surprised too."

"It's neat," Stefan mustered, and his mother nodded fiercely. Dinner went on just as quiet as before except once or twice his father muttered "school" under his breath like it was a joke. Stefan pictured his mother at a desk like his with a whole lot of other ladies—but they'd be too big to fit. Stefan stifled a giggle, pretending it was a cough, and then really did start coughing so bad he had to get some water.

Why would you go to school if you didn't have to, unless you were a teacher?—and sometimes he didn't think his daddy liked going there either, even though he didn't have to do homework, real homework; looking at somebody else's work couldn't be as hard as having your own to do. And his father didn't even have to go every day or stay all day either—Stefan was in school more.

If his mother went to school she wouldn't be home as much. Maybe she didn't want to be.

Suddenly Stefan felt real scared—what if his daddy had gone away because of him? And his mother too? What if it was all his fault what happened? He'd never thought that before; it could be why everyone was so strange, why Sasha didn't tell him the truth.

"But I didn't do anything," Stefan whispered.

Stefan couldn't concentrate at all the next lesson. Sasha corrected him very patiently, but after only about twenty minutes. Sasha put a hand down on his.

"What's wrong?"

Sasha's hand was so big; Stefan wished he were big, so he could play without any mistakes and people wouldn't lie to him or tell him to wait for anything.

"You're shaking," Sasha said, putting an arm around his shoulders. "What happened? Is something—" Sasha hesitated, "—something wrong at home?"

"He doesn't like me," Stefan muttered.

"What?"

"That's why he left—he doesn't like me." It sounded so much like the truth Stefan wanted to cry, but that didn't make you feel better, and only babies cried anyway.

"Why do you say that? Come, let's sit on the couch and you can tell me."

"The lesson—"

"You can learn that line next week. Now tell me."

Sasha's big pale face was so kind, like one big smile. It came back to Stefan how once he used to think Sasha was like a magician, mysterious, but he didn't think that now, not really.

"That's why he left," Stefan insisted.

"He *loves* you."

"Who says?"

Sasha frowned. "I say."

"*He* never does."

"Your father isn't like that; he wouldn't say it."

"He says other stuff—lots."

Sasha shook his head. "It's different to say you love someone. Harder."

"But he's my daddy."

"I know," Sasha nodded.

"And he went away." Stefan felt real nasty, like he'd stuck a stick down an ant hole to break it all up.

"People have to go away sometimes. Love has nothing to do with it. . . ."

Stefan stared at Sasha until Sasha glanced away.

"And Mommy's going too," Stefan produced, triumphant. "She's going to school."

Sasha smiled.

"No, *really*," Stefan pressed.

"When?"

Stefan shrugged. "She didn't say, but she is." He was sure his mother would do it, though he didn't know why yet; her face had been too steady when she mentioned it, like when something hurt and you didn't want anyone to know.

"I wonder why she—" Sasha broke off and went to make tea and get chocolate milk for Stefan.

His mother was going to take a test to see if they would let her in—not at his father's school but another one downtown. It was still strange to Stefan that anyone would want to go to school when they'd already been there, but his mother said lots of people did it, so he guessed they knew why. Maybe when you were older, fun was different than when you were still in school. He hoped he would never want to do it, though. "Once is enough," he'd told Scotty.

His mother was talking more—she had all sorts of papers and booklets she even read at dinner, read to them, but mostly to his father who explained whatever she didn't understand, which was hardly anything compared to the stuff Stefan missed: like "credit." He thought that was when you didn't pay for something, but it was also what they gave you for taking courses; maybe it was like a pass to take more, like sending in jar labels to get a cup with a neat picture on it. The questions he asked seemed to annoy his father, who even said once, "Please—we're figuring this out," so Stefan only asked his mother when they were alone.

Sasha brought his chocolate and some cookies.

"What will she study?" Sasha asked, settling into his chair.

"School, I guess." He hoped she didn't have any mean teachers like Miss Zimmer. Were teachers ever mean to grown-up students? Maybe they couldn't be.

"Will she take your father's classes?"

"She's going to another school."

Sasha fell silent.

Stefan downed his milk and fiddled some with the glass while Sasha sipped his tea.

"Well," Sasha brought out, smiling. "I think this is a good thing. It will give her something to do."

That word again—why did people have to "do" things more than they did already?

"You must help her," Sasha announced.

"Me?"

His uncle nodded very slowly. "She'll be nervous, and there'll be all that work she's not used to."

"But she works at home."

Sasha laughed. "It's not the same, you know that. What about cleaning your room and doing arithmetic homework? Aren't they different?"

"They're both yucky."

Sasha came over the night his mother went to take her exam to keep Stefan company. It was beginning to be vaguely reassuring to Stefan that adults had to take tests and worry about them too, just like kids. Even Sasha and his father were nervous and it wasn't their exam. His mother was quiet and a little sick-looking when she left for the bus; his father had a night class and would be bringing her home.

So he and Sasha watched TV, Sasha looking at his watch now

and then to say things like: "She's just starting," and Stefan felt almost like he was with his mother—tests scared him too. Sometimes he even went all blank and didn't know anything he could put on his paper.

"Of course she'll pass," Sasha assured him. "She was a wonderful student back home, she went to the university before— And our schools were much harder than yours here. Your father says so, and he would know."

Harder? Stefan quailed; if schools were harder in Poland he bet the teachers were meaner.

Later his mother came in talking: "It wasn't bad—it really wasn't bad," she kept saying, perched on the arm of the couch, hands smoothing her skirt, straightening the collar of her blouse: restless, excited. Her face was as red as if she'd been in a cold place and her eyes were very big.

"It was an essay—" Here she went on to tell about the test in detail, hardly any of which Stefan understood, but he knew from her voice and hands and eyes that she was happy.

His father stood in the arched living room doorway, smileless, looking very serious in his blue three-piece suit.

Sasha leaned to take his mother's hand. "So it was good?"

His mother grinned and it sounded to Stefan like what she said next was the same as before.

His father went to change.

"Are you thirsty?" Stefan asked; he always was after a test. She smiled and he went to the kitchen to get iced tea; he hoped this was what Sasha meant by "You must help her"—would he have to vacuum too and things like that? When he brought her the tea she was still on the couch arm, but saying something different.

". . . and of course the coffee wasn't very good (thank you) but I thought if I could make myself sit down and actually drink it I would relax and he said, 'Are you taking the exam too?' and he was even more nervous—he couldn't drink anything." She shook her head, sipped from the glass.

"Not even bad coffee?" Sasha murmured.

"Not even that."

Stefan sat further from his mother than before; she was so strange tonight—all speeded up and beautiful, and it awed him.

"He told me how important it was for him to pass and come back to college to go on to business school and he was so nervous it worked on me much faster than the coffee because I had to be less nervous than he." She glowed now. "And I did. I helped him be less nervous too."

Stefan wondered who she was talking about.

"He's very nice," his mother added in a different voice—one he didn't know.

"Who is?" His father walked in and stood near her, put a hand on her shoulder.

"I should go," Sasha said, adding a kiss and a "Congratulations."

"Who's nice?"

"Leo. A student I have met." She rose to walk Sasha to the door. Stefan followed; the good-byes took a long time, he thought. When Sasha finally left, his mother turned from the door looking closer to the way she usually did: pale, quiet.

Stefan tried to think of something "You must help her" to say, but nothing came because his father stood there in the foyer like a guard with a gun, so Stefan just hugged her real quick when he said good-night. He didn't hug his father.

It was a good thing for his mother if she was so happy, but not a good thing for his father; Stefan couldn't tell why, unless his daddy thought she might be going to school to get away from them.

He knew that every summer for years Sasha had been going to Rockaway where he was the only roomer in a house near the beach owned by a woman whose husband had left her a piano she didn't play. The piano was small, Stefan remembered from a day visit last year, and a little buzzy, but Sasha didn't seem to mind giving up his Baldwin.

"It's a relief not to have lessons. All that running around." Sasha told him the three months off were perfect; in the first he got used to the change, in the second enjoyed it, and in the third waited to go back. Sasha returned brown and shiny; Stefan remembered one summer—he must've been little—when he was afraid to say hello to Sasha because he looked so different.

"Won't you miss me?" Stefan asked near the end of his last lesson before Sasha left for the summer. The ride to the beach seemed hours long to Stefan, long and hot, through places he didn't know that just made him tired, and last year they only went twice.

Sasha shook his head. "I won't miss you at all." Stefan didn't know what to make of the grim words. "Because you're coming to stay with me."

"What!" He grabbed Sasha's arm.

Sasha nodded. "As soon as school is finished."

They didn't really go anywhere summers, except for little times, because his father taught during the summer too, and Stefan had envied kids who wrote about places when they had "What I did last summer." His father said in the summer you could "take advantage of the city," but to Stefan it was mostly nasty and hot, and even though he liked museums, they sometimes made him tired because there was too much to look at and not enough places to sit down, and the bathrooms were scary and far away.

Sasha stood to turn up the small air conditioner.

"It's not a joke?" Stefan had to ask.

"No joke. Your parents think it's a good thing."

Sasha had two rooms at Mrs. Mannion's, so it would just be him and Sasha all summer.

"It's like a birthday," he breathed.

Sasha closed the piano lid. "People have many birthdays," he said. It sounded so nice Stefan didn't ask what it meant.

He could hardly wait for school to end; he tried doing his work faster to make it go quick but he couldn't; the days were sticky, and as annoying as flies you couldn't catch. There were lots of fights at school and kids forgot their homework; Miss Zimmer even yelled at them once for not listening—that just made things hotter. His father was in a bad mood most of the time; his father would come in from class pulling off his clothes as he headed for the bedroom.

"Why doesn't Daddy take off his tie before he gets home if it's so hot?"

His mother looked up from a book list. "I don't know," she said. "He doesn't."

Looking at his father drag at his tie, forehead dark and shiny, made Stefan uncomfortable. He tried staying out of his daddy's way without making it look like that's what he was doing, just in case his father got mad and decided not to let him go stay with Sasha. Stefan was afraid to choose anything he wanted to take—it might be bad luck, and also he didn't know how, really. He guessed his mother would do it when he had to go.

She was different. She spent a lot of time reading ahead for September; the living room was peppered with her books—but it didn't really take her away. She answered his questions like she heard them better now. When he asked her why she wanted to do so much work, she told him it was like his piano and he began to understand. Also, the way his mother walked and stood and smiled was so much lighter he was convinced she had fun with all those hard-looking books. Once, when she wasn't around, he picked through them, careful not to lose her place anywhere, but they were all much too old for him, full of words he could just guess how they sounded but not the meaning.

"Do you want to be a teacher like Daddy?"

She smoothed her hair back with one hand, the other fiddled with a book she opened and closed. She sat so straight in the fat brown chair it looked like a throne.

"I don't know. I didn't think so far ahead. Wouldn't that be something. . . ."

He talked to Sasha in Rockaway twice on the phone before the end of the school year, feeling sad each time when he hung up, even though sooner and sooner he'd go out to be with his uncle the whole summer. The last Friday did finally come and Stefan wanted to pack his things for the next day's drive before he ate dinner.

"There's time," his mother assured him, making him sit down at the table. His father was at school doing late work and Stefan chattered freely about going.

". . . and there's a piano there so I can keep playing."

"I know. You've told me. I saw."

"Can we pack now?" Stefan pressed after dinner.

"No dessert?"

He raced to his room before her, flung open the closet and began pulling things.

"Wait, why don't you sit there and help?"

So she packed for him, asking sometimes what he wanted, neatly folding a huge pile of clothes into a not very big brown suitcase. Into another smaller one she placed books and Scotty and anything else he remembered.

"You can always call when you need something," his mother said matter-of-factly and Stefan suddenly felt sad to be leaving, even though his parents said they'd come visit. He kind of wished his mother could come for more than a visit, but she had lots of work to do, and it would be better just him and Sasha, Stefan guessed. When she finished he wondered if it was dumb to take Scotty, and was thinking it over when his mother stood the bags side by side near his door and went out to the living room.

She was always reading now—all kinds of books followed her around the house—as soon as she ended one she began another, and sometimes she read a few at the same time. This particularly impressed Stefan, who didn't know you could do that; he read his books straight through, even if he didn't like them: it was "good discipline" his father said. He wished he was grown up enough so his mother could talk about her books to him like she did to that new friend of hers, Leo, who phoned her sometimes.

His father didn't like discussing books when he wasn't at school and didn't have to. Stefan thought also that maybe his daddy didn't like his mommy's books, because he saw his father pick up one from a chair once like it was nasty and put it on the floor when he sat down. But Sasha said his father was always irritable at the end of a semester.

Stefan had trouble sleeping most of the night—he kept waking and thinking he needed something but didn't know what and in the morning he ate breakfast only because he had to. The food didn't look any good at all. His eyes felt scratchy and in the car he fell asleep, so he didn't know if his mother and father talked any more or less than at the kitchen table. His parents both wore white; it was like being at the beach already.

All the houses on Mrs. Mannion's street were wide and old with cracked steps and bushes; he almost didn't remember which one it was, and then they stopped in front of a green one with a gray roof, white shutters. "This one is Sasha's," he thought, scanning the porch. Stefan waited until they were parked, and even then he was suddenly reluctant to leave the car, he didn't know why.

He followed his parents up the broad high stairs, embarrassed, confused, almost like it was his first day at school. There were no lights on and it looked real dark inside, unless that was just because of the sun being so bright. His father knocked twice and called hello.

Maybe it's a mistake, Stefan thought. Maybe he's not here.

His mother looked down and up the hot deserted street. "Sasha?" His father opened the screen door and stepped inside. Overhead Stefan heard some noise and Sasha appeared at the top of the narrow stairs.

"I fell asleep," he called, grinning. "Sorry."

The little dark hallway was too crowded for all four of them; Sasha led them into a large fancy living room that was so thickly rugged and curtained and planted Stefan felt he was inside a pillow. He sat on the plainest-looking chair; it wasn't next to any little table full of stuff he might break or knock over.

His father told Sasha all about the ride: which roads they took, where traffic was bad, where it was good, how long they'd been driving, even about an accident Stefan must've slept through.

His mother sat on a nearby chair which was all carved and red, nodding at Sasha and at him too, but he guessed she was really thinking about one of her books. The room was packed with all kinds of pictures and lamps and boxes like it was a store, but his mother didn't seem to notice.

Sasha was wearing white too and already had gone darker from the sun. Stefan sat and listened to the men talk, full of this new room, of the beginning of his vacation—and of seeing Sasha again.

"Why don't you try the piano?" Sasha asked him. Stefan started. "Where is it?"

"Down there," Sasha pointed, and Stefan trotted out to find it, stopping when he remembered where it was.

The piano stood in a bedroom. Stefan stared and stared at the shiny white piano opposite the large pink-covered bed. He couldn't go in—it looked too private. He stood in the doorway upset; how could he ever come into this room and touch the piano? It wouldn't be right. He turned away; there was something about this that made him feel all wriggly.

"I didn't hear anything," his father said as Stefan hovered in the doorway, embarrassed.

Stefan looked down at the rug. "I forgot it's in somebody's room."

"That's all right." Sasha smiled. "I go in there all the time." Sasha rose, but his father insisted that instead of listening to music they walk to the beach.

"I'm tired," Stefan groaned, making himself yawn.

"Let him stay—he has all summer." Sasha ruffled his hair. So he went upstairs to the room that'd be his and when he heard the screen door and then the creaking stairs, he realized that he was very tired. He went right into the combination bedroom-kitchen and curled up on the bed.

"We're going now," he heard his mother say, and it was dark in the room; he almost couldn't see her.

"We went for a long walk," she said vaguely, sitting on the bed. "Very long."

Stefan wanted to say something about the work she was going back to at home, something that would help her.

"I miss you," he said. "I mean—" He thought he was going to say "I'll miss you."

His mother leaned down and gave him a quick good-bye kiss and then left the room. He followed her out down to the porch, where Sasha and his father sat in blue-painted high rocking chairs.

"Good," his father slapped the chair arms and stood. "It's a long ride."

Stefan hesitated and then moved to his father.

"Don't get sunburned," his father nodded at him.

And they were gone—the car just went straight down the street and turned right and that was it.

"You must be hungry," Sasha said. "Mrs. Mannion made us a nice dinner."

"I'm sorry I wasn't here when you arrived," Mrs. Mannion said at the kitchen table, motioning him to sit. Stefan did, but he had trouble looking at the meat loaf she dished onto his plate: she was so pretty and pink—like her bedroom—or a toy—not like a real lady. Even her voice was pink.

Sasha dug in and Stefan tried eating; once he started it was easy and soon more interesting than Mrs. Mannion, or almost.

"You must feel free to practice," she remarked after a short silence, "Whenever you like."

Stefan coughed.

"Your uncle does," she said with a smile at Sasha.

He watched Mrs. Mannion eat; there was something real slow about her. He'd thought she'd be old and skinny—somehow he didn't remember her as blonde, and big where women were.

"Mr. Mannion used to play for me before retiring," she said after another pause. She went back to her meat loaf.

Stefan flushed—it made him funny inside still to think of where the piano was.

"He's dead," Sasha mouthed to him, and Stefan was more interested in Mrs. Mannion; he'd never known anybody with a dead husband before.

"I enjoy when your uncle plays," she said, bringing her napkin up to her mouth and making little dabs there. She rose with her plate and Sasha's and sort of drifted across to the dishwasher. Stefan tried to finish quick.

"Don't rush," Sasha leaned back in his chair, stretching his arms.

"Perhaps a nice sit-down before dessert?" Mrs. Mannion suggested, and they proceeded out to the porch.

He liked Mrs. Mannion, even though she was a little strange. She called him "my dear" like it was his name. She got up real early, at five o'clock, to do exercises, she said, and went for long walks he didn't know where, and was always lying down for naps.

"It's hard work staying healthy," Sasha winked.

Mrs. Mannion didn't much like the beach; except for the exercises, she was very quiet, came upstairs only when Sasha asked her, so he and his uncle were often alone. Once he got used to the sun, Stefan spend hours every day on the beach, making sand castles—grown-ups were always coming over to help and he thought they had more fun than he did—swimming (Sasha had taught him last summer), and just lying on his blanket or chair. Sometimes he and Sasha went on the boardwalk to eat junk and play lots of games so they could win some kind of prize. They were right near a library so he had plenty of books to drag to the beach or out onto the porch; his favorite was *The Three Musketeers*, though—his own copy. He read it twice more the first weeks he was there.

There were other kids on the block but nobody asked him to play, and Sasha was enough. He practiced now every day and he was used to where the piano stood; having one whenever he wanted was the best part of being there with Sasha. The sound wasn't very good—it was almost like there was sand inside, but after a while that didn't matter.

Sasha seemed different here, besides not being so white anymore; his uncle was quieter, like someone who'd been tired out or sick and needed rest real bad. On the beach Sasha could lie stretched, big and silent, for more than an hour without moving, and when they went shopping with Mrs. Mannion or down the boardwalk or sat on the porch at night, Sasha said very little.

Maybe there wasn't much to say since most days were alike. One night they were out on the porch listening to the radio inside which wasn't much louder than the buzz of flies and things. The porch light wasn't bright enough to read by, but Mrs. Mannion could see enough to knit (she was always stopping to start something new and then stopping that)—she knitted as slowly as she rocked, almost like she was asleep. Sasha was asleep—it was easy out here at night with every sound as dim and far-off and peaceful as the ocean. When the phone rang Sasha jerked up and went inside. The screen door was something else Stefan thought he would never get used to: even with oiled hinges it screaked and thwacked like it wanted to catch you, and at first it'd annoyed and almost scared him, but now he didn't mind.

"Come talk to your parents," Sasha called, but Stefan didn't hurry; he could feel Mrs. Mannion's long glance over the top of her knitting spectacles as he crossed to the door.

Sasha smiled handing him the phone but Stefan couldn't. He told both of them he was fine. Sasha was fine, and the beach too. They were coming the next Saturday—all day.

"Don't you want them to visit?" Sasha asked, smiling curiously when Stefan hung up.

Stefan couldn't really answer; he did and he didn't—everything was so good just like it was. Even Scotty looked less faded. He blushed.

"I understand," Sasha nodded.

Stefan wished *he* did.

"Your mother," Mrs. Mannion said, when he was back on the porch, "Your mother is a beautiful woman."

Stefan felt pleased and embarrassed at the compliment.

"She is," Sasha agreed.

But Stefan thought Mrs. Mannion was maybe more beautiful.

"Very," Sasha said, like he was wondering why.

It was not so bad when his parents came; he rushed down the stairs to them and knocked into his mother. Her white hat blew off and danced down the street; he and his mother chased it, laughing, but he caught it.

"Thank you, sir." She took it from him with a little bow, her face red. And then she thanked him in Polish—"*Dziękuję*"—which sounded so pretty and soft to him: dzehnkooyeh.

"Your hair's—"

"Different, yes—isn't it pretty this way? Almost like Mrs. Kennedy."

He nodded, following her back to the car where his father stood looking impatient.

His mother had Mrs. Mannion show her all over the house, even the cellar, and asked about everything like she'd never been there before or it was some kind of special joke she had all by herself.

They had a very small lunch. Sasha and his father talked about money for something new in the car and his mother and Mrs. Mannion talked about dresses.

Upstairs, when he was done changing, he went to knock on the bathroom door to see if his mother was in her bathing suit and ready. The door was open a little, and he saw his father pushing her against the sink, trying to kiss her. She slapped him and Stefan backed off, ran down the stairs feeling sick.

It was good they didn't have to share a room, because Stefan had trouble enough after that Saturday falling asleep by himself. He lay in his bed listening to a tree that leaned near his window hiss and scratch; it was sometimes louder than all the things cricking and croaking at night in the little backyard. After a while in the dark he thought he could make out the wallpaper pattern even down to the last porthole on the sailboat that flowed in red-gold hundreds across each wall, and the refrigerator's cranky groans began to sound like a person's. He lay on his back, legs tangled in the sheets, smacking away the mosquitoes who got through his cloud of night repellent, feeling ugly about his parents. It felt like when he couldn't stop looking at a man or woman without a hand or leg; his father had told him never to stare but he always did when he saw a broken person.

When his father called a week later to say they were coming out again on Saturday morning Stefan realized the summer was beginning to be over: he and Sasha had a little more than a month left before he'd have to go back to school, have to give up the beach and the piano downstairs and reading books on the porch before lunch and the way ice cream tasted on the beach after he'd been really thirsty. When he tried thinking of his street in New York it came to him all blurry like through an old screen window. It would be hot there and not clean and quiet. He'd miss the huge Saint Bernard next door that Mrs. Mannion had told him found a black kitten under a car and brought it home "very gently." Now it carried the kitten around the honeysuckle-framed porch in and out of the sun—the heaving brown-and-white bulk with a scrap of black at its mouth. Stefan had visited there once or twice and watched the dog lick and lick its friend with a pink tongue as big as Stefan's hands, bigger, and twice the size of the kitten. Stefan would miss watching the kitten wander around the Saint Bernard's back, stumbling and confused.

He didn't ever want to go home. Sasha now and then said things like "It will be good to return," with a kind of face like he'd just smelled something tasty, but Stefan didn't answer. He read *The Three Musketeers* once more before his parents came. That Saturday morning he felt something peculiar when all four of them were upstairs drinking lemonade. His father looked all flushed and angry; they'd had a flat tire, and his father's white shirt stuck to him in ugly wet blotches. Sasha offered to lend him a shirt but his father wouldn't change, like he *wanted* to be uncomfortable.

"You don't write," his father said, holding the tall ice-full glass against his cheek.

"I call," Stefan said lamely. How could he explain what happened when he put the white tablet on the table and found a sharp pencil, how when he thought of things to say—like he went to the library yesterday—he sort of dreamed about them, sitting there awake, and forgot the waiting page.

"Well I want you to write me a letter. Anyone can call, it's too easy. You should learn how to write."

"I can write," Stefan sulked.

"Well then, write us a letter—I want you to promise." Stefan looked at Sasha who was near the window and glancing outside at the tiny backyard which was Mrs. Mannion's private place. His mother sat behind Stefan on the bed, reading a magazine she'd brought along.

"Why make a fuss? It's so hot," his mother murmured. Stefan waited for more, but the hot silence didn't break. Finally Sasha said, "Shall we go to the beach?"

Stefan didn't like the beach on weekends; sometimes it got so crowded he couldn't find Sasha when he came out of the water, but wandered in the blaze of umbrellas and blankets and beach chairs, looking for him. He'd be too embarrassed to yell the way little kids and even some grown-ups did. The last time his parents were here and he kept looking for them, his father said "Did you get lost?" when Stefan finally got to them. He didn't want to have that happen today.

"Can't we just sit for a while?" his mother wished, pushing at her hair.

His father snorted. "You came out here to sit?"

"Oh, please." His mother rose, the magazine hanging open from one hand. "It's too hot." She trailed from the room, her thin green dress rustling, and for some reason, Stefan thought of Mrs. Mannion.

"Where are you going?" his father called in Polish; his mother didn't answer. Stefan heard her on the staircase, and then the screen door whined open and closed.

"She is impossible," his father began, but Sasha coughed and his father said nothing more.

Later, when they were trailing back from the jammed frantic beach (Stefan hadn't even tried to get to the water), their beach chairs trickling sand and sometimes scraping the sidewalk, Stefan noticed Sasha and his father talking very quiet—really his father talked and Sasha nodded. It looked like something important. His mother walked ahead of them, the white beach jacket blowing around her; the white suit was new and kind of tight, Stefan thought, but he liked the big straw hat and dark glasses. She was very beautiful today, not like a mother much—maybe that was

85

what made things funny and different. When he caught up with her she was climbing the porch steps.

"We'll both be in school," he said.

She turned. "School?" Then she smiled and crossed to the door; he rushed to hold it open for her. "School" she said again, real soft, like it was a dream.

"Do you mind if Stefan plays for us?" his mother asked Mrs. Mannion in the kitchen after they'd all showered.

"No," Mrs. Mannion slid a heap of sliced carrots off a cutting board into a pot. "Why should I?"

So Stefan sat down to play a new little Bach piece Sasha was teaching him, but instead of sitting across in the kitchen like everyone always did, she followed him into the large pink room.

"How lovely," she said, perching on the edge of the bed, legs crossed, arms out and back to hold her up. It made him nervous for her to be right behind him almost. Also he heard Mrs. Mannion in the kitchen and for some reason saw in his head Sasha and his father talking, so he made lots of mistakes playing.

"Lovely," his mother said, stroking her hair, and he hated that she lied: he knew it was bad, he wasn't a baby.

"Can I help?" his mother asked, joining Mrs. Mannion.

"Why yes." Mrs. Mannion rinsed her hands.

Stefan drifted out to the porch where his father was talking to Sasha in Russian, and Stefan remembered in a hot way how the bad things were always in Russian. Something bad was going to come, but there was no place he could run—he didn't have any friends here. He pulled the screen door shut when he went inside so it wouldn't make all that noise and tramped upstairs to listen to the radio until dinner.

"I like my own bed," his mother repeated after dinner; Sasha had suggested they stay the night.

"I'm tired," his father said.

"And where would we sleep?"

"My room," Sasha said. "I can put a cot in Stefan's room."

"It's too much trouble," his mother sighed. She sat all stretched

86

out on the porch swing like she was going to sleep there. "Let's go home."

"Well, if we're going, let's go." His father stood.

Mrs. Mannion came out then with a small foil-wrapped package which she handed to his mother: "Some brownies for the ride home." She and his mother stood smiling at each other.

"Come on," his father ordered, and they all said good-bye at once. His father looked impatient, and muttered something to Sasha Stefan couldn't hear. When his mother kissed him good-bye and followed his father down the steps into the night-quiet street, Stefan felt very sad.

"She gets more and more beautiful," Mrs. Mannion said, sinking into a chair to knit and rock. "Your mother."

Sasha came back from walking them to the car. "It's warm tonight," he said, taking a seat.

A few days later Stefan got his first mail of the summer: a postcard of the Empire State Building. On the back his mother had written "I don't know why I have never been here before," signing it "All my love." He didn't show it to Sasha, he didn't know why; it made him feel wonderful to get mail from his mother but also funny, like she wasn't supposed to write him or something.

"What a pretty card," Mrs. Mannion said, finding him on the top porch step. "From a friend?"

"My mother."

"It's fun," Mrs. Mannion said, straightening the row of chairs, "It's fun to sightsee in your own city."

His mother had seen the State Building before, a long time ago, Stefan remembered Sasha telling him about it. Why did she forget? And why did she go again? It must've been for fun, grown-up fun, the kind he didn't understand.

He didn't think about it much more that day because one of Sasha's students called after dinner to find out when Sasha was coming back to New York.

"You've had a good time, haven't you?" Sasha asked before he went off to sleep.

"Real good." But that wasn't enough, especially now that they'd be going home in a few weeks. "The best time."

Sasha smiled good-night.

A week after, Stefan was getting ready to go back to the beach when he heard a familiar-sounding car drive up. He stopped changing and moved to his door. Sasha was out on the porch talking to someone. A man. His father. Stefan couldn't mistake the low voice under Sasha's. He was suddenly real afraid; it was the middle of the week and his parents hadn't called they were coming. He crossed to the top of the stairs and listened; he couldn't hear his mother's voice. Stefan edged down the stairs, from just inside the door he could see his father sitting on the steps all hunched over. Sasha stood two steps down; something was wrong in his face.

They weren't talking, not even in Russian.

Stefan opened the door and they both looked up at him. The door creaked shut as he stepped out onto the porch, terrified by he didn't know what.

"Where's Mommy?" He advanced to the edge of the porch; his father's face was as white as Sasha's used to be.

"She had work to do," Sasha began, "She's—"

"Your mother and I have decided to live apart," his father said, clearing his throat.

Part Two
Separate Lives

5

"I don't understand how you can watch so much television and do well at school." This was as close as Sasha ever came to criticizing, but it was close enough for Stefan.

Standing behind him, Sasha was peering at the TV screen where Jethro of the Beverly Hillbillies was trying to impress a girl with how smart and brave he was, while he was dressed as a pirate. Sasha didn't watch this or any of Stefan's favorites—"I Dream of Jeannie," "Bewitched," "Get Smart," "Lost in Space."

"It's so vulgar," Sasha added, as if he hadn't said it before.

"Vulgar," meant "American," of course. And vulgar was everything that Poland, that Europe was not. When Sasha talked like that, it made America seem like a very small and ugly place. And because Sasha was always so vague and unrevealing about his life before America, the label "vulgar" had even more power.

Stefan's mother's approach was a little different. When she was over here, she would ask, "Isn't there something else you'd rather watch?"

It came out sounding very polite, like his mother was at some kind of tea party, but it was a dumb question, Stefan thought. Once he'd said, "If I wanted to watch something else, I'd watch it," but she almost slapped him she was so angry. "Don't *ever* talk to me like that!" she stormed, and he realized he was crossing a line that was very clear to her, but not to him. He was supposed to treat her the way *she* had been supposed to treat her parents, the grandparents he didn't know, had never seen a picture of, and couldn't ask questions about. As if they were criminals, and had done something so shameful that their names and faces were blotted out forever. "I'm not your servant!" his mother had added, and he thought later, they had servants, or they knew people who did. It seemed an important piece of information.

"Don't you have homework?" Sasha asked him now.

Stefan shrugged and drank some milk. "Did it already."

He didn't turn from the screen because he knew what Sasha's expression would be. It was the same look his teachers mostly had. They said they couldn't figure him out, because he didn't seem to care much about his work, sometimes didn't even seem to pay attention in class—yet he maintained a 95 average in all his classes, making him one of the stars of Junior High School 152's accelerated two-year special sequence.

"It must be because you read so much," Sasha concluded, going off to the kitchen.

Was that it? Was that why his grades were so high? Or did he just not care enough to *fight* school, to fight giving himself to other people's unimportant demands, since he had gotten what he wanted.

When his parents finally divorced after three miserable years of separation, Stefan had said it over and over: "I want to live with Uncle Sasha."

All through his mother's and father's angry and pleading conversations with him, with each other, with Sasha, that was all Stefan had cared about. It didn't matter to him that his mother and father couldn't live with each other. It didn't matter that his father now had a beautiful faculty apartment near where he taught at Columbia, or that his mother promised to buy him his own piano now that she had a job in a publishing company, where all the languages she knew were useful. He wanted to live with Sasha. Sasha would not leave him, or ever be strange and distant. Sasha could be trusted.

His father had shouted: "But you're my son. *Our* son! You *have* to live with one of us!"

His parents had given him a choice, without expecting that he would choose something they didn't like. Too bad for them.

"And Sasha's apartment is too small," his mother had added more reasonably. "There's not much room."

Even at 11, Stefan knew that wasn't really true. His uncle could get a Castro convertible for the little room that was his study—Stefan had seen the advertisements on TV—and Stefan could sleep there. But he knew something more important. There was room for him with his uncle in ways there could never be with his mother or father, not anymore. They weren't the same and everything was messed up. It was like the clown marionette he got for one birthday. Packing up to move to Sasha's, he had found it forgotten at the bottom of a toy box. The hands and feet were so tangled in string that he couldn't fix it. He threw it out.

"I want to live with Sasha." He said that so many times they had to give in.

"I didn't know you could be so stubborn," Sasha said to him when it was all over, when his parents were finally divorced, and Stefan felt released into a different life.

Was he really stubborn? Or was it being quiet, and waiting because he didn't care what anyone else said to him, he could keep looking at them but feel protected by music inside of him, music that drowned everything else out—the glorious full sound of a triumphal piano and orchestra filling the world with noise like in Liszt's orchestral transcription of *The Wanderer Fantasy*. He had first heard it in its original piano version with Sasha. It was music that made him feel defiant and safe.

Like in his first year of junior high, at 152, when other seventh grade kids, kids he didn't know, made fun of his name, and called him "Steffy" and "Stephanie." He never winced, or shouted back at them, or even looked like he'd avoid a fight if it came to that—and eventually they gave up, because it wasn't interesting enough. He understood that reacting in any way would have given them the power to torture him until he escaped to high school. He had already seen kids beaten up, pushed into lockers, tripped in the gym showers, smacked hard with school books on the clangy gray metal stairs. He had discovered a whole world of cruelty existing beyond the reach of teachers and parents. It was like quicksand in movies, trapping you, drawing you under. Slowly.

And just a nickname could stay with you forever—like poor Elizabeth in grade school, who made the mistake of bringing a week's worth of tuna fish sandwiches for lunch. She was still, five years later, in a new school, often taunted with the name "Tuna Face," even though she was pretty and did not smell like her Flintstones lunch box had.

"Are you hungry?" Sasha called from the kitchen. "No?"

They had eaten dinner just a few hours ago, at 6:00, which was when they ate dinner every evening, watching the CBS news on the small TV in the kitchen. But Sasha seemed to think that part of taking care of him was always asking if he was hungry. It was strange.

His mother, and sometimes his father, at first had suggested to Sasha that they move to a larger apartment, but Sasha said he didn't mind sleeping in the study and letting Stefan have the larger bedroom, that there was more than enough closet space, that the apartment was rent-controlled and very cheap—so why move? Sasha said lots of things, mostly because he wanted to calm everyone down, Stefan decided.

Stefan just said, "I like it here." This was where he had first learned to play the piano, this was where he had discovered he had an aunt who was dead. Even having been hurt here when he fell and hit the piano made him feel it was a place he couldn't give up.

"Do you have a lot of homework?" Sasha called from the kitchen.

"I told you—I did it."

Sasha was always expressing amazement that Stefan had so little to do for school, unlike himself back in Poland. But Stefan didn't care, because it gave him plenty of time for what he really loved: reading. Every week he went to the library and came back with a pile of books—mysteries, science fiction, history books about French kings or long-ago European wars, books on dolphins, lost civilizations, magic tricks, UFOs, secret codes, ESP.

Sasha sometimes said, "Maybe you read too much?" But he never sounded that convinced. The reading didn't affect Stefan's grades, and when Sasha wondered if he should try to make more friends, Stefan just shrugged. He didn't hate the kids at school, he just didn't like anyone too much, and didn't want to have to talk to people about his parents, and why he lived with his uncle.

Stefan didn't like talking about himself, and even more, he didn't like it when English teachers asked for autobiographical narratives or anything like that. He wanted then to invent things, and sometimes he did, imagining himself a Polish count, defending his castle against invaders—hairy Mongols with cruel eyes and wild armor, or endless marching ugly Teutonic Knights. He would be noble and brave, fighting despite terrible wounds, waving his flag and wielding his sword without ever falling from his horse.

The phone rang, and from the way Sasha lowered his voice, Stefan knew it was probably his mother. His father hardly called now that he had given up Columbia to take a teaching job at the University of Michigan.

Soon Sasha would get off the phone, come in, sit down, and pretend to watch the television, waiting for Stefan to ask who had called, which Stefan usually did, eventually, after he got tired of waiting for Sasha to just say it. Though sometimes Sasha would wait a day or so before telling him his mother or his father had called. She was calling more often now that she had moved to Brooklyn and came to see them less than when she had lived at their old apartment here in Washington Heights. Or see *him*.

Because he figured that she and Sasha probably got together a lot, and Sasha didn't talk about it.

He turned off the TV and went to his room, shut the door, turned on the radio, which was usually tuned to WQXR. Stefan liked listening to rock stations, but not at night, not in his room. He couldn't fall asleep with Cream, Jefferson Airplane, or even the Beatles—the music kids at school listened to and talked about—no matter how low the volume was.

He lay down and stared at his Abbott and Costello poster with the "Who's On First?" routine that always reminded him of a dog chasing its tail. And sometimes reminded him of himself.

The last movement of Beethoven's *Emperor Concerto* was playing, and Stefan lay back, letting the music take over, take him away. Briefly, he thought of reading something, but decided not to. He hoped Sasha wouldn't knock on his door to see how he was doing, or ask if he wanted to play chess. After his mother's calls, Sasha was sometimes too attentive, as if he felt guilty or something, felt like he wasn't doing enough.

Sasha did plenty. Stefan knew that his parents paid for clothes and other stuff, and that the allowance he got came from them too, but Sasha added to that, and cooked for him, gave him lessons whenever he wanted them, took him to concerts and museums, to Rockaway every summer, and—this was the best part—mostly acted like they were having a quiet kind of adventure that would have a happy ending.

Stefan didn't want more attention from anyone.

At school it embarrassed him that one teacher had called him a walking encyclopedia, because he was afraid the name might stick. It was in social studies and the teacher had jokingly asked if anyone knew who the Brazilian president was.

"Costa e Silva," Stefan said, without raising his hand. It just popped out, but Mr. Fischer didn't mind. Everyone turned to look at Stefan and he blushed, which made some kids start to laugh. But what could he do? He always knew the social studies answers, especially if they were about current events. He read the *New York Times* every morning. Was that such a big deal?

He sometimes made himself *not* answer questions in class, just on tests, to avoid being looked at. That was why he hated gym class. He could climb up the thick rope suspended from the gym ceiling, win for his team at volleyball, outrace other kids (Mr. Hessman said he had "natural ability")—he was basically good at all that stuff. He was skinny, he was fast. None of it mattered any more to him than schoolwork did. When he was playing basketball or passing a football, the coach would shout at him, "Get excited! It's not a *job*, boy—it's *life!*" But he never passed into that realm of commitment and freedom.

He listened to other kids brag about how tough they were, how many push-ups they could do, and listened to others complain about how boring gym was—and none of it reached him. Sometimes guys would congratulate him, or slap him five, but he hated to be cheered, hated guys calling out his name, urging him on. It was as bad as dreaming he had to be somewhere fancy, and didn't have the right clothes, or *any* clothes. He wanted to be left alone. In some ways, it was as awkward as being made fun of, called a sissy. That could never happen to him, not just because he was good, but because he knew sports stats as well as anyone in class, could correct guys about batting averages—if he wanted to. He read it all in the newspapers, heard it on TV. He just didn't care.

Which was what his father had done, eventually. His father had tried taking him to ball games and movies every week during the separation and after the divorce, but it was terrible. First his father would pick him up, and Stefan would have to stand there awkward in their apartment foyer with its black and white linoleum squares, waiting for the typical stupid little conversations his mother and father had. Like they were supposedly friendly. He had always wanted to scream, or jump up and smash the carriage lamp on its twisted chain, but they talked—like people in his French class forced to make up a conversation out of brand new vocabulary words.

"We're civil," his father said proudly, more than once.

"That's what they called a *war*," Stefan blurted out, and his father almost smacked him.

After the separation and then the divorce, knowing that both his parents were coming to a school play or holiday show he was in had made him so anxious he always expected to throw up. But he couldn't say "Don't come," because he craved the appearance of a normal family, a normal life. Yet he didn't know what to say afterwards, when they both congratulated him. Only Sasha seemed relaxed enough to smile naturally, and hug him as if he meant it.

Until he moved in with Sasha, spending time with either one of his parents alone was terrible, whether it was shopping, or watching TV, or sitting in the park and watching the barges on the Hudson, waiting until dark for the lights of the George Washington Bridge to string along to the Palisades. Once he was with Sasha, he felt better, he had his own home, and both his mother and his father were the visitors, and they had to be nice to him. That didn't just mean buying him presents, it meant not yelling or acting too weird.

But then the whole divorce was weird, because no one could really explain it.

His parents had not been clear. Yes, his mother had met another man, but he was just a friend, and that wasn't really it, even his father said so. It was more like they finally gave up hope.

"Everything was . . . so chaotic after the War," his father said. "So much confusion, refugees, everywhere ruins, everyone dead—" But to Stefan it seemed that his father was talking to himself, answering his own questions and accusations. And Stefan imagined a time bomb that had taken years to explode. But it did explode. And nothing could change that, nothing could keep his parents together.

"It's the War," Sasha kept repeating.

"No it's not," Stefan said. "It's them. It's *their* fault."

Sasha stared at him.

And Stefan felt full of power, full of himself, like he could say *anything* he wanted, like he was Godzilla crushing all of Japan with his enormous clawed feet.

Some kids at PS 98 had felt sorry for him, Stefan knew. A couple mentioned it. He told them to shut up. Their parents must have found out. Why couldn't his father or mother have died of a heart attack instead? That wouldn't be so embarrassing.

And when he entered junior high, it was briefly worse.

Mrs. Schulberg, his English teacher, took him aside one day, her face unrevealing as a bird's, to tell him he might want to write about the divorce, to explore his feelings.

"Why?" he said.

She squinted, looking very silly in her lace-collared blue dress. She was skinny, with short dark hair, and had an archipelago of moles down one side of her face.

"Why?" he asked again.

"Well, Stefan . . . writing can be, can be—"

"Therapeutic?"

She winced. She had already told him that even though his reading scores were so high, he used words in his compositions that were inappropriate for his age level—words like "phantas-magorical" and "supernumerary." "I know what they mean," Stefan had said, because he did, but that didn't seem important to Mrs. Schulberg.

"Writing can be *good* for you," she said now. *"Helpful."*

Stefan said, "I think my parents need to write about it more than I do."

And maybe they did. His mother was furious that he decided to live with Sasha.

"I knew I shouldn't have had a child! I didn't want to! Not after everything—" On the brink of revealing something, on the brink of filling in miserable gaps in what he understood of the past, his mother stopped, blushing, head down, ashamed of herself.

"Sorry," she said, shaking her head back and forth. "I'm so sorry." And she tried to hug Stefan. He fled for the bathroom and locked himself in. They were at home, but the white tiled bathroom felt cold, like a prison.

"Your mother's sorry," Sasha called from the other side of the door after a while. Stefan was sitting on the floor, a towel crushed to his wet face. He had screamed into it at first, and then cried. But nothing helped.

"No she's not," Stefan growled. "She's just *embarrassed*."

Both his parents were embarrassed, he was sure of that. It was like a Perry Mason show—he had seen the crime, he knew, and he was going to jump up in court with the truth. They were afraid of him. *He* could explode too.

By the time the divorce was finalized, his father had admitted he was looking for jobs outside of New York, because staying wasn't "comfortable."

Go to hell, Stefan thought. I hate you.

He hated his mother too, maybe a little more, because she tried to pretend that nothing had changed, that she hadn't left him, that she loved him just as much as ever. Even though there was this Leo guy Stefan supposed she was "dating." Just the idea of it made him sick, and he refused to meet Leo.

Sasha was knocking on his bedroom door now.

"What?"

"I'm going to bed," Sasha called. "Did you set your alarm?"

"Yes!" It was always set, he had never missed getting to school on time, but still Sasha asked, as if we were acting out his idea of what living with a teenager was supposed to be like. It was annoying, but it was also kind of funny.

"Good night," he said, and heard Sasha's echoing good night followed by the bathroom door closing.

Right now, being in his room made him feel kind of lonely. He got up to turn on the desk lamp. He pulled down the window shade with no regret, because all you could see was another wall of the building, pierced by windows, a grimy closed courtyard if you looked down, and boring stone decorations along the roof if you looked up: dumb flowers and designs. From his old bedroom window he had seen Manhattan stretch out towards the Bronx. The view had been full of red, gold, and brown apartment buildings rising and falling over hills that he knew from his school teachers had been claimed by Indians and then Dutch farmers long before the English, and then all the European immigrants who came much later, immigrants like his parents and Sasha.

His old building had filled half a city block. It had massive cornices and leering griffins, but it wasn't the highest spot in the city. Teachers had told him that the Cloisters in Fort Tryon Park, a few miles north, stole that honor. And he loved the Cloisters, the battlements that made you feel you were really in the past because all you could see at most spots was trees, the enormous cold hallways and wide worn stairs, the big rooms filled with armor, chests, and tapestries whose colors were so bright they looked fake. This was *his* past, he felt, something beyond his parents' lives in America, something more powerful. Whenever he took a school trip to the Cloisters, he came away wishing he could be one of those beautiful serious-looking angels in fancy robes. But despite all that, on his old hill he used to imagine *it* was the highest place in the city. He could then feel sorry for anybody who wanted to live downtown or off in flat and dreary Queens which his mother had once told him was built on garbage.

Their old building had been built on history, not far from the crowded and very old cemetery used by Trinity Church, a high mysterious walled space full of big dark trees, tumbled grave-stones, and ghosts, he used to think. On the thick stone wall at one corner was a plaque commemorating a battle of George Washing-ton—a shiny plaque, like it had just happened.

The dark lobby of the building he'd grown up in, three steps up from the outer hall, three again from the street, was walled and floored like a castle. Its mirrors reflected a heavy peeling table where people rested their packages while they waited for the scarred paneled elevator. He loved listening to it sink and sigh like it was alive and seventy years old. At night, because his parents' apartment was right next to the elevator shaft, the heavy murmur came to Stefan distantly through the thick walls. It was comforting, like somebody in a rocking chair.

Sasha's building didn't have the same romance for him—it was newer, much smaller, and even the mailboxes weren't heavy and brass, but skinny aluminum-looking things. He didn't talk about this with Sasha, didn't even think about it much, except at night.

He missed the archways of his parents' apartment, the parquet floors with the design along the edge that Sasha explained was a

"Greek key." He missed the high ceilings, and the moldings where the walls met the ceilings, and the ones that made rectangles and squares on each wall. They were a reminder of palaces where he knew the frames would be filled by paintings, but empty and painted the same color as the rest of the wall, they seemed like sad and quiet ghosts. He missed the glass-paneled double doors between the living room and dining room, the cupboard that filled one corner of the large square foyer. It had always seemed a little mysterious, because its doors were glass, but little thick curtains hung inside—which seemed strange and inviting. It was basically for junk, but Stefan had always loved rooting around in there, and when he was little, had even tried crawling into it.

He curled up now, imagining what it would be like to do that, to crawl in, close the doors, to have light penetrate the curtains, but nothing else except the sound of the elevator, filling the shaft, rising slowly, pushing air up to the top. He would have all his favorite toys and books, and his dog Scotty, and he would sleep without dreaming anything that made him wake up.

The radio was playing the *Goldberg Variations*, which always made him fall asleep, so he got up to go wash his face and brush his teeth. Sasha had left the light on in the bathroom, like Stefan was a little boy, but Stefan had stopped complaining about it. It wasn't so bad, really, that Sasha was taking care of him even when asleep.

Looking into the mirror, Stefan wondered if he was more like his mother or his father. He couldn't tell, and he didn't want to ask any of them. He wet a comb and tried parting his hair on the right, then the left, then the back. Then he just stuck it in and made faces at himself for a while before he yawned and decided he was probably tired.

He headed for bed, glad that Sasha did not nag him about staying up late, or reading, didn't announce lights had to be out at a certain time, or that he had to be in his room. At school, kids were always complaining about things like that. These were conversations he didn't join, because he didn't want anyone to think he was bragging about Sasha.

He liked being up when everything was quiet in the apartment, and he could admire the paperbacks he had begun buying with his allowance: the Edgar Rice Burroughs *Tarzan* books, books by Isaac Asimov, Arthur C. Clarke, and Robert Heinlein. This was really a new thrill for him, made even better after Sasha had said, "You're building quite a library."

Their public library a few blocks away was his favorite place in the world. He loved the big fat globe lamps that hung down from the ceiling but were so large they seemed to hold it up. And he loved the dark old shelves filling every possible space—high shelves, low shelves, big, small, along walls, in the middle of rooms, almost like a forest of books—and everywhere colored book spines or book jackets shouting at him for attention.

He wanted his room to feel like that, walled with books, a castle of books.

And he would be its knight, with the Polish eagle on his breastplate, fierce and triumphant.

Stefan liked reading about Poland, even though its history was mostly very sad. Especially it being "The Christ of all Nations." That was a picture which made him feel like he did when he was about to throw up—sweaty, heavy, cold. He did not want to think about anybody, anything nailed to a cross, tortured and bleeding. His parents and Sasha felt the same, he had figured out. And besides, they didn't believe in any religion, which sometimes made him feel weird. Like singing Christmas songs in school, and wanting to see the store windows, especially at Macy's. He understood that Christmas, and everything connected to it, was "vulgar"— maybe the most vulgar thing about America. But that made him feel a little guilty when he got Christmas presents, and when he figured out what to get for all of them.

"It's just lies," his father had told him many times.

Stefan never shared this with kids at school; besides, most of them were Jewish in the special track at JHS 152 and they talked about their Hanukkah. He knew that his parents and their parents had something in common. Because the Jews had also suffered in the War, just like the Poles. And the Jews were brave, also like the

Poles. Only Poland still wasn't free, because of Russia, but the Jews had their own country which nobody had taken over, not yet.

He fell asleep thinking about Israel, and the United Nations, and the Straits of Tiran, all of which had been in the news lately.

"I betcha the Jews get their asses kicked, I betcha they get *fried!*"

Stefan was in homeroom, and Eddie Morrice, the class clown, had been blabbing about Israel and the Arabs. He was always making noise or calling attention to himself, and was frequently sent to the principal's office. He was a math and science whiz, and loudly bored in those classes. He mimicked teachers behind their backs, made jungle noises like elephants and wild birds. All the guys knew from the showers that his was as long as a toothpaste tube. And Eddie had once, on a dare, taken it out in homeroom, in the back row, and put the end of it on his desk top for a second or two. Stefan was a row over, and had felt disgusted, excited and alarmed, remembering bathing with his father as a little boy, and wondering what it would be like to stuff so much into his briefs every morning. In the john, Eddie loved to flick his penis around after taking a leak, splashing anyone he could.

"No they won't!" "Bullshit!" "You're crazy!" Guys were yelling at Eddie, Jewish guys, mostly—like little Ronnie Stern and red-faced Michael Gross. And even some of the girls were shaking their heads and muttering.

From the newspaper that morning, Stefan had gathered that a war was imminent, and it made the June day seem hotter and heavier. Sasha was asleep when Stefan got up, so they didn't talk about the news, but Stefan thought about it on the bus all the way up through Washington Heights to 152 in Inwood. He tried to remember something he read once about Winston Churchill and World War II—didn't he say "Brave little Belgium" when it was attacked? Stefan thought of Belgium, and poor Poland, betrayed by the Russians and wiped from the map in 1939 one more time, Germany crushing it in only three weeks. *Three weeks!*

How could a little country like Israel stand up to all those Arab armies?

"I'll bet a dollar," Eddie was saying. "I'll bet *two* dollars," and soon he and other guys were snaking their pinky fingers to clinch the bets. The bell rang and they headed for their seats.

"Can Israel win a war?" he asked Sasha at dinner, which they had gotten to late, because of the scary news from the Middle East.

Sasha looked pale, hadn't eaten much of his lamb chop or mashed potatoes, and had just picked at his salad. He shrugged. "They have to. They have no choice. It's win or—"

"Will we ever go to Poland?"

Sasha set down his fork, pulled at his shirt collar. "What?"

"Poland. Will you take me there someday?"

Sasha shook his head. "There's nothing left of where we lived—it was all bombed, destroyed, stolen. It's a graveyard, not a country. And the war hasn't made them better people."

Sasha had always been negative about Poland—like he was ashamed of it—but never sounded this depressed and discouraged. Was it connected to the Middle East somehow?

Stefan drank some more iced tea, and thought about what to ask next. He occasionally imagined himself and Sasha—and sometimes his parents, though usually not—being welcomed in Poland, welcomed home, dancing with folk dancers, eating sausage, and talking that language so very full of shushing sounds.

"My French teacher said a third language is always easier to learn than a second is. Since I'm doing so well in French class, why don't you teach me Polish?" It bothered Stefan that all he really knew how to say was *Do widzenia*, "Good-bye," *nie* and *tak*, "no" and "yes," and things like *Dzień dobry*, "good morning" and *Proszę*, "please."

Sasha sat back in his chair, frowning. "Polish, it's a useless language."

"Not if I want to go there."

"Why would you?"

"To see things, to be there."

"Poland is ugly. Go to France—your French is so good already. Go to France, live in France."

"Is it because of the Russians? Because of the Communists?"

Sasha nodded quickly. "Of course. Now, why don't we have some Jell-O—that should taste good today."

And Stefan brought out the cool green dessert dishes from the refrigerator.

When he was washing up, the downstairs bell rang, and Stefan knew that it was his mother—she always rang twice, and then twice again. Like it was a secret signal. Usually, he headed for his room if he didn't know in advance she was coming over, but tonight for some reason, he stayed in the kitchen at the sink, and didn't stiffen when she came in to kiss him hello a minute later.

"I'll take a cab home," she said to Sasha. "You'll come down with me."

"So, darling," she said, sitting at the metal-rimmed table, drumming a pretty hand on the Formica top. "How's school?"

He shrugged. "The same." And he suddenly felt awkward, now that the dishes were done and he had to hang up the dish towel and turn to face her. She looked as beautiful as always—even when the weather changed, his mother never looked as sweaty or tired as other women her age. Her white linen dress was hardly creased, and with her hair pulled back she looked very sophisticated.

He brought out a pitcher of iced coffee, which she loved. He had seen it there that afternoon, and wondered if Sasha hadn't prepared it for his mother.

She clapped her hands. "Lovely!" She held the cool clinking glass to her face, briefly, as if it weren't just refreshing, but something special and dear.

"Will there be a war?" he asked.

She sipped from the glass, eyelids flickering. "I think so."

"Will the U.S. and Russia be in it too?"

Sasha was off in the living room, playing a Chopin ballade, the rippling notes wafting in with the air conditioner in that room.

Stefan and his mother were silent, and he felt a sudden tension in her, like she wanted to say something, do something. Or maybe she wanted *him* to say or do—what?

"We need to be together at times like this," she brought out, and

106

he wanted to laugh at her. She was afraid, and he was supposed to make her feel better? What a crock!

"Let's go listen to Sasha," he said, and she followed him.

They sat on the couch, but not too close, and let Sasha fill the air around them with wave after brilliant crisp wave of Chopin, a clear potent sea of music. He was old enough now to know that Sasha's expression was better than his technique—perhaps because for him, it was just the opposite. But there was still something magical about having Sasha play for him.

He clapped when Sasha finished with a slightly mocking roll of his shoulders. Sasha turned and leaned back against the keyboard, his hands on the piano stool.

"Lovely," his mother murmured, as if she were in a museum opposite a painting. And imagining that, Stefan said, "Let's go to the museum next week." That always meant the Metropolitan.

His mother grinned at him and then at Sasha, and Stefan felt momentarily embarrassed that such a little thing could make her so happy.

They went on a Thursday, by which time war had been raging for several days. Stefan wasn't interested in any special exhibit. As usual, he just loved being there, loved the crowds, the enormous rooms. He roamed from hall to hall, consorting with Junos and knights, consoles and landscapes, surrendering himself to color and form: the lift of a marble chin or the light on a marquetry cabinet top jostling for attention in his mind. It didn't matter how long he was there, any time at all was like shoving his face into a bouquet of flowers—sweet, rich and strong. Tonight, he needed the distraction because of the war, which it looked like Israel would win. He spent a lot more time than usual in the Greek and Roman sculpture galleries. The gods and senators seemed in their shiny silence to have a message for him. He felt hypnotized, confused.

Sasha and his mother talked about it at dinner in the noisy museum restaurant, and Stefan felt very adult because they didn't act as if he wasn't there or couldn't understand, but asked him his opinion now and then, and talked to him too, not just to each other. It was kind of exciting, and he wondered somehow if this new war wasn't connected to it all.

His mother was flushed and sat with her head up, her chin high, as if she were Joan of Arc ready to go into battle alone.

"They *must* win."

"That's what Sasha said," Stefan noted, slicing into his steak. And he felt that his mother and Sasha probably believed in all underdogs everywhere. Stefan was very proud of them, but also a little concerned. Sasha hadn't been sleeping at all, and his mother was calling several times a day, like she was afraid that they could be separated even more than they were by the divorce.

His mother had even taken his hand when they crossed the street to the museum. Before he could snatch it away and complain, she laughed and lightly patted her cheek as if slapping it. "I'm sorry," she said. "An old habit."

"It's better than smoking," Stefan quipped, and she and Sasha eyed him with delight.

That evening his father called from Michigan.

"Are you okay?" he asked.

Stefan said "What do you mean?" His father's voice was as cool and unemotional as someone asking questions for a survey about dish detergent.

"The war. It's hard when you're young."

"There's a war in Vietnam, Dad. I watch the news, I read the papers."

"I know that—but the outcome there isn't doubtful. The U.S. can't lose, but Israel might."

"Even with wiping out the Egyptian air force?" He was prepared to disagree with everything his father said tonight. Maybe it *was* the war, or maybe it was just that he couldn't relax with both his mother and father, but had to be mad at one of them at least.

His father gave up after a while, asked some questions about his school work, and then asked him to get Sasha.

Stefan closed the kitchen door when Sasha was on the phone, and went to play something to drown out the sounds of their

conversation. He chose the last movement of a Haydn concerto—
the *Rondo alla Turca*. It was fast and noisy enough.

All week, Stefan had found himself practically ready to cheer
every time he heard something good about Israel. Kids at school
were jubilant, and he felt swept along. Well, most kids. Some
looked annoyed or even ashamed, especially Eddie, who knew he
had probably picked the losing side, and would have to settle a lot
of debts.

Stefan almost felt sorry for him, and the night that it was clear
the war was over, was a miracle of victory, he imagined having
Eddie over, and playing for him, or something. And he found
himself before bed remembering Eddie in the gym showers one
time after a volleyball game that he and Eddie had basically won.
Eddie had slapped his back and rubbed it, calling him Champ. And
then, stepping away from him and everyone else, Eddie had swung
out his incredibly long penis, flicked it up to his belly past his navel.
"Look!" he shouted, "My cock's a clock. It's midnight!"

He dreamed something very confusing, about crossing the Sinai
in a tank with Eddie.

6

Because his father was in Michigan, there were only two people to hassle him about his hair. Sasha just looked at him, fighting obvious disappointment. Like he was wondering what he had done wrong or something. Stefan's mother wasn't that subtle.

"Every time I see you," she would say cheerfully. "Your hair's longer." She sounded as bright and surprised as someone whose carpet had sprouted daisies.

"That's right, Mom."

"Do you *have* to grow your hair long, just because everyone else is?"

"Everyone else isn't. Lots of kids at school have short hair." By which he meant crew cuts or styles like Dick Van Dyke, Opie in "The Andy Griffith Show"—dumb haircuts, he thought, hick haircuts. His was long enough now for a shag cut, and it looked great, though getting it styled was more expensive than a regular cut.

He had grown his hair longer not to be like anyone at school, anyone on TV, or even any rock musicians. What had inspired him was an older guy in high school who lived in his building, someone who barely said hello to him, but did nod at Sasha. That was Louie del Greco, who had the only Italian name on the buzzers or mailboxes. It was very exotic plopped in with names like Steinmetz, Goldenberg, Kravitz, Romanovsky, Mermelstein, Kedeny.

Louie played baseball, and Stefan often saw him twirling his bat on the way to or from a game, flushed and eager, or sweaty. Probably because he was Italian, Louie always looked like he had a tan. In fact, even in the winter Louie looked as dark as Stefan did at the end of a Rockaway summer. Louie's mother talked to Sasha and to him, but it was just neighbor talk—about stores or kids getting into trouble, the landlord, the lazy superintendent—talk that was meant for the lobby, the elevator, or waiting at the mailboxes for the mailman to finish.

Stefan had been covertly studying Louie, studying how he dressed: the type of beads he wore, the scarves, the hip-hugger bell-bottoms, the dark-brown suede fringed jacket. All his clothes were really cool—maybe because his father owned the cleaning store a few blocks up on Broadway, and Louie *had* to look good. Ever since Sasha had let Stefan go shopping to Korvette's and Macy's by himself when it wasn't a question of something like a winter coat, Stefan had been choosing clothes with Louie in mind. Louie was shorter and stockier than he was, but that didn't matter. He would imagine Louie there standing next to him in front of the mirror, saying, "Groovy" or pointing to a really cool shirt, pushing him away from belts that weren't wide enough and had buckles that were too small. These images were helpful because he felt good buying something he thought Louie would approve of; he felt mature. When he had shopped with his mother or Sasha, their standards for what was nice always seemed arbitrary, and he felt much younger than he really was, like he should be stomping his feet and saying "I want it—I want it!"

Because Louie was older, always with kids his own age, Stefan was surprised to get on the elevator with him one day after school and have Louie say, "Do you want a job? Part time?"

"What?"

"You know, J-O-B. You do work, you get money. Sound familiar?"

The elevator stopped at the fourth floor, and Louie got out. "Come on," he said. And Stefan followed to his black apartment door. "It's at my dad's store."

Stefan knew that Louie's mother sometimes worked there too; it was where he and Sasha took their clothes. He usually didn't see Louie in the store, because Louie was at the back, pressing.

Louie waved him into the apartment, and Stefan had a strange feeling that he was in a dream. The apartment was almost exactly like his and Sasha's, two floors up, but instead of opening to the left off the little foyer, it opened to the right.

"Want some doughnuts?" Louie headed into the kitchen, which was much more crowded than Sasha's, full of appliances, shiny copper pans, flowery wall plaques, plants in little pots, hanging kitchen gadgets, and dish towels. The colors were all red, green, and white.

"The Italian flag," Stefan murmured, sitting down at the small table covered with a red-and-white checked cloth.

"Pretty smart," Louie said, bringing out a gallon of milk, two big glasses, and a bag of chocolate Hostess doughnuts—Stefan's favorite.

Louie put on the kitchen radio, and they listened to a station play some Beatles songs from *Rubber Soul* and *Help!* They ate almost silently, grunting a little at each other when one wanted more milk. Sasha would hate how Louie ate, Stefan thought: noisily, with his mouth opening. And he slurped up the milk, almost sucked it in.

"He'd pay minimum wage," Louie said, abruptly setting down his glass so hard Stefan thought it would break. "It's not hard stuff. Just putting clothes together with the tickets after they're pressed. I do the pressing." And Louie held out one dark arm and made a muscle. His bicep was big and hard and veins ran across it as clearly as highways on a map. "Baseball camp," Louie said. "Every summer."

Following Louie to his room, Stefan felt envious—what did he do with his summers? Just went to the beach and read books.

There were few books in Louie's jammed and slightly smelly room, which was overflowing with clothes, dirty sneakers, baseball mitts, crumpled underwear, trophies, and lined with posters of the Yankees.

"My mom tries to clean it up, but I won't let her." Louie sat down on the floor, pulled a game out from under the bed, wiped dust from the cover. "You play Risk?"

And they launched into a hectic silent game, the little colored wooden squares surging back and forth across continents. Louie played like he was gambling, eyes on the board, tongue protruding sometimes, forehead scrunched. When he rolled the dice, he closed his eyes like he was praying, and kissed his fist. It was contagious, it made the game seem even more vital and earthshaking than games usually were. Louie's hands were grimy, his nails ragged— but they were large, larger than Stefan's. And when they hovered over the brightly colored board they made him think of the hands of a Roman god about to cause havoc on Earth.

That was what Louie looked like! With the clear dark eyes, wide-jawed face, and strong body, he was like the gods you saw in gladiator movies, or in picture books about mythology, or at the Metropolitan Museum.

"Hey—it's your move," Louie was saying.

Stefan had been imagining Louie in one of those short belted tunics that only covered half your chest.

"Are you deaf, asshole?" Louie asked, pushing at his knee.

"Fuck you!" Stefan said, pushing back, half-joking. And when Louie tried to hit him, he grabbed Louie's hand and they were soon rolling on the floor, wrestling, with pieces of the game scattering in every direction. Stefan was trying to do something, he didn't know what, trying to hold Louie down and keep him there, as if Louie were his bed at night, the lights were off, and he were

113

pressing into the sheets. Louie stopped struggling, and lay there underneath Stefan not moving, eyes half-shut.

"*Moron*," Louie said softly. "I was winning!" And he laughed, dark hair smeared to his forehead and face by sweat.

Stefan got up, turning away because of the stiffness in his pants, and he pretended to be interested in a trophy.

The front door slammed, and Louie called, "Hi Mom, we're down here."

Mrs. del Greco was standing in the doorway, surveying the room strewn with Risk pieces. Stefan turned to say hello, and she nodded, asked how his uncle was, and then said, "One day I'll just set a big fire in this room. That's the only way to clean it out."

"Gimme a break, Mom," Louie said, but Stefan saw that it wasn't serious, since he and his mother were smiling. Stefan wished he could be so relaxed with his mother.

"Will you stay for dinner?" Mrs. del Greco asked. "It's just lasagna."

"Wow. We never have lasagna." He looked at Louie, who nodded.

Stefan ran upstairs to leave a note for Sasha, and when he went back down, he helped Louie clean up, or at least put the Risk stuff away, back under the rumpled bed. They played cards and listened to Bob Dylan on Louie's eight track.

Stefan asked, "You *like* him?"

"He's great, man."

"But he can't sing."

Louie shook his head like he was very adult, and Stefan dropped it.

"I bet you like the Monkees," Louie sneered. "They don't even play their own instruments!"

"But the show's funny."

"It's *jive*."

"Your dad's late at the store," Louie's mother said when she called them to the kitchen.

"He's always late," Louie griped, sitting down and grabbing for

114

milk. His mother slapped his hand and they both laughed. Stefan sat opposite Louie, waiting.

"Go ahead, boys," Mrs. del Greco said, waving a spatula. "Start."

And they did. Everything was terrific, Stefan told her: the salad, the lasagna, the garlic bread.

"So skinny," she said, shaking her head. "Does your uncle feed you?"

Stefan started to answer, but realized it was a joke.

"So how come we never see you in church?" Louie's mother asked.

He shrugged.

"You're not Protestant, are you? Poles are good Catholics like us. They love the Holy Father."

"We're not religious."

"Who? Your parents? Your uncle?"

Stefan looked away from her friendly curiosity; what he'd said sounded childish and empty.

"Listen, you have to believe in something—no matter what you get in life." And she shrugged, as if referring to her own troubles— whatever they might be.

After dinner, when she shooed them out of the kitchen, Stefan briefly explored the apartment, which actually was larger than Sasha's, with a separate dining room crowded by swollen, dark, shiny furniture. "We use that for Sunday dinner," Louie explained.

The whole apartment was so full of chairs and lamps and pictures and statues of saints and Jesus and vases with plastic flowers it was like a store, or even a warehouse. It reminded him a little of the crowded chaotic Indian Museum further down Broadway not far from where he used to live.

Everything at the del Greco's seemed connected to the past. "Oh yeah," Louie might say, when Stefan picked up an ashtray— "That was my Great Aunt Teresa's."

They played some more cards, and then Stefan went home, his head buzzing with everything they had talked about, with dinner, with how he and Louie had wrestled.

"Did you have a nice time?" Sasha wanted to know.

"It was okay," Stefan dropped, reluctant to reveal anything at all. Then he mentioned the possibility of working in Mr. del Greco's store. "Just now and then," he said.

Sasha was seated at the piano, a steaming mug of tea on the small round-topped table within reach of his long arms.

He nodded, considering it. "If you want to."

That was what Sasha said about almost everything, as if he were unwilling to challenge Stefan, cautious of starting a fight.

"I'll go talk to Louie's father tomorrow," Sasha said.

Stefan shrugged. "Cool."

Del Greco's Cleaner's was on the west side of Broadway, just a block over from Fort Washington Avenue, but seemed very distant. Fort Washington was quiet, lined with large old trees that formed a canopy over the street, while Broadway was much wider, noisier and kind of dirty, with papers and stuff flying around when there was a breeze, and occasional dog turds in unexpected spots. The store was in a one-story building. On one side was a small bookstore that sold magazines, comics, and all the daily papers. On the other was a lady's shop, called a *corsetière*, that always made Stefan uncomfortable when he passed. The high narrow cleaning store was painted sky-blue inside, and stretched far back. Despite the air-conditioning, it was always warm or hot where Stefan started working near the cigar-shaped pressing machine and the steamers. Still, he liked feeling hidden back there behind the squatty beige cleaning machine and dryer and their companion bins, and behind the long oval two-leveled conveyer belt clothing rack that was a toy to him no matter how many times he pressed the controls to put away a finished ticket.

He liked working there, the order, the precision of shifting newly pressed clothes from the pressing line to his own, bringing white tickets back down from the counter, putting them in numerical order and clipping them to their little metal hangers, arranging ties, slacks, completing tickets, bagging them, and hanging them away was a steady source of achievement. And it was different. He worked almost without thinking, his own movements part of the heavy whoosh of the air-conditioning, the thunk and roar of the cleaning machine, the thud, stomp, clank, and hiss of the pressing machine. It was a very private world back there his three afternoons a week. A younger neighborhood kid did the deliveries, and Louie seemed to be there almost every time he was; when Mr. del Greco did the pressing instead of Louie, Mrs. del Greco was at the front, taking in clothes, running the high gleaming register, laughing with customers as if she were at some fancy but friendly hotel. She knew everyone's name, and spoke a few words to people in different languages: French, Spanish, German, Russian.

When he told her how impressed he was, she shrugged. "It's not so hard to say shirt in five languages. We talk clothes, it's no big deal."

Mr. del Greco was easy to work for: a large, red-faced cheerful man, who never lost his temper even when things broke down, a pair of pants was somehow lost, a stain didn't come out, a pipe broke. He looked just like Louie, only fatter and wrinkled, with less hair. Stefan envied how Louie and his father could tease each other a little, almost like they were friends.

The best part, though, was working with Louie. Louie didn't talk much when he pressed, and it made Stefan feel very adult to share the companionable silences punctuated by the scrape of metal hangers across the bar in front of him, the roll and rip of plastic bags. He liked being behind Louie, watching the broad strong back and shoulders in the sleeveless white T-shirt, the large hands that made the pressing machine seem puny. Stefan had tried, but he couldn't pull the levers all the way down as easily as Louie. Louie didn't make fun of him, though.

When he was done, Louie would pull off his T-shirt and wipe his chest and under his arms. He had some dark hair in his armpits, and more across his chest, which was very thick and tight—from all the baseball, Stefan figured. That chest made him feel scrawny by comparison. He was totally flat, skinny, but with a boy's body, not a man's.

They sometimes went down Broadway to the Greek place for

pizza, competing as to who could shake on more Parmesan and red pepper, and eat his slice without sneezing or choking. Then they usually went to Louie's apartment. Sometimes they did their homework together. It was strange to be taking classes that Louie had already had with the very same teachers. The assignments didn't seem to change at all. Being friends with Louie made him feel confident about when he would go to George Washington High School, or "Gee Dubs," as Louie said it was called.

"But don't you want to take the exam for Music and Art?" Louie asked him. "I thought you said you were good at the piano. *That's* the school to go to."

Stefan shrugged. After years of playing, he had come to realize that he would never get much better, never become a *pianist*, but would always just play the piano. Hearing Rudolph Serkin perform *Pictures at an Exhibition* at Carnegie Hall a year ago had convinced him that he should let his music be a hobby, something he liked, not anything to live for or dream about.

He thought of explaining this to Louie, but decided, for now, to just say, "Sometimes it's boring."

"What about Bronx Science?" Louie asked.

"With all those nerds?"

"Yeah," Louie said, "That would be pretty gross."

Stefan did not say that what really mattered to him was staying as close to what was familiar as possible when he went to high school. He knew where George Washington was—but thinking of taking a train to the Bronx or to Music and Art scared him. Either choice took him out of the two neighborhoods he had grown up in, and he didn't like that.

"Okay!" Louie said, slamming down a history book. " 'Nuf of this crap! Risk? Monopoly? Or maybe," he sneered, "Scrabble for the walking encyclopedia?"

"Don't call me that! I told you I hate it."

Louie sat back against his bed, arms crossed. "I could call you a dictionary. Dick, for short. How's that?"

Stefan enjoyed the teasing—it was strangely exciting, especially since it always wound up with their struggling and wrestling, like now, only today he ended up on the bottom, and Louie, who was heavier than Stefan had imagined, held him down, his arms pressed into the dusty carpet.

"Lemme go!"

"This time," Louie drawled, like a cowboy, and they soon settled into a game of Broadside, one of Stefan's old favorites. He loved the little red and blue plastic ships with their sails, the islands with cannons. It was like being in a pirate movie, where he could leap onto an enemy vessel and battle his way to the treasure.

"I like Louie," Sasha said now and then, though nobody had asked him. This time, it was at breakfast.

Stefan just nodded.

Louie had come to dinner a number of times, and Stefan was right that Sasha wouldn't appreciate how he ate. He caught Sasha's half-amused frown when Louie used two fingers to push food on his plate, but neither one of them mentioned it.

Sasha said, "Maybe he might want to come to Rockaway next summer? To stay there a weekend or two. We could put a cot in your room."

Stefan did not look up from his cornflakes, but ate more slowly. "Maybe," he said.

The idea excited him so much that he thought of it all day in school, at lunch, even in bed at night. Sleep-overs were for much younger kids, but as soon as he started working in the cleaning store, he imagined Louie sleeping over at his apartment. It could never happen, which made the fantasy more precious. But Rockaway—wouldn't that be like a sleep-over? They'd be in the same room all night, would stay up and talk, and eat potato chips and listen to the radio, make fun of kids at school or people they'd seen at the beach, play cards, wrestle.

"I'm glad you're working," his mother said on the phone a few weeks after he started his part-time job. "It's good experience. And Sasha says you have a new friend," his mother chirped.

"Jeez, Mom, I'm not a two year old."

There was a dangerous silence, and his mother hissed, "Don't ever use that tone with me."

She was always going on about his "tone" he told Sasha afterwards. "What am I, tone-deaf or something?"

Sasha peered at him, and then started to laugh. "I hope not," he said. "After all those lessons!"

Sasha's laughter kept Stefan from saying he wished Sasha hadn't said anything about Louie. He wanted to keep that private. But he knew that pretty much everything that happened to him got passed on to his mother and even his father. It wasn't like spying exactly, which was what Stefan had felt it to be when he was younger. It was more like the price Sasha probably had to pay, to keep things going, since it was all so unusual.

"Your mother's in *New York?*" Louie had asked, amazed.

"Brooklyn."

"Shit, that's New York! Even Staten Island is New York. I thought both your parents lived in Michigan, or were dead or something." Louie frowned, obviously trying to remember what he'd heard. "I mean, you live with your parents unless they're dead, or crazy, or in jail. So how come?"

He wanted to tell Louie, to be able to tell Louie, everything. But it didn't make sense to him, didn't really add up. There were too many blanks—like why they sometimes seemed to hate the Old Country even though they were always comparing America to it, with America generally losing out, why they had no relatives, why his father and mother seemed to enjoy the distance from each other and from him—well, at least he couldn't exactly see that they were suffering.

"It's all fucked up," he said, feeling hopeless.

Louie reached over and stroked his hair.

Stefan thought he might start crying, and he felt ashamed of how good it was to have Louie's hand touching him. He broke away. "Don't do that!" he said. "I'm not a baby!"

"No?" Louie was at him, tickling, going "Coochy-coo" and Stefan didn't laugh, couldn't laugh. He got angrier and angrier, feeling ridiculed, and fought back until Louie rolled onto his back

120

and Stefan was on top of him, feeling hard in his pants. He closed his eyes because Louie was silent, motionless, and he started rubbing his body against Louie's.

"I know what you want," Louie said quietly. And the soft voice seemed to crackle like a short-circuiting plug.

Stefan didn't understand. He couldn't move.

"Let's go into the bathroom," Louie said, getting up, brushing off his black chinos.

Stefan followed him and when he tried to shut the door, Louie put his arm out, stopping it. "Keep it open, so we can hear."

Hear the front door, Stefan realized, briefly frozen by the image of Louie's mother finding them there, just standing there, but red-faced and breathing hard, ready for—

Louie unbuckled his thick black belt, unsnapped and unzipped his pants, pulled them down with his white shorts. He was squinting, breathing hard.

"Touch it," he said.

Stefan had seen lots of guys in the showers after gym, had watched them soap up and get harder, gotten harder himself. But there was always a wall between them—as if the spray from the shower heads was impermeable, some kind of force field. Now, he was standing only a foot or two away from Louie, who was getting hard. Louie's was even darker than the rest of him, fatter than Stefan's, though just as long, hanging down in front of large round balls with a little hair on them. Louie pulled his short-sleeved shirt off as if he were opening curtains on a stage, tossed it into the bathtub, where the gold and green paisleys looked like fish swimming in the white porcelain.

"Touch it," he said again.

Stefan felt as exhilarated and free as if he were in the Super Bowl, returning a punt all the way down the field for a last-second touchdown. He pulled his own pants and shorts down, held himself out as if to say they were equals in this moment.

Louie moved closer, and so did Stefan. They both reached out and soon they were leaning into each other, pulling, stroking, licking their hands for moisture, bringing them back. Stefan kept

121

wanting to laugh out loud, to shout with relief that at last he was living the fantasy he had hardly let himself know was coiled inside of him like a snake, waiting to spring. He felt Louie's balls and back, the tight round behind that quivered underneath his hands, as Louie sighed and shifted from foot to foot. Louie's hands were very warm and heavy wherever they rested.

"Faster," Louie said, gritting his teeth, and soon he splattered all over Stefan's flat hairless belly. Louie fell against him, moaning a little, held him tight at the waist as Stefan rubbed up against him, harder, harder, imagining they were back on the floor, or in bed, and he too felt himself explode like wild and pounding drums, gluing himself even more tightly to Louie's body.

He couldn't speak.

With his pants still down, Louie hobbled over to the sink to get some tissues, and they wiped each other off as if it were just a spill at the kitchen table. The smell in the air—sweat and something else—was so intoxicating. Stefan wanted to just sit on the edge of the bathtub and breathe it in and in.

But what was he supposed to do or say now? Surely Louie knew—he was older, he was in high school.

Louie told him to get dressed, so he did. Louie ran cold water into the large round pedestal sink, half-filling it, and leaned down to dunk his face. He splashed in it like a dog digging its snout into a snowbank. Stefan handed him a towel when he was done.

"Thanks," Louie said. And they went back into Louie's room to play some cards. Stefan didn't ask if anything was wrong, because Louie wasn't acting different. They kidded each other, talked about the card game, sitting there cross-legged on the floor as if nothing different had happened.

But upstairs, Stefan felt like he was a stranger. He looked at the Degas ballet dancer prints in the living-room, at the shining friendly piano, at everything that was familiar and welcoming and felt himself alien, alone. This was the biggest secret he had ever had, and he guessed from Louie's silence that in a way it even had to be a secret from themselves—it wasn't something to talk about.

He was alone in the apartment, because Sasha had gone to see a neighbor down the block, and that was okay with Stefan.

He thought of when he first moved in, and some questions about a pregnant lady they saw at the library led Sasha to take out some books on sex for him. Stefan had read through the complicated books in a haze, as if it were all less real than *The Hobbit* or *I, Robot* which he was reading at the time. Even when he had started to wake up wet in the crotch at night, and had discovered how much fun it was to rub himself into his sheets and feel a little burst, he had not really connected all that with the books he'd read.

But this was different. This was sex, it had to be, even though he couldn't remember reading anything about two guys together, with their pants down. He felt like Henry Hudson discovering the widest river anyone had ever seen, mysterious and frightening, but leading him onward. He wanted to do it again with Louie, he wanted to see Louie naked—as naked as all the guys he realized now he'd always tried not staring at in the showers—like Eddie Morrice, who really looked like he had a skinned hot dog hanging down there, and Eric Stone, who guys joked about, because the end of his was covered over, with something like a little hood that made it pointy. Eric had to pull it back, to wash completely, and Stefan had been fascinated at the small temporary ring of flesh.

Blushing, he couldn't help wonder what Sasha looked like without clothes—he'd never seen him in anything less than a bathrobe—and now he squeezed his eyes shut as if he could squeeze the picture right out of his brain. He went to the piano to lose himself in playing, it didn't matter what. But even the grave opening of the Mozart *Fantasia* couldn't wipe away the images of naked men: teachers at school, all the guys in his class. He imagined them lined up and frozen like statues or trees, and they were all *his.* He could move among them, touch anyone anywhere, do whatever he wanted with them.

What he most wanted was to be with Louie again. And he was, that night, lying on his back after Sasha was asleep, and Stefan had put away his book, *The Time Machine.* Pulling with both his hands, cupping his balls, he imagined Louie there, smiling, guiding him, applauding as he splashed his own face.

A few nights later, after their homework was all done, Louie came up to his place so they could watch *Ben Hur*. Sasha was off giving a late lesson.

They gobbled pretzels and popcorn. Stefan had seen the movie before, been excited by it, but sitting there now with Louie he understood his excitement for the first time. It wasn't just the battles, the trumpet calls, the costumes and huge pillars, even the vicious chariot race. It was Charlton Heston, slim, dark, hairy, almost naked.

"You can see his dick," Louie muttered, waving at Charlton Heston's loincloth in one scene.

"Wow."

Stefan imagined himself in the sea-battle scene, rescuing Louie as a Roman, and drifting on a large raft with him. They would hold each other, and touch, and later, picked up by the Roman galley and returned to Rome, they would be bathed by slaves, perfumed, combed, massaged, and dressed. They would feed each other, drink from the same goblet, and at night find themselves in a room swathed in silk and cloth of gold, where they would spend the whole night together.

"Would you want to do it with him?" Stefan asked, when there was a close-up of Charlton Heston.

Louie shrugged. "You're enough for me."

Stefan forced himself not to fling his bowl of pretzels into the air with a shout. He just stuffed some more into his mouth and chewed.

"Those Jews," Louie said at one point, shaking his head.

"What about them?"

"They killed Jesus, dummy! That's what."

Stefan remembered Sasha explaining this question to him years ago. So now he said: "The Romans did it, and it's wrong to blame the Jews." His words sounded stiff, rehearsed, and he wasn't sure he meant what he said.

"That's not what the Bible says. The Bible says they did and they knew it and God's always gonna hate them. Haven't you read all that?"

Stefan was too embarrassed to say he had never opened a Bible, not even in the library or a bookstore. He always felt a vague unease around one—something in Sasha's attitude had communicated itself to him. And once his mother had said, "More people have died because of that book than any other." It left him feeling that somehow the book itself was as dangerous as kryptonite for Superman.

"You're so stupid, sometimes," Louie concluded, and Stefan had to quietly agree. "Aren't you worried about going to hell or anything?"

Stefan felt on safer ground. "My Uncle says he's seen hell, and it's on earth."

"Like where?"

"In Europe, in the War."

"Was he a soldier?"

Stefan fell silent. He didn't want to reveal the vastness of his ignorance and be mocked even more, but he didn't want to lie to Louie either.

Luckily, there was a key in the door, and Sasha let himself in.

"Hi, boys. What are you watching?"

Ben Hur, they chimed.

Sasha nodded and went off to the kitchen.

Thinking of Charlton Heston, Stefan said, "It should be Ben Him, get it?" And he dug his elbow into Louie until he admitted that it was funny.

Watching movies at home wasn't as much fun as going to theaters with Louie, walking down to the RKO Coliseum at 181st Street or to the smaller Loew's at 175th and Broadway. He liked passing all the different apartment buildings and stores on the way, anticipating the popcorn, the orange soda, the Chuckles, Jujubees, and sitting next to Louie in the dark, legs almost touching, arms sometimes rubbing on the shared armrest, breathing in Louie's smell, which seemed heavier in the dark, like he was some kind of rare flower in a book. They liked to sit in the very last row downstairs, with the balcony hanging down over them. Each theater was kind of like a castle to Stefan—enormous, drowning in velvet, with marble stairs and railings, gold paint, angels, ornate balconies, and statued alcoves. Sasha, of course, did not share his enthusiasm for all the decoration.

Their favorite movies were anything with James Bond, and afterwards, on the walk home, they would play out their favorite parts, showing off who could remember more details, imagining having secret briefcases and pencils that were cameras. Watching Sean Connery with his shirt off made him think now of Louie, and when 007 was grappling on-screen with a Russian lady agent or someone in a bikini, Stefan saw all the details differently. It was him and Louie in the lavish hotel suite, the enormous bathtub, the stretch of sand, kissing.

He wanted to kiss Louie, but was afraid. He wouldn't do much of anything until Louie did it first, or made the silent suggestion, because this was a game he was afraid might break up in an argument over the rules—like when you played Risk with a bunch of kids, and there was always some kind of fight.

The first time they lay down on the bathroom floor in Louie's apartment, Stefan was surprised, partly because it was uncomfortable—his knees and elbows got rubbed too much and he felt cold—but also because he'd imagined it, and it was coming true. It was really just as exciting as standing up.

And then, a few days later, when he and Louie were in the cleaning store, Louie beckoned him over, and just put his hand on Louie's pants, which were bulging. Louie didn't talk, or even smile. He closed his eyes until the bell over the front door jangled and someone came in to Mrs. del Greco's cheerful greeting.

That same day, up at Louie's, they didn't go into the bathroom when Louie put down the model aircraft carrier they'd been looking at. Louie slipped off his loafers and socks, stepped out of his pants, his shorts, and sat on the edge of the bed, cupping his hands under himself.

Watching this, Stefan thought of the picture in Sasha's Gauguin book of a native woman holding a platter of fruit, her breasts large and round.

"Why don't you put it in your mouth?" Louie suggested, and Stefan got down on his knees, crawled closer, bent over, eyes closed, imagining he was James Bond or Charlton Heston or with one of them, confident, controlled. He did what Louie wanted, a little, then Louie did that for him, then they lay on their sides on the floor and tried it together, but it was too complicated and Stefan ended up climbing onto Louie like other times, and they were both quickly done.

His fantasies at night were now much clearer, full of details, smells and sounds, and especially dialogue. Because he could say whatever he wanted to in his head, and do anything—like kiss Louie, take a shower with him, wash his back and shampoo his hair. He imagined the two of them on the beach at Rockaway sometimes, in the blistering heat, with no one else there, and just to cool off, they would go back under the boardwalk, where the sand was shaded and almost cold to your feet. And no one would see them.

And sometimes he imagined himself and Louie in Europe, Poland mostly, discovering Stefan's ancestors, the homes his family had lived in. Everyone would be nice to them, and they would stay in something like a ski lodge, with a big fireplace, and heavy goose-down comforters, and no one would suspect anything, no one would think anything funny about two guys in one bed.

Stefan thought that Sasha was beginning to look at him differently, especially when he'd just got back from spending time with Louie, or just after Louie had left. It was like the times he had broken something—a small vase, or eaten more doughnuts than Sasha had said was okay. And Sasha was looking at him, waiting for a confession. That was very different from the way his father used to yell at him and bluster, but it wasn't exactly better. He almost felt like he was eating a big dinner and a pitiful dog was staring at him, wide-eyed and hopeful, unwilling to budge, until he had to break down, had to give it something from his plate.

But he wouldn't talk about what had happened between him and Louie.

"You've become good friends," Sasha observed, idling through the Sunday *Times* one afternoon, inspecting all the announcements of concerts and recitals.

Stefan grunted his agreement.

"It's good to have a friend," Sasha said.

"Right."

Stefan was reading a long and kind of confusing article about China's Cultural Revolution in the *Times* magazine.

"It's good to have *many* friends."

Stefan looked up, but Sasha was holding the paper in front of his face.

"Why many?"

"Variety," Sasha said after a moment, turning a page.

"You once told me that Americans make too much out of having lots of friends, and being popular."

That stopped Sasha, who could only say "Really?"

"And you don't have that many friends," Stefan wanted to add, because he'd always been puzzled by that absence. Somehow his parents and Sasha had cut themselves off not only from the past and Poland, but from *everything*.

The next time he was alone with Louie, in Sasha's place, Stefan felt a little defiant. Being with Louie was more than just being together, it was proving something to Sasha—though Stefan didn't know what.

So when Louie pushed him down by the shoulders onto his knees, Stefan plunged his mouth forward more hungrily than any time they'd done the same thing.

"Sweet Jesus. . . ." Louie said, his hands clutching Stefan's hair. He didn't pull away, but started to thrust so quickly that Stefan knew his efforts, his rebellion would be complete.

"I'm—"

But before Louie could finish the sentence he collapsed against Stefan, shuddering and sighing, "Oh, shit, oh, shit."

Stefan let his mouth be filled before pulling back. He swallowed, eyes closed, feeling warm and calm, until Louie made him stand up, and licked at him like he was ice cream.

His library books always took precedence over what he had to read for school, and so homework assignments, no matter how complicated, and tests didn't ever seem important or real. He knew he could basically whip through his material after lingering in a book that he had chosen.

But he had trouble reading now. He kept putting his book down, especially if he was reading in bed. Either Louie was in the story, or he just remembered Louie's hands and mouth. They got together every chance they could, even slipping into the bathroom at the cleaning store sometimes, just to touch each other.

Louie had gotten him to watch "The Man from U.N.C.L.E." and Stefan often wished he could go off on adventures with Illya Kuryakin. He felt like a secret agent, living two lives. He was keenly aware of Sasha's schedule and noises and everything that could possibly interfere with him and Louie. Sometimes they did things twice in an afternoon, which by bedtime, when Stefan relived the experience, would leave him sore and a little swollen.

He found himself having crazy fantasies that weren't just sex. In one, he and Louie went to Michigan, which he had never seen, except in snapshots. Stefan's father played a vague role—like leaving them his house for the summer or something like that. And they would go swimming and lie around in the nude, get suntanned. Or he and Louie could become famous—at something— and wind up rich on Park Avenue, drinking champagne on a green velvet couch, surrounded by books and paintings and photographs of themselves in gold and silver frames. There would be a piano, too, a long white one, and whenever Stefan played, Louie would sit next to him, turning the pages.

That truly was a fantasy, because the one or two times he had played for Louie, his new friend didn't even try hiding his yawns, didn't look embarrassed when Stefan stopped and considered glaring at him.

He wanted to give Louie something, something no one else could give him.

But Stefan didn't know what that might be.

"Are you feeling well?" Sasha was asking on and off, looking ready to put a hand to his forehead.

"I'm fine!"

"Because you seem . . . distracted lately. Maybe you should do things with more people, make other friends."

Stefan knew that Sasha and his parents had been very worried about his heavy reading, his unwillingness to spend a lot of time in the park with other kids, to do after-school activities. Trying to make friends had always seemed pointless and humiliating to Stefan—which was why Louie was such a blessing. Louie had sought him out. Louie *liked* him.

A few weeks before Christmas, Louie started joking about "stocking stuffers." At first, Stefan didn't get it, and when he did, he felt abashed at being so ignorant. Then he was afraid that he might be misinterpreting what Louie meant, but Louie held up a finger which he shoved into his fist, and Stefan was too excited to object or ask any questions.

"You first," Louie said one afternoon, up in Stefan's bathroom. Their pants were down, and Louie turned around, bent over and braced his hands on his legs.

"Get some Vaseline or something, smear it on," Louie directed. "Ow! Lower."

Stefan was amazed at the ease with which he slid inside Louie, at the warmth and tightness. He leaned over, clutching Louie's chest, but before he could get used to the sliding and pulling, he gave way with a gasp.

"Wait a minute," Louie said, when Stefan tried to move away, and when he did wait, it shrunk and plopped out by itself.

"My turn," Louie said, but even with lots of Vaseline, it hurt and Stefan had to make Louie stop. "Then gimme your hand," Louie said, and they were soon washing up at the sink.

Because of what they had planned for the afternoon, the bathroom door was closed and looked. Stefan almost yelled when Sasha knocked on the door. He hadn't heard Sasha come home.

"Who's in there?"

"Me and Louie."

"What are you doing?"

"Washing up."

Sasha tried the door, which Stefan hurriedly unlocked.

"Hi," Louie said, calmly drying his hands.

"Why was this door locked?"

Stefan couldn't face his uncle, who looked shocked and disappointed. He pulled the plug from the sink to let the soapy water gurgle out.

"I'm going to make some coffee," Sasha said, leaving them there in the doorway.

"Got to help my mom with something," Louie said, and was gone.

Stefan drifted into his room, furious at himself for having locked the door, at Sasha for being home early, at Louie for suggesting what they had done. "It's his fault," he heard himself saying to Sasha, if the secret came out.

But Sasha didn't say a word about it that day, the next, or any other time. As if he had silently agreed with Stefan that nothing had happened.

And instead of feeling completely relieved, Stefan thought, "Something else not to talk about."

7

Because Sasha and his parents had always seemed even more distant and preoccupied than usual during the Christmas season, Stefan had never felt much different, even though he knew he'd be getting presents and it meant vacation from school. He couldn't feel like celebrating, because it was the time of year he felt most detached from other kids at school, who were almost stupid with excitement. Even the Jewish kids had something to look forward to with Hanukkah, which seemed a lot like Christmas to Stefan, only with less decorations.

When he and Sasha bought their Christmas trees on Broadway, and strung them each year with lights and popcorn, it seemed like an obligation they were fulfilling, a kind of job.

"Do you miss your parents?" he asked Sasha one Christmas Eve.

"What?" Sasha's eyes were wide.

Stefan explained: "Because it's Christmas."

"I always miss them," Sasha brought out heavily, and his sadness kept Stefan from pushing for more information. The past was like one of those stupid and depressing mazes: he could get past the entrance, but no further. And what lay ahead was frightening and confused.

Stefan's presents had gotten better and more numerous since the divorce, but he still had never enjoyed the cheeriness he was now discovering with the del Grecos. First of all, their cleaning store was hung with large wreaths, ribbons, and glittery MERRY XMAS signs and cardboard Santas. The store window had a flashing little tree, fake snow, poinsettias, and a plastic sleigh with reindeer. And Mr. del Greco gave customers a choice of five different store calendars with Christmas or winter scenes. Working at the back of the store, Stefan was practically pelted by all the cheerful holiday greetings of customers and the del Grecos. It was like they were all on the way to an incredible party—one that *he* hadn't been invited to.

The del Greco apartment was a wonderland for Stefan. It teemed with little plastic and porcelain Santas (with sleigh and without) on bookcases, shelves, the television, the refrigerator. There were big red velvet bows on all the doors, and smaller ones on picture frames, the backs of chairs; sleigh bells on the doorknobs; red and green candles, thick and thin, nested in beds of plastic evergreen throughout the house; brass angels hung from all the light fixtures; cloth elves grinned from unexpected corners; all the house plants had miniature tree ornaments; and electric lights were strung around each window not just so they could be seen from the street, but also in the apartment. On the front door there was an enormous fragrant wreath studded with pinecones and tiny red bows. The tree in their living room was so thick with tinsel, white satin bows, glass and china ornaments, glass snowflakes and stars, gold and green lights it seemed impossible that it could bear all that weight of festivity. Everything was bright and hot and shiny. And the manger scene on the dining room buffet was so complicated, so full of dozens of realistically painted figures and animals—it was as elaborate as the most fantastic model railroad set you could imagine. It had belonged to Mrs. del Greco's grandmother, and hearing that made Stefan ache for something, anything, from his own grandparents. But there was nothing, not even a photograph.

"You know," Louie said, "My mom kind of goes crazy at Christmas."

The sheer number of big and little ornaments everywhere amazed Stefan, and made his and Sasha's little tree and their halfhearted attempts to decorate seem even more pathetic. A few times, he had considered bringing Sasha down to see all the decorations, but he could imagine Sasha's pained attempts not to be impolite, while inwardly he was gagging at the display of so much American vulgarity—as he would see it. Sasha would be appalled by the music box shaped like a chimney, with Santa on top of cotton snow.

But Stefan didn't think Louie's mother was vulgar or crazy. She was *happy*. Whenever he was at Louie's house, Mrs. del Greco was cheerfully baking cookies, pies, cakes, planning meals, marking things off a giant list on her refrigerator door. Dressed in skirts and sweaters with Christmas themes and colors, she hummed or sang, danced a little when the radio played a Christmas song, and seemed almost like a girl Stefan's age. She talked about all the upcoming Christmas specials on TV, and she laughed about how much work she had to do.

"How come you're so gloomy?" she kept asking Stefan. "Have you been a bad little boy?

It would have been embarrassing to say that he had always been kind of gloomy at Christmas, and that he sometimes wondered if someone in his parents' family had died at Christmastime—forever overshadowing what was supposed to be a time of joy.

Mrs. del Greco was rolling out some dough on a floured counter. "Are you afraid Santa will leave coal in your stocking?"

At the mention of "stocking," Stefan looked down at his plate of brownies, wondering what Louie was thinking. Wondering if Louie was afraid his parents would find out about their "stuff" and keep the two of them apart.

134

"Well *I* know what'll cheer you up! Christmas dinner with us. We're having a turkey with all the trimmings—fantastic, huh?"

He nodded eagerly, then glanced at Louie, who said "Sure" and smiled.

At home, he asked Sasha why they never made so much fuss at Christmas.

"Because it's vulgar here, cheap."

"But you had Christmas in Poland, so why did you stop celebrating, really celebrating?"

Sasha shook his head. "It's too complicated."

"Why won't you talk about the War, about what happened to you before you came to America, about our family, about *anything?*"

"Who's been asking you all this? Louie?"

Stefan gave up, because he didn't want to risk arguing about Louie in any way. Since Sasha had almost found them in the bathroom, he had been very careful to mention Louie as little as possible—even though that was pretty strange, since they spent so much time together, after school, at the cleaning store, going to movies on the weekend. But he had Louie come up to his apartment less than he went down to Louie's.

What Stefan was most afraid of was a call from his father, or a visit from his mother and a humiliating quiet interrogation. And then Mr. and Mrs. del Greco would come in and everyone would be talking about him, dragging his secrets into the light. The more stuff he did with Louie, the clearer it seemed that this was all something forbidden and forbidding. Louie resisted Stefan's few attempts to ask how he felt about their stuff. When their pants were down, they communicated with grunts, or just shifting each other's hands in some way. Afterwards, they didn't smile at each other, touch or talk; before, there would be the tension as each seemed to wait for the other to start the wrestling, or just say, "Let's go into the bathroom."

He wanted to know more about Louie. He wanted to know if Louie had done things with other guys, and which guys, which things, for how long, what was it like. He wanted to know if his own feelings were a surprise too. If Louie had also never really thought about touching a guy so clearly until after he had already done it. But he didn't want to annoy Louie, to act like an obnoxious puppy pawing at you, too eager to play. Louie was older, after all, and Stefan kept expecting him to suddenly turn around and call him a jerk, an idiot, a kid, and say he didn't want to hang out together anymore. When he saw Louie with friends from George Washington, Stefan felt intimidated and shy. Even though Louie didn't ignore him then, said "Hi!" and waved, Stefan felt excluded. In a group, Louie seemed alien and powerful. It was kind of like the museums at Audubon Terrace on 155th and Broadway. It was a superlong block that stretched down to Riverside Drive, formerly the estate of James Audubon, a teacher had told Stefan. Now, it was covered with big stone buildings that had red-tile roofs like in Italy. There was the National Geographic Society, the Hispanic Society, the Indian Museum, the Numismatic Society, and a bunch of statues in a sunken court at the center. The sidewalk was some kind of reddish stone or brick—and when he thought about it, it was very strange that all those buildings were there, looking so foreign and unknowable right in the middle of everything else. Yet Stefan had passed it all the time growing up. That was Louie too; he was already used to Louie, but when he kind of stepped back, Louie seemed a little mysterious and out of place.

Louie's mother was full of questions about Stefan's Christmas. "We had some Polish neighbors back years ago, the Sobieskis. They made vodka with peppercorns in it for Christmas, and put straw under the tablecloth for Christmas dinner."

She waited, and Stefan said, "We don't do that."

"What's the straw for?" Louie asked.

Stefan guessed, "The manger?"

"Of course!" Mrs. del Greco seemed as pleased as if Stefan were her own son and had passed some kind of test. "So that you're eating with Joseph and Mary and Christ. Will your father come in from Michigan?" Mrs. del Greco went on, and when Stefan shrugged, her silence clearly indicated she disapproved of the curious arrangements in his family.

Once or twice his father had come back to New York at Christmas, but it was terrible and awkward. Like Stefan imagined it would be for an American ambassador finally going to Red China, recognizing that it existed. They did talk at the holiday, though. His father called to find out if his presents had come (they were always at least a week early), and to tell him about the snow in Michigan or something equally stupid. His father talked about cross-country skiing, and tried to make Michigan in winter sound as glamorous as Switzerland, but Stefan had never been convinced. On the map, the part of Michigan his father lived in, the lower peninsula, looked like a glove or mitten, and he could never picture that without imagining the glove closing, squeezing and crushing where his father lived in Ann Arbor. His father rattled on about what a terrific football team they had, and had even tried to get Stefan to come out for the Ohio State game—supposedly a nationally significant event. But Stefan always refused, despite Sasha's disappointment, and even his mother's "Are you sure?" He told his father that college football was boring. His father said, "Well, maybe next year."

His father was apparently doing very well at the university, Sasha informed him, had gotten tenure and been promoted to full professor, was doing everything right, and Stefan hated his success.

"His work is getting attention," Sasha said more than once. "He wrote a book. . . ."

"So what? Lots of people write books."

His father had sent him a copy, inscribed: For my dear son. Stefan had ripped that page up and thrown it out, even thought of burning the book, but it was too thick, so he just tossed it into a pile of junk at the back of his closet.

He usually let Sasha decide what Christmas presents to buy for his father and mother; they signed the cards and gift tags together, though Stefan didn't much care what Sasha bought. Sasha always got him new albums and sheet music; his mother bought him clothes, pretty nice clothes; his father sent lots of books—European classics—like the complete works of Jane Austen, stories by de Maupassant, Russian and French novels that Stefan read in a blur if he did read them at all, unable to disassociate the gift from the giver, but intrigued by books he knew from Sasha were *important*. And they were books Sasha and his parents had read before the War.

Louie asked Stefan which Christmas carols he could play.

"None? Then what good's a big piano if you can't use it?"

"I use it plenty," Stefan said, forced into a lie.

"But you can't play any carols. Or any songs, either, I bet."

"Oh, like 'Blowin' in the Wind'?"

"Don't goof on Dylan—"

"He's a jerk with a big nose and a shit voice."

Louie seemed ready to pounce on Stefan, but perhaps because their wrestling always led to something else, he held back.

All Louie did was say, "You're weird."

Sasha had actually asked him more than once if he wanted to play any contemporary music, like anything from *My Fair Lady* or even the Beatles. But these questions were always somewhat careful, as if Sasha were afraid Stefan would say Yes!

To learn new music would have meant that playing was still as much a part of his life as it had always been. But it wasn't. He still listened to classical music on the radio and on Sasha's hi-fi—but his tastes had changed. He had come to like the cynicism and playfulness of Poulenc, who Sasha thought "shallow." What they *could* share was Stefan's love of Russian composers like Borodin, Khachaturian, Stravinsky. The wilder and more Orientalist, the better for Stefan, because it all took him to the Poland that was only in his imagination. Like whenever he heard the sleigh bells in Prokofiev's *"Lieutenant Kije Suite"*—and imagined himself hurtling along a snowy street, reins tight in his hands, sitting there triumphant in a huge fur coat and hat. It was a picture inspired by watching *Doctor Zhivago*—a movie that Sasha had called *"Dr. Kvatch."*

"What's that?"

"Kvatch? Trash, sentimental junk."

"In what language?"

"German."

And Stefan remembered the trouble over *Winter Eyes*, how his father had said he hated Germans.

And while Sasha played and taught German music, he must have hated them too. Because he was always inspecting things they bought in stores—like clocks, knives, kitchen gadgets—to see where they were made. If the label or markings said "Made in Germany" or "Federal Republic of Germany," Sasha didn't buy it. And if he forgot to check, and found out afterwards, he always returned it without a qualm.

"I won't support them," he said simply. "Not after the War."

In his slight reading about modern European history, and about World War II, Stefan had come to understand a little the hatred that Germany inspired not just in the Poles, but in many nations. Yet Sasha's embargo on German goods struck him as something different, something more personal than history.

"You can come to midnight Mass with us," Louie said about a week before Christmas. "It's pretty cool. They close all the lights right before midnight, the choir comes in holding candles, then you hear the organ. It's really cool—"

Stefan wondered what he could say that would hide his ignorance about churches and what went on inside of them.

"Do you believe in God?" he asked.

Louie thought a little. "Not like my mom and dad do. They're *serious.*"

He wanted to go to church with Louie, to plunge into something joyful and holy, instead of treating Christmas like it was almost a punishment.

"Go," Sasha said. "I can't stop you."

"You want to stop me?"

Sasha shook his head, as if already weary with the effort of explaining—but he had explained nothing.

"Maybe Mom would come. . . ." Stefan said aloud.

But he didn't get a chance to ask her.

His father called the day after Louie suggested midnight Mass. Whenever he heard his father's voice on the phone, he wanted to hang up, or smash the phone against the wall, or just hold it away from him, so that his father couldn't come any closer.

"Are you okay?" his father asked. "Enjoying New York now? Have you been on Fifth Avenue yet?"

And Stefan briefly relaxed, remembering the years that he and his parents had gone to Fifth Avenue just to see how many people were there. It was a wall of faces and fur, wool and leather coats, punctuated by store shopping bags that seemed alive as they eddied in the constant surge of more and more people. They would buy those big hot salty pretzels from stands whose owners wore black gloves with half the fingers cut off. They would watch the skaters at Rockefeller Center, where the tree seemed more like a monument than something that had been alive—as heavy as Atlas nearby holding up the world.

"Not much," he said, wondering how he could let his father know that he was recalling something pleasant, without seeming like he had forgiven his father for any of what had happened.

After some idle questions about school, Stefan said, "Should I get Sasha?"

"Not yet. I have to tell you something."

"What?"

"I'm sick. I had a heart attack, a small one, but the doctors think it'll get worse."

"Worse?" It felt good to grab one of his father's words.

"Much worse."

"Oh."

"Maybe I should talk to Sasha."

"Sure," Stefan said, and called out for Sasha, who came in from the living room, face a little tight, since he had obviously been listening and knew who it was.

Stefan felt very cold, like he might start shaking. He went to his room, crawled under the covers without turning on the lights, and forced his mind to go blank, forced himself to sleep.

But Sasha woke him up not much later, just by sitting on the bed. Stefan felt the pressure, and rubbed at his eyes. "What?"

"We should go to Michigan." Sasha's face was hard to read now. "It's heart trouble."

Stefan looked away.

"He could die," Sasha said, as if repeating himself.

"So what?"

Sasha stood, blinking furiously, hands clenched. "He *is* your father. No matter what."

Sasha suddenly looked kind of old to Stefan, battered, heavy at the waist, his hair thinning and receding, old and defeated. But Stefan didn't care about hurting even Sasha's feelings. "You go," he said. "I'm having Christmas with Louie's family."

Sasha just walked out.

They didn't talk for a whole day, and it was much worse than Stefan could have imagined. While silence from his father or mother was something he welcomed, Sasha's silence was cruel and unbearable.

"Why do I have to go?" he finally asked, sitting down next to Sasha at the piano the next evening.

"What if you never see him again? What if he dies and you always wish you did go, did see him? This could be your last chance." He looked away. "You don't always know when you'll see someone again."

And Stefan suddenly felt a peculiar surge of pleasure. It was almost as if the possibility of his father's death was a gift, a sure thing. If he *did* go, he would never have to see his father again.

"What about Mom?"

"I called her this morning. She's worried about you. But—"

"—she doesn't care either."

"No. That's not true. She just can't see him."

And Stefan felt himself to be braver than his mother, as if she were a general in World War I avoiding even the sight of trenches, the mindless charges and bombardments, the land mines leaving bits of flesh on barbed wire. Instead, she was safe at headquarters, safe and warm. While he and Sasha were headed into the unknown.

"You'll go?" Sasha asked, hands on his shoulders, looking into his eyes.

"I'll go with you."

It was snowing when their train left New York, and so Stefan passed through "America"—which Sasha had promised he'd see a little of—as if it were all just a painted backdrop in a movie. It didn't matter if there were cities, fields, factories, hills. It didn't matter that they passed through states he had never seen and never even thought much about. New Jersey? Pennsylvania? Ohio? Those were names from history books, names from the news or maps. It was all unreal and annoying.

"Your father is ill and you're going to see him?" Mrs. del Greco had said. And she smiled tearfully, as if this were some longed-for fulfillment, as if Stefan and his father truly meant something to her. "I want you to take something with you." And she gave Stefan several Christmas tins of brownies (dark chocolate and light), frosted cookies in the shape of Christmas trees, and Russian tea cakes.

Louie said, "You want your present now?" He had bought Stefan some James Bond books. Stefan shyly handed over his small package for Louie. He had blushed at the store buying the black shiny beads when the clerk asked if the "love beads" were for his girlfriend.

"Cool," Louie said, carefully slipping them over his head onto his neck.

Louie was unemotional about the trip, but Stefan didn't know if that was because his mother had embarrassed him by her extra baking and her tears. Before he left, he wanted to secure some kind of admission from Louie, a promise, an indication that he was important to Louie. But he couldn't be sure what form that would take and he didn't know how to ask Louie for comfort or advice.

"I hope your dad gets better," Louie said.

"I hope he dies," Stefan shot back, half because he did, half because he wanted to shock Louie. But it didn't work.

"You are *weird*," Louie said. And he didn't even say anything about Stefan missing Christmas with them.

Right before he left, he tried writing Louie a poem, but he could only come up with four lines:

We wrestle and touch, so close are we
It's been much less than a year
And between us friend is a mighty wall
That's built up of our fear.

He wanted to say more, to move Louie, but he felt powerless to find the words that could describe what was going on inside of him. This wasn't like the stupid little English assignments he never had any trouble with—this was something real, and he couldn't do it. He couldn't communicate, he could only feel miserable. He made a copy, then tore up the original, and tore up the copy too—though he knew he could write it down any time. How could he forget it?

On the crowded stifling train, he read a library book, or tried to. It was a novel called *Another Country*, all about black and white people, and sex, and racism, and music. It was very confusing to Stefan. He kept thinking he was just around the corner from understanding it, but he never exactly did. Yet he was excited, because for the first time, he was catching glimpses in a book of someone a little like him, someone who wanted to touch another guy. And there was something alive in the characters that made all the other books he had liked seem childish and dull. Sometimes he would stop and repeat a phrase or description softly, imagining that he had written the words.

"Isn't that a little advanced for you?" Sasha frowned when he saw the title on the book spine.

Stefan shrugged. "I have a twelfth-grade reading level. And the writing's very fine," Stefan went on, echoing a phrase he had heard Sasha use once on the phone. Sasha nodded, almost smiled. That seemed to have distracted Sasha, though Stefan thought his uncle was probably upset by the rush to get tickets, and the smelly noisy uncomfortable train ride. Stefan had seen lots of movies set in England or France—mysteries, comedies—and the trains were always beautiful and romantic. But this train was just a dump on wheels, and he shut it out as best he could.

"That's all you brought?" his father asked at the snowbound station, pointing to Stefan's one suitcase. His father wore a heavy overcoat, thick boots and glasses, and a Russian-style hat.

"We're not staying long," Stefan said.

"Let's get going," Sasha said. "This is terrible." The snow was whirling around them as if they were nothing more than figures in a snow globe. "Why are you here? You should be home. Why didn't you let us take a cab?"

"I didn't think you'd get one," his father said, huddled over against the wind, looking smaller and frailer than Stefan remembered him. "In this weather. . . ."

Driving slowly through the snow as thick as fog, Stefan had a sense of a very small town, and he felt hemmed in.

"You told me they call this the Harvard of the Midwest," Stefan said from the back seat of his father's black Chrysler New Yorker.

"That's the school, not Ann Arbor itself."

Stefan had somehow expected Ann Arbor to be as big and impressive as Boston looked in pictures and films—but Ann Arbor struck him as pathetic, a frontier outpost that could be easily swept away, destroyed.

His father kept talking about different landmarks as they drove, and Sasha asked polite questions that made him sound like he was an explorer. He half expected Sasha to ask about chief minerals and major exports next.

His father's house was up a long hill and in the middle of a circle of other small homes. It was all stone, with small many-paned windows, a smoking chimney. Like something in a fairy tale, Stefan thought: the witches's house, hunched over, keeping its secrets.

They parked in the driveway and hurried inside, where it was almost too warm. His father was breathing hard, and stood with his coat on and hands at his side for a few minutes, as if surprised he had made it this far. Sasha took his coat, and Stefan wanted to sneer at his father's clothes which looked like a parody of what a professor would wear: corduroy pants, turtleneck, loose cardigan with leather elbow patches.

His father held out a hand to Stefan, who just stood there.

"Do you smoke a pipe?" he asked his father.

His father started. "Is that a joke? No, I don't smoke. I can't."

Stefan moved from the tiny hallway into the living room, and beyond to the kitchen and dining room. Each room was full of built-in wooden cupboards, and thickly trimmed near the floor and up at the ceiling in the same gleaming wood which also made up the window frames and the staircase. It was like being in a box.

He turned to see Sasha and his father embracing the way Eastern European leaders did on TV—with large showy gestures that camouflaged their real feelings.

"No Christmas tree," he said aloud.

After a silence, his father said, "There wasn't time."

And Stefan looked away, embarrassed, knowing Sasha was probably glaring at him, trying to get him to simmer down.

"I'm as tall as you are," he said to his father, who smiled and nodded.

"How about something hot to eat? The food on the train must have been very bad."

Sasha headed for the kitchen, where the windows were steamed over. "It wasn't really food," he said. "The *idea* of food, an image."

Stefan sat at the round table. "The sandwiches were okay," he said, more to be contrary than anything else. And he glanced around the kitchen, which seemed blank and unrevealing.

"I just moved in last summer," his father said, lifting the lid of a pot on the stove. "That's why things seem a little bare."

It was as if his father had read his criticism.

"I had planned on taking you on a tour of the campus and a drive, but I think we might have to stay in for a while. They're predicting a lot more snow." His father stirred the pot and closed it. "Let me show you your rooms, and then we can eat."

On the way to the stairs, they passed his father's small study, which barely had room for a leather couch and chair opposite the long crowded desk.

Heading up the staircase, his father said, "Sasha's right near the stairs, you'll be with me," and Stefan wildly thought his father wanted to share a room with him. Then he realized from the way his father was pointing, that he was at the end of a hall, by himself, but next door to his father. The room was about the same size as Sasha's back home, and very bland—like a room in a department store advertisement. Stefan put down his suitcase by the bed, avoiding too long a glance at the window, where the thick snow lashed and eddied.

"You could lie down, if you want."

His father stood in the doorway, hands in his pants pockets, looking as tired as Sasha. It's me, Stefan thought, it's me being here that makes him sad. But why should that be true? Why couldn't he have the easy relaxed connection that Louie had with his father, who was always smiling at him, saying, "You make me proud. Just like I knew you would." And Louie wouldn't talk back or make a joke then, just nod, accepting the praise like the honest gift it was. Why did Stefan have to have this stranger as his father, this man who wanted something from him and seemed disappointed because he knew Stefan fell short.

"I slept on the train. But I'm still tired."

His father showed him the bathroom, and the linen closet for extra blankets and pillows. Stefan closed the door and slipped out of his clothes in the warm anonymous room, dropping them in a pile near the closet door. Just getting undressed made him think of Louie, and defiantly, he got into bed imagining Louie already there. He rolled onto his stomach and rubbed and rubbed away, glad that he would be messing up his father's sheets.

When he woke up it was dark and he felt sweaty under the thick down comforter. He pulled out his bathrobe from the suitcase and went to shower. The large shiny bathroom was neat, he had to admit—black and white tiles everywhere, and the tub was raised off the floor on a little platform set into an arch. He took a long time showering. He dreaded having to emerge and face his father and Sasha. And he enjoyed the hot water covering and massaging him from six different spray heads.

Toweling his hair dry, he stood nude in front of the long mirror, comparing his body to Louie's, comparing his face to his father's, and Sasha's.

Something smelled great when he headed downstairs.

"Goulash," his father said, setting a place for Stefan. "We've already eaten."

Stefan wolfed down the delicious stew, wiping the plate with bread several times.

"Aren't you thirsty?" his father asked, and Stefan shook his head.

"You're just like I was as a boy. I could eat and eat, but I never gained weight." His father leaned back against the sink, beaming. Was the smile for Stefan or for the memory of himself?

Sasha was sitting opposite Stefan, and he held a shot glass up to his nose, sniffing. Then he sipped from it.

"Vodka?" Stefan asked, intrigued because Sasha rarely drank.

"You want some?" his father asked, reaching for a bottle on the nearby counter.

Stefan shrugged, momentarily sated. He pushed his chair back, and looked from his father to Sasha and back. He couldn't help imagining his mother there, too—as if the family they had been had been transported to this out-of-the-way little house.

"Cool shower," he said.

"It's not original. It was added in the late Thirties."

"You own this house?"

His father nodded.

"So it's mine too?"

"In a way. It can be."

Sasha rose to pour himself more vodka, and Stefan's father said, "Let's sit by the fire." Stefan dutifully followed the two men to the living room, which was furnished with thick-armed chairs and couch covered in a maroon material with gold threads running through it. The rug was maroon and gold too. The room looked warm.

His father took the poker hanging by the open fireplace, stoked the fire, the light flaring across his face. He did look sick to Stefan: thin and even a little frail.

Sasha was on the couch, eyes closed, head back, and when Stefan's father sat in the chair opposite Stefan, Sasha snored, lightly.

They both smiled, and Stefan looked away, into the fire.

"I like it here," his father said.

"How'd you know I was gonna ask you that?"

His father shrugged. "You're my son."

"That doesn't mean anything."

Eyes down, his father said, "That's true, I suppose."

Stefan suddenly felt sorry for his father. It was almost too easy to score points off a man who might be dying.

"Dad, are you really sick?" he asked quietly.

His father looked up, surprised, perhaps, by the change in his voice. He nodded. "Maybe I was too quick to call you. But I was afraid something *could* happen, and then it would be too late."

His father explained about tests he needed to take, and the details blurred for Stefan, who felt overwhelmed to be there, to be talking to his father without harshness and distance. If only it could always be like this—sitting by a fire, warm and comfortable.

"What about Mom?" Stefan asked.

"How do you mean?"

"Do you ever talk to her?"

"We are very cool," his father brought out, and the words sounded like something he had memorized.

"Where'd you learn English?" he asked. His father frowned. "Because the way you said cool, it sounded like you were from England or something."

"Well, you know Poland and England had very close ties before—"

Stefan had read about Poles who had escaped the Nazis and fought with the British. "Were you in the Polish Legion?" he asked, excited, sitting up, leaning out of his chair.

His father sighed. "No. I was not a hero. I didn't have a chance."

"Then what were you? Why is everything this great big secret, and nobody wants to tell me about the War?" Stefan almost went on to ask his father if he had been a traitor or a spy, but he was suddenly afraid of his own eagerness.

Sasha snorted and sat up sharply, blinking, looking around. "I was asleep?"

"Coffee?" Stefan's father asked Sasha. And he looked at Stefan too, eyebrows up.

"I don't drink it much," Stefan said, getting up to go to the bathroom.

"No coffee for me," he heard Sasha say as he left the room. From the downstairs toilet, he could hear his father and Sasha talking loudly, but it didn't exactly sound like an argument. What language were they using? It wasn't Polish or Russian, it sounded a little like German. Dutch? Why would they be talking in Dutch?

When he opened the door he heard Sasha hiss, *"Shah."* No one spoke.

"I'm going to bed," Sasha finally said. "I'm exhausted." And he gave them both curt good night nods.

"I have some work to do," his father said, face flushed, and Stefan found himself moving towards his father, to take his hand. Instead, he threw his arms around his father and squeezed, thinking all kinds of wild thoughts. He would come to college here in Michigan and live with his father. But before that, he would tell his father about Louie, tell him everything. His father would understand, he would have to understand.

"Oh, Stefan," his father said softly.

Stefan said good-night and headed upstairs. But even though he knew he was tired enough to sleep until the next afternoon, he couldn't. He tried jerking off, because that sometimes made him sleepy, but he didn't want to leave where he was, even in fantasy. He found his robe, belted it tightly, and crept to the door as if there were ghosts lying in wait outside. The floor was cold, colder out in the hallway, and the house creaked. He realized that he hadn't been hearing clanking radiators like back home as he made his way to the top of the stairs. He could see a light from his father's study.

In the doorway, he saw his father slumped at the desk, head buried in his arms.

"Daddy, are you asleep?"

His father looked up, and Stefan was appalled to see that he had been crying. It was his heart attack, Stefan thought.

"Sometimes I wish I were dead," his father said, wiping his eyes with a sleeve.

Stefan felt pulled into the room as if caught by an undertow at Rockaway. He shivered when he sat on the leather chair, and his father pointed to an afghan on the couch. Stefan got up, wrapped it around himself and nestled into the chair.

"What does my life mean? I grade examinations, give lectures, read papers at conferences—but it's all false."

He must be drunk, Stefan thought, looking around for a bottle. What else could account for all this? His father was talking to him as if they were equals, as if he knew who his father was. Or maybe it was something else, maybe his father was talking as if he wasn't there, talking to himself.

"I don't know how else to say this," his father said, head high. "But to say it, is so terrible, so terrible. . . ."

"What, Dad? Say what?"

Covering his face with both hands, his father murmured, "I am Jewish. Your mother is Jewish, Sasha is Jewish. We were born in Poland, but we were never Poles, not really. Not to *them*."

"I'm *Jewish?*" Stefan said, and he laughed because the words were so ridiculous. "You're crazy," he said.

Now his father sat up straight, and looked right at him. "No, I'm stupid. I thought we could protect you. That's why we couldn't stay in Europe after the War. We came here, to hide, to change our lives. But I couldn't protect you against myself. I had to tell you. I couldn't face dying with such a burden."

"I'm Jewish?"

His father shrugged.

Trembling, Stefan pictured himself grabbing his father out of the chair and beating him against the wall, over and over, until he denied it, denied everything, said it was a joke, a mistake, a test.

He shut his eyes, but what he saw was worse: The No-Jew Club, and the argument about *Winter Eyes*, the anxiety about Israel's war, and the perpetual sadness at Christmas. It was like a horror movie, with everyone huddled in a deserted farmhouse, hoping they could escape the creature, but finding out that the creature had always been *inside*, disguised as one of them. Everything had been false from the beginning.

"You lied to me. You always lied. You and Mom and Sasha. I *hate* you," Stefan shot, but the words didn't have any power to destroy his father, which was what he most wanted.

His father just nodded. "I know."

"No wonder Mom always bragged about how her English was so good—it *had* to be. And that was Yiddish, wasn't it?" Stefan said. "When you and Sasha were talking before, loud, and you thought I couldn't hear. So what did you do when I was little— wait till I was asleep to talk Yiddish?" And he felt horribly excluded at the thought, cheated and fooled. He wanted to rush out into the snow and bury himself and never come out, never return.

"No. We didn't risk it. We grew up with Polish and Russian too, so—" And his father seemed on the edge of a smile, as if pleased he could maintain the front for all those years.

"I want to get out of here!" Stefan fled from the door, but at the first window he saw, he stopped. The snow was piled high, getting higher, falling thick and fast, almost to the windows. The one road he could see was like an iceberg—a huge block of white. Stefan stalked through the living room and back, turning on lights. "I want to get out of here."

Sasha was coming down the stairs, face as rumpled and creased as his dark blue pajamas.

"You bastard," Stefan said to him. "You could have told me anytime. I feel like such an asshole! All those Christmas trees! And the fucking presents! And feeling sorry like a jerk because Louie's parents really knew how to celebrate. Of course they do! It's their holiday!" He was shouting now, arms crossed, beating at himself with clenched fists. His father and Sasha stood side by side and he imagined the roof caving in and crushing them.

151

"Why didn't you tell me?" he snarled at Sasha.

"That was the agreement. If you lived with me, I had to hide everything."

Stefan stopped pacing, his arms dropped to his side. So he hadn't even won the battle to live with Sasha. That too was a lie. They had let him believe they were giving in.

"Why did you do this to me?"

"We wanted to save you," his father said, pale and shaken.

"From *what?*"

Sasha hesitated, looked at Stefan's father, who nodded. "From the past. We were all three in concentration camps. That's where your grandparents died, and almost everyone else from my family, your father's."

Stefan rushed for the phone. "I'm calling Mom!" But there was silence when he picked up the receiver; he banged it down and listened again. Nothing.

"The snow," his father said. "It must be the snow."

Stefan ripped the phone from the table, yanked until the cord came out of the wall and then hurled it into the fireplace. Its bell rang, and ashes and bits of wood splattered out onto the rug.

"Oh, Jesus," he said, starting to cry.

He was trapped.

Part Three
Connections

8

"How come you never talk to anyone?"

Stefan shrugged.

Jenny grinned. "See what I mean?"

"I don't know," he brought out, wondering how long Jenny would make him stand there in front of her building. He was safe from being invited upstairs, he knew, because her mother didn't like company. Jenny leaned back against one of the low ornamental gray stone urns that made the Exeter—already grim and worn, its beige brick dark brown with filth—look more depressing. Jenny had been on the city bus with him but on the other side of a knot of Catholic school girls, all plaids and cursing, so she didn't talk to him until they got off.

"You sure you don't know?" Jenny asked, meaning more than he wanted to understand.

Stefan shrugged again.

"See you tomorrow," she sighed, striding off into her building. Her legs were very long, he thought, moving off down the crowded block; little kids on and off pushcars were screaming for attention. He crossed Broadway to his quieter, cleaner block and fell into a more even, less anxious step; it was never until he was actually very near home that he began to feel safe. Leaving school, on the bus, or at any point between school and home, disasters flitted at the edge of his thoughts, teasing him almost: cars lurching onto the sidewalk, masonry tumbling off a roof edge, someone gone crazy firing a gun out into the street. They were all much the same to him—sudden, final. And so when he stepped into the beige marble lobby, keys ready, opened the heavy glass-paned door to the coffer-ceilinged and pillared inner lobby, he no longer expected that "anything" could happen.

The building was safe—riding the elevator was safe—coming in and hearing Sasha with a pupil was safe. He would close the kitchen door and make coffee, leaf through a magazine, half-listen to the radio, check the calendar if a concert was coming up. Most months had at least one red circle—it was these, mostly, that pulled him from day to day. Once, in the school cafeteria, some classmates had been discussing what they believed in. And as assertions and questions hung over their table thickly, like cigarette smoke, he thought that all he believed in was that things went on. He didn't know what that might mean, completely, but he knew it was true for him. He wondered then what Sasha believed in. Music, probably.

"So? How was your day?" Sasha would join him in the kitchen for coffee and they'd exchange their days. Then there was dinner, which Sasha still insisted on making by himself ("It relaxes me after a day of false notes"). Stefan would play sometimes, or read, or something. His life had been like this all the years he'd been living with Sasha since the divorce, his father's illness and recovery, and his mother's remarriage: ordered, repeating, with the only change the advance from grade to grade, and that didn't mean very much because he did no better and no worse year after year. Even his playing didn't seem much improved.

And Sasha was not his father, not that Stefan ever said that to anyone, but he never said anything else either so when Stefan was with Sasha and they met someone from school or their parents, it was always "Hello, Mr. Borowski." Stefan didn't make introductions or correct the mistake.

They looked enough alike to be anything.

But this was all upset when Stefan heard from his father or saw his mother and her husband.

"Why does he write?" Stefan asked once, staring at the postcard his father had sent from Mexico to wish him a happy fifteenth birthday. Sasha, who had been trying to smooth out a passage in a Liszt transcription, went silent at the piano.

"I don't know why he writes," Stefan said evenly, holding out the card as if hoping it might disappear on its own.

"I won't read it," Stefan went on, answering Sasha's unasked question. He dropped the card on the coffee table and stretched out on the couch; Sasha went on searching at the keyboard. Stefan did not ever read his father's letters, and he didn't write back. For a day or two after something came for him in the mail he would be very strange: he couldn't play—the dumb shining keys infuriated him—and he couldn't really see or hear things around him, as if he'd become less real than usual, hardly filling the space he took up. This was when he hated anyone talking to him and would want to choke anyone who bumped into him on the street or in class. But the hatred wasn't real either because he could see all around it; it never surged through him, in command, but was an isolated little dagger somewhere inside.

It all went away soon, though, and he could play again, talk to Sasha, do his homework, even stand around with other people.

"You're so serious," Jenny liked telling him when they were in a crowd.

"I guess."

"No really, you are. Like a poet or something."

"I don't write any poetry." He winced, remembering the poem he had tried to write for Louie.

"I didn't say you *were* a poet," she laughed, shaking her frizz of blond hair. Jenny was almost as tall as he—thin, big-nosed, with large green eyes, and with so many freckles that friends called her "Red."

"And even writing poetry doesn't make you a poet," Jenny continued instructing him, wriggling her shoulders as if she'd tasted something she wasn't sure she liked.

"You mean there are poets who don't write?" Stefan asked over the laughter of some of Jenny's friends. They'd all been clustered on a corner near the high school trying to decide what to do or not do that Friday night. These decisions usually took at least an hour; Stefan never made suggestions, just went out later if he wanted to, or stayed home if not—it didn't much matter what he did. But he didn't mind. George Washington was up on a hill, and he liked the way being there made him feel isolated from the city, protected in a way. It was also a bigger building than the small brick apartment houses nearby, like a medieval castle surrounded by a shabby village.

"There must be," Jenny asserted, perching on a car fender.

"What do they do?" he wondered, aware that he and Jenny were being watched.

"They *live*," she murmured.

What the hell did that mean? Jenny wouldn't tell him, even when they got on the bus by themselves (everyone else lived near school).

What did that mean? Did he live? Did Sasha? Well, Sasha had his students, and music, that was living. And Stefan had music too, though not in the same way as Sasha—it was rich and full for him, but not life itself, and hadn't been, for years.

He had Sasha too, he supposed. No, that wasn't true—they were *with* each other. Together. That was as much as two people could be, together—you could never have someone. He guessed that was another thing he believed, maybe even more than that things went on.

He was also together with Jenny, and had been—on and off— since sophomore year, though in a way he didn't really understand; in a group kids tended to drift to each other, leaving him with

Jenny—it was natural enough but it made him uneasy. He didn't know what to say to her, or if he even wanted to say anything to Jenny. Since the other kids were mostly her friends it didn't matter too much. He would walk along with her, in the midst of laughter and long repeated jokes he never tried to add to in case someone would mock him, not really comfortable, but not all that uncomfortable. Sometimes he'd have to talk if a question came at him.

"Well Stefan's dad is nice," someone once said at the end of a long jostle of complaints about their parents.

Stefan flushed. "I guess," he admitted to the ring of question-filled eyes; it was as if they had to believe in at least the *idea* of a decent parent. Stefan couldn't disappoint them: "He's very nice."

They moved off, contented, massing at the corner. Most of their time seemed spent on corners.

"What makes parents weird?" Jenny asked herself. "You think it's they never get over how incredible it is, I mean having a kid and everything? Think of it." Jenny laughed.

He didn't want to. Sasha was good to him and that was all he cared about. Sasha had never spanked him, didn't argue with him, wasn't strict with curfews, but then Stefan never really pushed Sasha, had no need to test the limits of Sasha's tolerance because he knew they were great, knew that Sasha wanted peace at home as much as he did—demanded it, even: silently, but without wavering. So Stefan listened to kids at school complain about their parents with dread; it fascinated him to hear arguments reargued, see confrontations acted out, and it scared him too. He didn't know why, didn't want to know why, but he still listened.

Even Jenny had trouble at home—her mother didn't want her wearing jeans because "only sluts" did (that made him flush, especially the triumphant mocking way Jenny brandished the word and laughed), and her father yelled at her when she was late. Stefan didn't like it that anyone was mean to Jenny, though he'd never been able to tell her that. It made him angry, and when he saw her parents around the neighborhood he wanted to tell them to stop it.

That was probably the time he most strongly felt a need to

speak—usually he spoke in reply to people or because it was expected. Most of what he did was because it was expected, even playing sometimes. He didn't always want to sit at the piano; there were days when its gleaming silent bulk was like a weight on him he couldn't escape, when his fingers rebelled and wouldn't listen, wouldn't play, wanted to smash at the keys, fling the music up and out into the room. Days when one more trill would make him ready to slam the lid down on his own hand to stop.

He wanted to stop, often, but couldn't—things went on no matter what you wanted.

At school he did what was expected, too. He liked being lost in ranks of guys doing squat thrusts or in a class gripped by an exam no one had expected to be so hard. He didn't want to be singled out for attention; he avoided competing, challenging anyone. No—he didn't have what his seventh grade homeroom teacher had called "punch" and "fight." He didn't want to fight anyone ever; his fights were over, he felt somehow, though not sure what that meant.

Except that he hadn't won.

Sasha did not ask him to have "punch," did not push him like other parents did, except at the piano perhaps, and that was done with more charm than coercion. There was a silence between them, one that absorbed everything that'd happened before Stefan came to live there, and deadened any echoes of that time. Sasha's carefulness was so natural by this point that it was no longer a question of tact but the way the two of them lived.

So without anyone pushing him, Stefan did what he had to; it was simple maintenance, like dusting: you wiped it away and then it returned and there was no real change, no meaning, just the cycle.

In his senior year even more peace signs appeared around school: on jeans, knapsacks, dug into the track, scratched onto book spines, smeared on walls and doors. Jenny and her friends bristled with the word and the sign; conversations became harsher, less specific, directed at unseen parents and Stefan had no connection with the clustering in hallways, the walkouts, the petitions. George Washington High School—a huge granite-porticoed thirties building with lawns and wings and marble used as freely as wallpaper—seemed to him to be at peace. Even at lunchtime or between classes, the shuffle and calling and bells sounded dim, suggestive, fading off into the quiet of high ceilings. Sometimes walking up the long curving concrete path to the main entrance he pictured himself as a tiny plastic figure in an architectural model—he did little more than give scale. So the cries for peace in a way barely disturbed the school that was built over the ruins of a Revolutionary fort, or near them (no one seemed to know which). Yet Stefan himself was disturbed; he wanted to enter into this world that was so clear and possible. Jenny knew what to do and feel and say, and he didn't.

He didn't know what to say the afternoon he came down an empty hallway to find two guys wrenching off a radiator cover and hurling it out a waiting window onto the roof of the girl's gym. He could only stare as the strangers fled. He knew such acts were "in protest" because anything out of the ordinary that happened at school now was against the war in Vietnam.

"They were frustrated," Jenny explained when the guys were suspended.

He considered that.

"Because nothing is helping," she went on, pulling at her hair. Jenny would sometimes lapse from her hard optimism but he didn't point out how she was inconsistent; that didn't seem very kind.

"It's not that I think it's all right," Jenny continued, "But I understand."

And *he* didn't, was the unspoken comment. Jenny didn't act as if she really expected him to be with her on this or any other issue, and she didn't try to convert him as some of her friends did (he listened to their arguments very carefully, nodding, finishing sentences, even). He could not find in himself the still sure conviction that Jenny and growing hundreds of students at school had. The draft wasn't too far away, people warned him when he wouldn't sign a petition or join a committee.

161

"I was thinking of some friends I have in Montreal," Sasha said one afternoon, smoothing his hair back as he stepped to the piano.

"What?" Stefan barely glanced up from that week's issue of *Life*.

Sasha went through some music. "If you're drafted."

Stefan stopped reading.

Sasha looked round. "You can always go live in Canada," he explained matter-of-factly.

"I won't get drafted. The war'll be over." He couldn't imagine it.

Sasha sat at the piano, quiet, thoughtful. "It's good to have somewhere to go," he said. And Stefan didn't disagree; he could feel Sasha thinking of other times, other years.

Sasha began to play the slow movement of a Mozart concerto Stefan didn't particularly like, so he went into his room. He remembered how the piano's large night shadow had reassured him enough when he was younger. Stefan no longer venerated the piano or felt entranced by Sasha's playing, which he'd come to see was not brilliant—far from it—warm perhaps, and certainly Sasha's line was always singing, but Stefan had heard too many fine pianists to be able to fall under the old spell. Sasha once told him he used to listen "like an animal gaping at fire" but that seemed far away now. He was familiar with Sasha's playing, as Sasha must be with his too; it had taken on the air of atmosphere, was as much a part of the texture of the day as a shower, or the traffic whir from Broadway.

Also he didn't stay to listen very often because he was beginning to have trouble looking at Sasha.

Sasha was getting old, and it made Stefan afraid, angry, to see where at the crown of his head there was a thin spot, to watch the white hands that were now blotched and sometimes swollen. Sasha coughed in the morning, badly, got tired a lot, seemed bent and heavier and worn, as if unkind hands had plucked at his flesh. It was horrible to Stefan because he had never noticed until recently— and it was too late.

Though what he could've done about it, he didn't know.

* * *

Jenny wanted his help organizing the demonstration that would begin the week-long student strike; Jenny talked about it constantly, more and more thin-voiced and pointing, though at who or what he couldn't say. It was unpleasant to see her transformed by a force that didn't touch him, worse—that pushed a cause between them. Jenny seemed dismally unlike herself, blurred by signatures and buttons. He began to miss her almost, especially when they were together and she launched on a new set of plans and provisions.

"Don't you care?" Jenny finally asked one afternoon.

He couldn't answer, partly because the question was too large, partly because it was harder than ever to speak to Jenny when she was more like a committee than a girl.

"I don't know," Jenny shook her head, but smiled at last, as if there might be some hope.

Even Sasha had heard: "Will you demonstrate next week?"

Stefan hesitated; no one had asked him and he guessed everyone assumed he would—even lots of teachers would strike.

"I don't know."

"You shouldn't, there might be trouble."

"How?"

"Other demonstrators. The police."

"But this is America," Stefan protested weakly, remembering the bloody students at Columbia University.

Sasha nodded. "That's what they always say—but look what happens!"

Stefan squirmed, uncomfortable with Sasha's anger.

Sasha noticed and didn't go on. Later that evening Sasha asked: "Have you signed any petitions?"

"No. Why?"

"It's good not to," was all Sasha said as he left to visit a neighbor. Stefan suddenly was ashamed that he hadn't signed anything, hadn't helped Jenny.

The next morning he told Jenny he'd stay for her meeting after classes. That same morning a fight broke out in the cafeteria, "about the war" people were saying, but that only made him more determined to act, or at least help those who could. It was strange to be contemplating such a step, especially since a voice in him that would not be stilled murmured all day that it wouldn't make any difference what *he* did.

Most days, after the last period, school emptied as quickly as if there'd been a bomb threat; people just melted away and the only sound was the slide of pails and slushing mops, sometimes vague distant pounding that might be a hammer. Stefan saw no one on the way down to the meeting on the first floor. He stopped at one of the cool cavernous toilets that were ludicrously ceremonial in size. As he unzipped his fly he heard the door, and a rush, and then he couldn't breathe—a hand closed over his face and then another punched him in the back. He fell, or was pushed against the urinal, utterly unable to move or shout—even in his mind—as a hand pulled at his pants and he felt far away, wondered what would happen next. He was aware of pain, someone hit him again, but he could do nothing to help himself, not even hope he would not be hurt more.

He was kicked and punched and it was over: the same rushing noise and then the door. He lay on the small-tiled floor, eyes fixed on the white hexagons locked into each other. He noticed that a hand—his own—was slowly reaching back to where the other hand—not his own—had pulled at his pants. Stefan waited for the hand to tell him what it found: a back pocket hung loose where his wallet had been. So it was a mugging, he thought, beginning to make sense of why he lay on the floor of this dim huge toilet, still unable to move. Something in him had stopped working; Stefan did not know what that was. He had broken down—been broken down, more than mugged. No one had hit him since his father, and even his father had not hit him so many places, or kicked him either. But he had been too small then to be really hit, Stefan supposed, wondering when he would begin to feel the pain he was sure now clamored and twitched through his body—he couldn't hear it, though, could only guess at its existence: if someone hit you there was pain whether you let it call your name or not.

Could one person have done all that?

Held his mouth and arms—yes his arms had been pinned, he remembered that—and pushed him down and kicked him all at once? Could one person have done all that? Two—it must have been two.

This was more than a mugging; he had been attacked. Would they come back?

Stefan was now afraid, and the fear brought him up on his knees, which trembled, unable to hold up the stricken body. "Listen to me!" he yelled inside, but it didn't help; he fell over, and now the pain—in his side, at his neck, in one leg—struck and made him writhe. He would throw up or faint but nothing saved him from the outraged burn and flare. He was more helpless now than before because now he struggled and there was no chance of winning. He dragged himself to a urinal, shoved his head in, reached up with one aching arm to pull and pull at the handle, drenching his head in the water. He twisted round and leaned back against the urinal, his useless crying body stretched out on the floor. The mirrors over the row of sinks weren't long enough for him to see himself, though why this should matter now he had no idea.

He probably slept, because the cool hall-like bathroom seemed darker to him. This meant he had to get up—"But I can't," he thought and yet arms and legs began to work together as if they didn't believe him—and Stefan gradually rose from the enamel floor to stagger across and lean on a sink. So much hurt that he couldn't decide where to place a hand first, where to look. His face was pale but unbruised, perhaps his mouth was a bit swollen? No—he was himself, unchanged; his hair lay sodden and ugly across his forehead. He dried himself with paper towels, pulling the hanging pocket completely off and then wondered where to put the scrap of denim. There—he'd left his books perched on the edge of another sink; he opened a binder and lay the pocket inside.

His shirt and jeans were wet and grimed; he couldn't do much about that. As for the soreness, that too was beyond him. He gathered up his books and edged to the door; it would not be so bad if he moved slowly. And so he crept out into the hall to the nearest exit and outside where the darkening sky gave him courage, or something, because the pain was less vicious. At the bus stop he tried to look ordinary, but one or two people stared at him, and when he pulled himself onto the neon-lit bus he could feel stirring and turning. He fell into the furthermost seat.

A small parrot-faced woman two seats down leaned toward him. "You are all right?" she asked, face wide with concern. He nodded, and she nodded, and if he didn't sleep on the way home, he did something very like it.

Sasha called hello from the living room where he sat at the piano talking on the phone. Stefan somehow got to the bedroom, stripped off his clothes with loathing and plunged into the bathroom to shower. He could not touch himself but merely stood under the hot stream that wasn't hot enough or strong enough to stifle the shame he could sense spreading in him.

If he could cry—he hadn't cried since that night at his father's house in Michigan. . . .

He was very near breaking through, but pulled back in terror, hid in the less dreadful pain of what had happened, of what he could bear.

He toweled his hair and eased into his bathrobe.

He sat on the toilet seat, exhausted, afraid, wanting to be alone; why did he have to go out there and face Sasha? If he could just go away for a while, lie in silence on a beach somewhere, stupid to anything more than heat, or sit by a tree-ringed pond to watch the water wrinkle and swell: *days* like that to wipe this one from his mind. It would only make the attack more frightening to tell Sasha, and more real.

Sasha knocked to tell him dinner was ready.

Stefan took some aspirin and emerged at last, glad he had no visible bruises. He tried to walk normally to the kitchen table.

"You're all right?" Sasha asked, and Stefan's eyes blurred—he was on the bus, on the floor.

"Stefan—" Sasha leaned over him. "Are you sick? What happened?"

In front of Stefan's face was a screen of white locked hexagons.

"*Stefan.*" Sasha grabbed him, but he jerked away.

"Don't touch me—don't touch me!" It was all confused; his father had hit him, but not like that, he didn't have a father. He heard a cabinet open and felt or saw Sasha bring a shot glass up to his mouth. The liquor burned him.

"I'm okay," he coughed, motioning Sasha to sit. "I'm okay." He breathed in to clear his thoughts. It was all very simple now. "I was beat up at school," he said quietly, and then even more quietly, because Sasha stared and stared: "I don't know who it was. After school, in a bathroom. I'm okay."

Sasha looked wild, stunned.

"I'm okay," Stefan repeated. "I wasn't hurt bad." After a moment he added, "They took my wallet." But Sasha still said nothing, didn't even move and Stefan almost wanted to strike him, make him talk so they could end this.

"Who?"

"I don't know."

"You must know."

"I don't." Stefan's hands were tight.

"What were you—?"

"I was in the *bathroom*." He had almost never been this angry at Sasha, who was white and old and pathetic. "I was pissing! Is there anything wrong with that?!"

Sasha shook his head.

"It's over," Stefan said. "I'm *okay*."

"These things are never over," Sasha dropped, beginning to come to himself; he rose to open the oven and serve dinner, leaving Stefan thankful for the silence.

"No one was around?"

Stefan shook his head.

"So you made no report? Good. Don't tell anyone." Sasha ate grimly, shoulders hunched, eyes fixed Stefan didn't know where. "Did you get involved with those demonstrators?" Sasha eyed him steadily, without accusation.

"Sort of, but—"

"That's what it is."

"But how could—"

167

"You can't expect to be safe when you do things like that."

"I don't believe it," Stefan said from reflex; their little table suddenly seemed menaced by forces that had left their mark on Sasha, and had finally claimed him too.

Sasha didn't finish dinner but went off to the living room where he sat in the dark, smoking the cigarettes he kept for guests. Stefan managed to eat—it made him a bit sick—but also it was part of a normal day, and the movement of knife and fork reassured him: it was good to be in control of something, even a plate of food.

Stefan went to his desk, turned on the radio and tried to do some work, but now he was unable to forget the big white-faced man out there lost in brooding, as if Sasha's pain was greater than his own. Stefan was calm, but he could make no effort to be more than that. He sat straight in his chair, hands spread on a book, picturing Sasha lighting cigarettes, filling the room with unseen smoke.

He went out later, stood in the unlit hallway. All he could see was the tip of a cigarette; the radio murmur crept out after him, as thin here as the smoke.

"Are you okay?"

A glass was set down.

"Sasha?"

"Go to bed."

"It's late."

"Go."

Stefan obeyed, closed the door behind him, stood waiting for Sasha to play, but no music came from the living room. He fell asleep on the made-up bed.

Sasha had left him a note on the kitchen table which Stefan almost did not want to read, though what could words do to him now?

"I will be late." No signature. He guessed what that meant: out all day. Stefan stirred his coffee, a bit surprised by the clattering spoon: it sounded the same, everything was the same. The morning had come and here he was about to go to class. Things went on no matter what happened; he didn't know if the thought imprisoned him today or was encouraging, maybe it just *was*, with no connection to what he said or did.

There were livid places on his body which he contemplated in the full-length mirror in the bedroom, trying to find out what they meant. Nothing came to him; the bruises, separate somehow from their pain, were complete, not to be understood. Here was something you really had.

He did not look around him as he dressed, found a way to hold himself that was less painful, and left. Outside, it occurred to him that the disasters he'd imagined hadn't been like this—the crashes were impersonal, accidents in which his part was minor. This attack was too specific, too much his alone; he had not shared the pain, the cool white floor, the bus ride—it was all in him and on him, and this was too much, unfair, ugly.

He waited for the light to change out of pure habit; what would it have mattered if he'd stepped off the curb, been struck and sent flying onto another car, a parked one? He was not afraid of that, he thought, beginning to feel a grim warmth. He was not afraid; he had been attacked, he knew what could be done to him, knew that he was helpless.

This was something he hadn't expected.

So, reckless, confident he could be hit by a real car on a real street, Stefan crossed before the light changed, registering that the DONT WALK sign had no apostrophe.

The buses were slow that morning and he waited longer than usual, alone. Cars hurtled down the quiet street as if daring someone to run out between them. For some reason Stefan noticed how cracked and uneven the pavement was, and where the asphalt wore thin over the cobblestones.

He saw Jenny crossing the street to him, her stride unusually tight and held in. She glared at him before saying a word.

"I was stupid to think you'd come," Jenny announced. He met her hostile glance without a ripple of trouble. What was her annoyance to him? Yesterday's attack drained the effect of anything Jenny could say.

"You don't care about anyone, nothing gets to you," Jenny

169

began, and he saw how rigidly she held her head, saw where her neck was tense and flushed. Their bus heaved up to the stop; Stefan wondered if Jenny would sit by him. She did.

Jenny turned sideways to face him.

"This is really important. It's more than just us, it's our *country*." She went on like that for a while, but the words which had never stirred him now seemed empty and unimportant. What did Jenny know about anything?

"You're not listening."

"I heard you," Stefan was obliged to say, though not exactly in self-defense.

Jenny sunk into a pained silence which he ignored; the bus filled and filled with loud students who seemed so confident and at ease. "Because they don't know," he thought, but it did not make him feel superior or kind. He didn't really feel anything today on this jerking laugh-ridden bus, anything more than the aching, and he was used to that. In his sleep something had happened, Stefan guessed; he had arranged himself in relation to the attack: there was balance inside, although he wasn't sure what that meant. Perhaps while Sasha sat up late, smoking, silent, watchful, his pain had passed into Sasha—could that be it?

Jenny said "Seeya" when they stepped off the bus, dismissing him; she moved quickly away up the block to school. Would she drop him altogether? He could ponder that without being upset; it didn't threaten him as it might've yesterday, before.

Later in the day, moving in a crowd towards the cafeteria doors he thought he heard someone hiss "That's him," but when he turned, there was no one behind him. He looked up and down the empty hall.

It was bad when his mother came over with Leo for dinner or drinks, even though this wasn't often. Stefan sat quietly, the rage he felt stiffening his hands, his neck, shooting through him like a pain. He drank no wine with them because he was afraid of relaxing.

"She's your mother," Sasha always said beforehand, as if that was enough reason to smile and say nothing that was the truth or even close to it. "I know it is hard for you," Sasha would also say.

And this angered Stefan: Sasha's understanding, because Sasha understood and yet saw his mother and Leo often, understood and called them, sent birthday and anniversary cards with "love, Sasha and Stefan" at the bottom.

Stefan wanted his mother as far away as his father was in Michigan—out of the city, out of his mind; he wanted to tear her name, her face from his thoughts, to be free forever of his past where it tangled with hers. But this was impossible when they both lived in New York, when now and then he had to sit down in the same room with her for a few hours, and even play for her, impossible when she and Leo insisted on sending him beautiful birthday presents: books he never read, clothes he never wore.

He felt like a pouty little kid when he was with them, and hated the feeling as much as he hated them for causing it.

It was always a shock to see his mother; she seemed softer and lovelier each year—only now could he appreciate that, see her not as his mother but a woman: graceful, well-dressed, with confidence scenting her smiles.

"You seem pale," she said, smoothing the folds of a coral silk dress. "Are you working too hard?"

Stefan could feel Sasha's warning him not to mention the attack. Stefan stirred in his chair, shrugged.

"Don't overdo it," Leo spoke up. "Enjoy being young, it sure doesn't last long." Leo laughed and toasted Stefan with his drink while seeking his wife's hand. Leo punctuated most of what he said by touching Stefan's mother, looking at her, for reassurance, approval—Stefan didn't know what—but he couldn't stand it or stand the way his mother brightened at these little contacts.

"I'll play something," Sasha announced, setting down his drink. He chose a loud showy piece Stefan didn't like or dislike.

He watched Leo listen to the Romantic clatter; Leo's long serious face disturbed Stefan. It wasn't handsome—that he might have stood—but very Jewish, fierce-eyed, maned with silver-streaked red hair too thick and wavy for a man. Leo was too theatrical looking, too attentive to his mother, and too nice to him. Leo always spoke to him as if they were old friends.

When Sasha finished, Leo clapped his hands together. "That was good," he said, like it'd been a hearty meal.

"Very nice," Stefan's mother smiled.

Sasha bowed his head to them.

"We should go soon," Leo said and Stefan sat up straighter. "I heard your school's going to strike tomorrow." Leo was addressing him; Stefan had to speak, but before he could get anything out, Leo barreled on: "I don't agree with them but I sure think it's good they're expressing what they believe. People should demonstrate." Leo nodded firmly at the room, and suddenly Stefan felt strangely that Leo—an American—was outside, was not quite part of the world he and his mother and Sasha knew: the simple optimism seemed childish, uninformed. Stefan almost thought Sasha was smiling.

"I don't like demonstrations," his mother said quietly. "I remember being in gymnasium and anti-Semitic marches, shouting. . . ." She paused. "Some of us were hurt." She breathed in.

"But that's different," Leo insisted. "This is America."

"Perhaps you remember McCarthy?" Sasha cut in, voice steely. Leo was silenced, but Stefan could feel how he didn't believe what Sasha said proved anything. How could his mother live with someone who didn't know what life was really like?

"Friends should stay away from politics," his mother brought out gently, and even Stefan smiled.

When they were leaving, Leo shook his hand and said "See you soon" as if the words meant something, and with an arm around his wife's shoulder walked to the elevator.

"He's very good to her," Sasha observed, contented. Sasha always liked to talk about them when they left, as if to keep them near. Stefan couldn't stand to; when they were gone he felt trapped, the apartment smothered him, but he knew opening every window would make no difference, none.

There was no one he could tell all this. When his mother and Leo left he usually went to lie down in the dark, though it would've

172

been best to run somewhere hard and fast till he couldn't think or breathe. Lying on his bed in the dark all he could do was think. There was no one who could listen and help him just by listening. He had tried often the last year to keep a diary of some kind, one in which he could loose all the feelings he didn't know what to do with, the feelings that scared and crippled him. He wouldn't need to journalize his days—he told Sasha that stuff—he needed to be able to write away the pain for just a few hours, but he could never start. Between him and the smooth white first page there was always something that kept his hand stiff and tight, refused it movement. So all he had was the darkness.

Once he'd half-thought to himself: "I'll tell Jenny," the words blurring themselves as they came to him. He could tell Jenny about himself—and a vision had formed: Jenny sitting opposite, nodding as if nothing shocked her, perhaps saying "You too?" about some things and perhaps she would take him into her arms, stroke the back of his neck, never once saying anything crude like "I understand" or "It'll be all right." Her silence was what he wanted, and for her to hold him after she knew who he was.

He'd almost told her once, something, he didn't know what, but had felt himself on the verge of truth. They were in the large half-panelled rec room of her building at a dark party that had turned darker and quieter as more couples stopped dancing, and worked themselves into corners. He and Jenny had kissed and snuggled and kissed some more, the rustling and whispering around them making Stefan feel he was in stereo.

"You're so quiet," she said, lying back in his arms; she spoke up to the side of his head; their hands were twined at her waist.

"I am." He had been thinking of Louie, whose father had sold his store and decided to move when Louie went off to UCLA.

When Jenny said nothing more, he wanted to ask her what she was thinking or say something himself that would break through the reserve he felt in her stiffened shoulders. It was strange how they could hold each other and yet be no closer—would sex be like that too, more isolation?

He could start with Sasha, say that Sasha was only his uncle, that would be a beginning. The words didn't come, and it was almost as if Jenny sensed some of this; silent, she moved up, waiting perhaps, but he said nothing, just held her. Then someone turned on the lights as a joke.

Now, because of the demonstration business and missing the meeting, Jenny didn't want to talk to him at all. He considered calling her to explain, but Stefan never got as far as the phone; it had become so tangled up in him that the words to cut through seemed nonexistent. Telling Sasha about the beating had been bad enough; Jenny would want to know everything, how it happened, what he thought and did. He couldn't share it with her, go through it again.

"She doesn't know," he thought grimly. For all her protests and hard-edged assurance she didn't know anything as simple as that beating; she knew petitions to be drafted and waved on every corner, meetings and rallies and slogans and cries, but she was still safe and untouched.

He had tried reading about the concentration camps, books he hid from Sasha. But it was all too horrifying and sick, a different more bestial war than the one fought with planes and tanks. And he couldn't imagine it was a movie with him as a wisecracking gunner. No, he saw instead the battered filthy bodies of Sasha and his parents, zombies on the way to becoming animals and then corpses. He gave up, he had to. He had also been sickened by reading about a Poland different from the one he had fantasized about. Seen through the eyes of historians, it was a country whose independence in 1918 had precipitated a whole new cycle of Jew-hatred. His childhood land of castles was a wasteland of ghettoes and concentration camps, and the menace wasn't just the murderous Germans, it was the ruthless Poles. As a little boy, written Polish had looked like a secret code to him, with mysterious combinations of letters like "gdz" and "czy"—but now any Polish word he saw was as horrifying as *"Achtung!"* How could his parents have ever let him imagine himself to be Polish, after all the Poles who had betrayed Jews during the War or cheered their slavery and death?

He was not going to be the one to tell Jenny about the brutality she had missed. Let her believe whatever gave her strength, let her dream of making a difference.

The afternoon of the demonstration Sasha was out, luckily. Stefan wouldn't have wanted to discuss it. Alone, he could sit at the piano in the still, warm room, playing not very carefully, just to be busy. It wasn't enough, though; his hands knew everything he played too well for his mind to get clear of the phantom crowds outside his high school gate, sprouting signs and peace flags, chanting, moving, circling the loudspeakered kid who today would embody what they believed; perhaps even Jenny would take a turn shouting encouragement, standing frizzed and wide-eyed at the center of a long oval, voice strained and believing.

So he tried to learn something new, a piece too hard for him. He forced himself from bar to bar for more than an hour, making only linear progress and not much of that.

The buzzer rang too early for it to be Sasha.

"Hi." Jenny stood at the door, flushed and hesitant.

He squeezed her hand hello without even knowing it, but said "Come in" very formally.

"Sure?" she asked, wavering.

"Come on."

Now Jenny brightened, entering with pleasure in her stride. Stefan brought her a soda where she stood with her back to the piano like a recitalist. She gulped half of it down, plucked at her T-shirt, which he noticed now was sweat-stained. Her sandaled feet were dirty and even the long fringe of her purple suede belt hung limp.

"How was it?" He sat in Sasha's chair.

"Great, tons of people, everyone's out."

"Trouble?"

"None." Jaunty, radiant, she plopped onto the couch. "Except it was hot. Where's your dad?"

"Good question."

"What?"

"He's at a lesson."

Jenny nodded and the following silence lay on him heavy, humid; something had to be said, to just go on from before would be a kind of lie—he didn't believe people could really forgive and forget when they were hurt. It happened too often to be talked away, cut too deeply. But he didn't know what that left.

Jenny launched on a long overdetailed description of the day, as if creating it for someone blind. She's nervous, Stefan sensed; so was he.

"Oh, there was a counterdemonstration," Jenny said. "It wasn't very big," she added, wavering between delight and tact. "People believe different things," she continued, softly.

"I don't know what I believe," Stefan brought out.

"I worry about you."

Stefan tensed; Jenny's voice was suddenly thick with something she hadn't said. He didn't look up at her though her tone demanded it.

"You're so cut off," she said. "Where *are* you?"

"Now?"

"Now—yesterday—any day. It's like I can only get next to you and that's it." Jenny looked tight, frustrated. He met her hard anxious stare, so fixed she could have been willing him across to her.

"That's not enough?" He spoke only because it was his turn; he had no idea what he meant. He had never talked to anyone like this, never felt the air between him and anyone so charged and frightening.

"You only kiss me when you're drunk," Jenny dropped.

"You only let me when you're drunk." It was silly, like a sandbox fight; he grinned at her and Jenny relaxed, pushed the hair from her face. "I'm not drunk now," Stefan went on, surprised at the ease with which the words left him.

"You're also not kissing me."

He rose and went to where she sat, drew her up into his arms; Jenny stroked his back, his hair. He held her, afraid of the open searching face he looked down at. Her eyes were so strange and green; usually when they were this close it was in shadow or darkness. Her white face shone up at him, guiding him down. He kissed her slowly, more slowly than ever.

In a minute she whispered: "Now play for me." Jenny pushed hair back off his ears as if to see more of him. "I'll sit next to you," she said, joining him at the bench. Stefan didn't know what to play, what he wanted to say to Jenny, who sat all appreciative and ready at his side. He was only used to sharing the bench with Sasha. He fiddled at the keys with one hand, the other going through the music on the stand.

The downstairs bell rang.

"Your father?"

He nodded and went to buzz, reluctant. When he turned back, Jenny looked so delicate at the piano, one thin hand up at the edge of a page, the other palm down on the bench. He didn't move, just stood and wondered what next between them, and when, how? Not here, Stefan thought, it would make him too nervous.

Sasha seemed very tired but smiled at Jenny and chatted before he excused himself.

"Your dad's neat," Jenny said at the door. "But not as neat as you." She kissed him good-bye and left with a little wave just as Sasha emerged from the bedroom, changed.

"I like her," Sasha threw off, heading to the kitchen.

Stefan tensed and went to the bedroom, closed the door, but he couldn't sit; he paced and then stood at the window glaring out at the street. He didn't want Sasha and Jenny together, didn't want them to talk to each other—it split him apart to stand with them both. Sasha knew everything, Jenny nothing. No, that wasn't even true, they knew him in different ways, and the two clanged and clashed inside him. He hated it.

"I have to tell her."

After dinner, Jenny called. "Meet me at Dooley's—people are coming by at ten."

He went to wash up and put on a fresh shirt. Sasha sat a bit stiffly in the living room, reading the *Times*. Sasha didn't really like him to go drinking, especially since he was underage, and also

Sasha didn't approve of the run-down neighborhood bar two blocks over, so Stefan always felt sort of guilty going there. Still, it was seedy enough, dark and narrow and quiet enough even when crowded to be interesting, romantic almost.

Jenny was talking to the bartender, a third cousin of hers, when Stefan entered. She had her hair up in a loose tendrilly bun and leaned across the bar looking much older than seventeen. They talked nonsense to Johnny for a while, Stefan playing with his seven and seven, stirring it more than drinking it. He liked the anonymity of Dooley's, the plain small tables and chairs, the bottle rows, the vague trophies, the funny signs he never read; it made him feel warm and private, alone with Jenny no matter who else was there or what jokes her skinny, stooped cousin made at the two of them.

Some regulars came in and he and Jenny retired with their drinks to a back table beyond the jukebox. Before they could really say anything, the crowd from school descended, on the way back from an early movie downtown, pulling over chairs and tables. The talk soon shifted to the morning's demonstration and Stefan drifted away from the excited involved figures; they relived the demonstration there at the back of the bar, all its tiny mounting successes, while up at the front. . . . No, how could he be sure those squat red-faced men up there were for or against anything? That was making it all too "Us" and "Them," too simple.

Stefan nodded and nodded, trying not to look inattentive.

Jenny stroked his hand under the table, placed it on her knee and held it there, as if to make up for not having been able to say much to him. He was concentrated now all in his hand under Jenny's, wondering if he really could feel each of her fingers or if that was just imaginary.

When the crowd broke up with promises of getting together on Friday night, leaving Stefan and Jenny at a table thick with glasses and wet napkins, Jenny said, offhand, "My folks aren't coming home tonight, they're with my aunt in Jersey. They called me before."

So this was it, he thought in Jenny's elevator a few minutes later;

he would not have to listen to other guys so blankly anymore; he would be one of them, really smile, really know. But it was strange, he thought while Jenny was in the bathroom, strange that they would make love—they were too close, and not close enough.

When she entered her bedroom in a simple pink nightgown, her hair loose on her shoulders, he flushed and felt hot in a way he hadn't before.

"What were you waiting for?" Jenny smiled, gliding across to where he sat on her bed. "I'll help you." She pulled him up and began unbuttoning his shirt. Stefan groaned and stroked her rear, pushing against her; he kissed her neck, her eyes, as she maneuvered him out of his shirt.

"So nice," she murmured, stroking his chest. It was easy, he thought, kissing her forehead, focused on where a tiny freckle hid just inside her hairline. He sat her down, crossed to the door, shut it and closed the light. In the dark he slipped off his shoes and socks and pants but kept his shorts on; it embarrassed him to bear this stiffness across to where she lay.

"Have you—?" He slipped into bed with her.

"Once, sort of by accident, that's why I use something." It was good that she'd been there before him. His hands roamed under Jenny's nightgown, feeling flesh and cloth at the same time— amazing that this was Jenny in bed with him, Jenny he crushed with a kiss, Jenny he explored with a shy finger, Jenny who moved against him in a way even his night phantoms never had. She was so hot, her face so hot and her hands stroking his thighs, up, down, closer, teasing, finally pulling at his shorts. Jenny did this, Jenny spread herself out for him, saying "I love you, you know I love you?" He leaned down to slide off his shorts. Jenny reached to guide him to her, and it was over, on her hand, he was horrified.

"Oh God, I'm sorry!" He plunged from the bed to pull on his clothes.

"Stefan." Jenny sat up, flung aside the covers.

He couldn't find his shorts; it didn't matter—he stuffed his socks into a pocket, grabbed his shirt and tore open the door.

"It's okay, we have all night," Jenny called, following, beginning to cry.

He plucked at the locks in the dark.

"Let me out."

"Stefan, please—"

He pushed her away and the door gave at last.

9

He slept without waking and Sasha was already gone when he emerged from bed. Straightening the sheets and making the bed seemed an ordeal, and it all reminded him of something, something he couldn't bother to track down through this morning's haze. When the bed was made, he settled onto it, dizzy perhaps; what he couldn't think of kept creeping up to him. He shoved it away with breakfast, the image of breakfast. He padded into the kitchen to brew coffee; usually instant was enough, but Stefan had to slow down, had to fill himself. He turned on the radio, loud, didn't listen as he scrambled eggs, merely moved behind the wall of sound.

He ate concentrating on chewing, on his fork, on the white café curtains. When he tried to wash up, though, his hands shook and, turning off the radio, he left the dishes to soak. He carried his cup to the bathroom, set it on the shelf near the cabinet and turned on the hot water to shave. But as soon as he looked at himself in the mirror, last night rushed upon him; he leaned over the sink head down, clutching the porcelain, forcing himself not to cry, not to break, struggling against it, his jaws so tight he feared a tooth would break, would spill from his mouth all ground and bloody.

The doorbell rang. He groaned and it rang again, sharply, his mother's ring.

It couldn't be. His hands loosened as the bell rang again. I won't answer, he thought, passing into the hall to stare at the door, which seemed almost to command him across to it. He peered out the peephole: his mother.

"I had some—" she said when the door opened, and then stopped, not crossing the threshold. "You're not at school?"

"No."

"Are you ill?"

"No."

"Sure?"

He opened wide the door as if that would prove he was all right; his mother stepped in.

"Sasha's at a lesson, I think."

She nodded. "I should've called first. I had some shopping to do downtown—I thought I'd come up here first." She smiled, looking very slim and elegant in a beige linen suit. He resented how beautiful Leo had made her, how expensively Leo dressed her; it always seemed somehow that the clothes, the discreet bits of jewelry were more Leo's than hers. His mother appeared to him costumed: Businessman's Foreign Wife. He could not get used to her brisk perfection.

"Could I have some tea?"

Stefan obeyed while his mother walked down into the living room and over to the windows.

"Your view is beautiful this time of year," she called like a tourist.

What did she want? He wouldn't ask her, but he was sure she wanted something, needed something. Stefan brought out the cup and saucer, setting them down for her.

"You're not going to change?" she asked, moving to the couch.

"Change?"

"From your pajamas?" She sat, took up the tea, crossed her legs. He glanced down at her shoes, they were alligator, probably, like her bag.

"I didn't shower."

"It's almost noon."

"I didn't know." He settled onto Sasha's chair, not looking at his mother. He hadn't expected to see her so soon after the last visit, but at least she hadn't come with Leo; alone, she was less upsetting, though sometimes she seemed so sharp and clear as to give him a headache—then, even her smiles were too strong.

"You're sure you're not ill?"

"There's the strike this week," he reminded her. "No one's going to school."

"Well . . . as long as you're not on a picket line where someone can see you." She sipped from the gold-edged cup, eyes down.

Stefan didn't even ask who "someone" was—why bother? He knew, and he didn't know, didn't care.

He watched her—his mother—a stranger—more a stranger than anyone ever could be just because she was so close to him. Today, luckily, he didn't feel as uncomfortable with her as usual; Leo's image didn't blur and waver with hers. Maybe he was used to how they lived.

"I heard from your father," she began, voice clear, direct.

And now there was someone else in the room with them. Stefan hadn't looked at any of the pictures his father had sent, not for long, anyway—the beaten-down man's face seared him even at that size. The hand holding the snapshot would feel heavy, full; the few times they'd spoken on the phone with hundreds of miles between them—and that not enough—his father's voice made no sense to him.

Stefan forced himself to remember when the last letter came from Ann Arbor, a month ago? As usual, Sasha had left it around for a few days; as usual Stefan hadn't read it.

"He's getting married." She nodded. "Not soon. Next year, in the summer."

183

"Are you going?" Stefan heard himself ask.

"No." She eyed him oddly. "Are you?"

"I didn't know," Stefan managed.

"I'm sure he'll send you the plane ticket if you asked—or we'll pay for it."

He hadn't asked his father for anything, or his mother, in years, not even for an explanation of what had gone wrong between them. When his mother had tried asking him what happened that night in Michigan, and tried explaining why she had lied about her past, her whole life, he had simply walked out of the room. She followed, but he refused to listen, and she gave up. But she had slowly allowed herself to become more Jewish, with Leo, and he thought she had been trying to entice him with talk of the different holidays. As if he were nothing more than a cat leaping up for a piece of fish dangled out of reach. It disgusted him.

She finished the tea now.

"I suppose I'm glad he's decided to be with someone," she said a bit heavily.

"Did Leo say that?"

She started. "Yes. How did you—?"

Stefan shrugged, wondering why he couldn't have slept through the morning, her ringing, why anyone had to tell him this. Couldn't he have found out some other way?—when he was older and didn't care, had his own life that was unconnected with theirs, a life that could protect and enclose him. His lack of freedom had never before hurt so much; he was tied to them even now, even after he'd lived with Sasha so long.

I have to go away, he thought carefully, as if fingering something that hadn't cooled, and wondered that his mother hadn't sensed what he was feeling, planning.

"Well, it's a good thing," his mother asserted.

"That's Sasha's line."

She laughed. "You're right. I'm sure that's what he'll say." She leaned forward. "Will you tell him?"

He hesitated; it was almost as if she wanted to involve him in

184

his father's marriage or draw him back to them, but he didn't want to even think about it, let alone tell Sasha.

"Of course I can call later," his mother said smoothly. Too smoothly?

His suspicion of her was so strong today he felt ashamed. It wasn't even her he suspected, but the gleaming assured woman she'd become, and Leo.

"I'll call anyway." She rose, took up her handbag.

So then he had to decide; he still didn't know what she wanted him to do. His mother crossed to the stairs, turned. "Why don't you come stay with us? Pick some weekend you're free."

He had been invited like this many times, but today he couldn't keep silent: the way she stood, one arm stretched out to the curved railing behind her, was too expectant, too kind, and yet somehow it wasn't real—the movement seemed chosen far too well, managed. But she was his mother; she hadn't mentioned him visiting in a long time. Away, he thought—he had to get away.

"How about this weekend?"

She grinned. "Yes? This weekend's fine."

He thought she might want to kiss him, but she held back, just nodded. "Call us." And she stepped to the door. "Tell Sasha I'm sorry I missed him."

" 'Bye," he called as she got onto the elevator. He felt like a fraud—or a liar. But he was going somewhere; even *their* house was somewhere.

Stefan didn't even get the chance to decide whether he would tell Sasha or not; his mother called later just as Sasha came in around dinner time, and the long conversation drifted gradually from English through Yiddish to Polish, with some spots of Russian too. Ever since they got back from Michigan, Yiddish had emerged from hiding. Stefan sometimes couldn't stand the sound of it—so unmusical and coarse compared to Polish or Russian.

"So." Sasha stood in the bedroom doorway. "This is news." Stefan turned his chair to face Sasha, who entered and sat on the bed.

"This is news." Sasha's eyes searched his. "She is a professor with him."

Sasha nodded. "It was all a long time ago. Maybe now. . . ." He shrugged.

Stefan didn't ask maybe now what; Sasha probably meant everything would work out for all of them. How was that possible? What happened now didn't erase all the previous years, the divorce, the secrets; you couldn't make times like that go away by trying to be someone else trying to forget or live differently.

"It will be a good thing," Sasha decided. "I'll make dinner. What did you do today?"

Stefan followed Sasha to the kitchen and they talked casually about Sasha's lesson, the friend he'd met for a late lunch. Stefan tasted and chopped and did the few other peripheral things Sasha permitted him to do.

After dinner Sasha said "I met Jenny's mother on Broadway. She's very against the strike. Too much." Sasha stirred his tea.

Stefan excused himself. In the bedroom he hunted in the small leather-bound address book for his mother's number; Sasha hadn't put it under Borowski or Greenberg (Leo's name). He turned the pages slowly, reading every entry, found it under Ann, but he only knew because of the address—he'd never thought of his mother as that and even when Leo called her "Annie" or Sasha said "Anya" it sounded very strange to him.

"Yes?" Good—it was his mother.

"Can I come tomorrow?"

"That's Wednesday."

"School's on strike all week," he said; she had to let him come tomorrow. He had to get away.

"Do you remember the directions?" his mother asked after a pause. "Or Leo could pick you up—?

"No, I remember how." Before he hung up he thought perhaps she wanted to say something else besides going over the directions with him, even ask why he was coming so soon, but all she said was "See you, then," and hung up.

Sasha was about to sit at the piano when Stefan walked into the living room.

"I'm going to Bay Ridge tomorrow."

"Yes?"

"For a while."

"Ah. The strike is all week?"

"All week," Stefan told him, going off to the kitchen, hungry again.

After breakfast, he wandered around the apartment, wondering at how small it seemed; Sasha slept, so he had to be quiet, couldn't turn on the radio or play anything, and would have to wait before he could pack.

Sasha seemed very far-off when he woke, rubbing his arms as if he'd been cold; Sasha hardly spoke to him, but went right to the kitchen for tea.

Stefan headed for the closet, made some quick choices, collected underwear and then dragged his duffel bag out from behind a box of old music; with it came his old dog. He stopped to give it a good look: the face was worn and rubbed and stuffing had at some time escaped out the back legs.

"I haven't seen Scotty in years," Sasha said from the door. Stefan thrust the dog back into the closet. He heard Sasha go into the bathroom to shower.

He felt very restless, torn between wanting to rush off to Brooklyn and a desire to just sit somewhere, not here, somewhere he wouldn't have to think or talk or listen. There probably was no such place, so it didn't really matter where he was, Stefan thought grimly.

He drifted to the piano and tried a Chopin nocturne he knew he was really too young and clumsy to play—the most he could do was mimic the music, not enter and join it. This was his problem even with much simpler pieces when they demanded not only facility and expression, but depth, the depth Sasha had sometimes, when there was no line between the player and the playing. Still, he had to sit at the keyboard now and then, and if he wasn't very good, he wasn't very bad either. "Your touch is light," Sasha had told him once; at the time Stefan took it as a compliment, but now he thought different.

"I'm going to shop," Sasha said from the foyer.

"I guess I'll stay in," Stefan said, trying not to show he was relieved to have the apartment to himself for a while.

"You'll be gone when I return? Then have a good time." Sasha nodded at him and left.

"He doesn't want me to go," Stefan almost said aloud, but why that should be he had no idea.

The train ride was noisy in the afternoon, with crowds of school kids appearing at different stops. Stefan wasn't used to the subway so the metal shriek, the roar into and away from one dirty platform after another seemed like being stuck at a party with someone who knew only one joke.

His mother's bay-windowed corner house was a solid brick square with a curved flagstone path and a wall of thick even hedge; it looked more placed, fully-built, than constructed. There were no big trees so it faced its two streets with wide casement windows, severe and plain-lined.

"Mr. and Mrs. Greenberg" the black letterbox read, not "The Greenbergs" or "Greenberg." This bothered him. He rang and looked around, hardly taking in what he saw—it was one of those pleasant tree-lined simple streets you passed through and forgot.

"You're early," his mother beamed, waving him inside as if she'd been waiting quite a while.

"I brought wine." He fumbled inside his bag. "Sasha picked it out."

"You didn't have to." She took the bottle. "This is fine. I can hardly tell them apart. I know which ones I'm supposed to like, Leo makes sure of that. Come put your bag away." She led him past the living room to the small brown guest room. "You seem very tall to me. Come sit in the kitchen while I put in the lamb."

He lingered, glancing around the warm room hung with family pictures. Near the window was one of him; he moved closer, curious, hesitant. In it he stood, very little, four years old perhaps, in shorts and T-shirt, staring down at his shoes, looking like he wanted to cry. It was taken on the porch of Mrs. Mannion's house in Rockaway.

"Stefan?" his mother called.

He trailed to the large pale kitchen where his mother fussed at the stove.

"Smells good," he said, sitting on one of the bar stools.

"I haven't done anything, wait." She closed the oven and set its timer.

"Now, what would you like? Seven and seven? Let me see." She fussed some more and then stepped across to him with a glass. He was pleased that they all let him drink wine and alcohol, that it wasn't something to argue about, even though he was underage. "We'd rather have you drinking at home, where you're safe," Sasha had said. But Sasha had to admit that Stefan going to Dooley's, only two blocks away, wasn't too bad either.

When he took the drink from his mother now he wondered if her hand wasn't shaking. "Perhaps I'll have one myself." She made another and joined him at the counter. He felt very adult suddenly, and worried for her, and this was strange. She fiddled with the edge of her apron. "I'm glad you're away from all that demonstrating," she brought out at length, looking him full in the face.

"Nothing happened."

"Still. . . ."

He nodded.

"Leo doesn't really understand," she said, and it was as if Leo were someone neither of them knew well, he was that far away.

Stefan nodded again.

"He thinks we're all free to believe what we want," she smiled, sipped her drink, set it down on the counter very carefully. "All of us."

"Can I help with anything?"

"Later. Tell me about school, and next year. Where will you go?"

Because his grades were so high, and his SAT's were 1400

combined, he'd been accepted at every college in New York he'd applied to, but didn't want to go to any of them.

"I don't know."

"The money doesn't matter, remember; we both want you to pick the school you like."

He didn't know if the "we" meant his mother and father, his mother and Leo or even her and Sasha. Stefan's grasp of his financial situation was as vague as he could keep it; there was money for what he wanted, which had never seemed to be too much.

"There's Leo," she said brightly, as a car door slammed. "He's early too."

Stefan went to wash up.

Four blocks away was Shore Road and then just across a footbridge he could be close to the water, lean on the plain black railing while traffic off behind him almost covered the lap, lap of littered water below; tiny sailboats flitted off near the rising mounds of Staten Island which bristled with as many buildings as trees. At least from where he stood it seemed that way. He ignored the sky-slashing curves of the Verrazano off to his left, and also the columned base of the Manhattan in the other direction. He stared at the green-gray-blue water, at the large slow dirty-looking ships, at nothing special, just stared. His mother had gone to shop and Stefan remembered having shared this view once with Sasha years ago, so he had come to the water. Sasha seemed very distant now.

The breeze played with his hair but hardly offered any glimpse of an answer as he eyed the ceaseless cutting little waves. Nothing seemed any clearer here—all that happened was that he'd changed places, nothing deeper, nothing more. No, that wasn't true; his mother was glad he'd come and Leo was heartier, more man-to-man. After dinner last night, while his mother was upstairs, Leo, from the deep shelter of a champagne-colored wing chair, had remarked warmly:

"Your mother's been through a lot," and shook his fine dramatic head in admiration. It was at once a very private statement and yet

190

public too and Stefan didn't know how to take it up, or if he even wanted to. He didn't want to resent Leo—or not completely—but how could he stop feeling a bit repulsed by his mother's husband? Leo liked him, yet the gap between them could only narrow, not close. And Stefan was jealous, because Leo must know exactly what had happened to her, his father, Sasha, and Eva, Stefan's aunt. Leo didn't have to live with lies.

Leo seemed determined not to notice any awkwardness. "Shall we go?" His mother had appeared all quickened, smiling, and they went to see a very silly movie, took a drive afterward.

Stefan was too tired this morning to think of what he'd left in Manhattan; he hadn't slept well because the room practically gloated at him—so many pictures of his mother and Leo, so many poses and grins; the walls were clamorous and disturbing, forcing him to face what had been a fact now for years. The walls were worse than the way his mother touched Leo's shoulder to get his attention, worse than the silences in which he felt something pass between Leo and his mother that was so intimate it stifled him.

"I don't want to go back," Stefan muttered, and then glanced round to make sure he was alone. Not back home, and not to that perfectly appointed house in which everything looked made of silk.

Once some friends of Jenny's at a party had discussed suicide, alternately boisterous and hushed; Stefan listened, not tempted, not outraged—the idea didn't touch him, somehow, was foreign and incomprehensible.

"If you were really low. . . ." he remembered Jenny having said thoughtfully. Was he really low now? How did people decide such big questions?

"You just do it," one of Jenny's friends had assured the room, and Martina knew because a cousin of hers had sealed his head in a large plastic bag.

He didn't want to go back anywhere, wanted not to take up his life again. Graduation was coming, and then a strange summer, he was sure—he dreaded this one. And he had to choose a college soon. Faster than soon.

And Jenny.

He broke away and stalked back to the house his mother lived in. "Would you like some lunch?" She already seemed less tense with him, asked questions more slowly. He leaned in the kitchen doorway.

"Maybe I'll read something."

"Most of the books are up in the study."

But he didn't go there; instead he drifted to the Steinway grand in the living room which glistened in the sun. Stefan played everything he could remember, not once stopping to see what music was in the bench.

"I wish I still played," his mother smiled, coming in to sit on the sofa near him.

"Does Leo?"

"No. It's really Sasha's piano, whenever he's here. Leo thought of it."

He nodded, thinking he should say something about how nice that was of Leo.

The silence in the room wasn't strained, but dead somehow, as if alone, the gulf between them became obvious, immeasurable. He didn't know what to do except play more, but that wasn't really for his mother, or even for himself.

"You're good. You should practice more—"

"To be a tenth-rate pianist?" he flashed.

She blinked, said nothing but "I'll start dinner."

He did go up to the book-crammed study, which, with its brown-gold couch and armchairs and ceiling-high shelves, looked like a club room—anonymous in a way, with nothing more personal than the names inside the books: Leo Greenberg, Fania Greenberg, Ann Borowski. Many just said "For Ann" with a date; he guessed those were from Leo.

Stefan settled into one of the chairs, stacking books on the arm, but he didn't begin to read. There was no noise out in the street, no cars, no bicycle bells, and certainly no voices. What did his mother do all day? He knew she'd finally earned a Ph.D. four years back—why wasn't she teaching, or something?

Was it simply that Leo was enough, a life with him enough? Stefan suddenly felt for the first time the urge to ask her; he could go downstairs and sit her down and say "Now tell me why you married him, what makes him better than Dad? And how could you lie to me all those years?" It could all begin there.

He flushed with the vision, but it was no more than that. He'd never said anything half so real to her, now wasn't the time to start.

He took the top book and began reading to drown out the rising clamor; he didn't dare unravel his past, their past. He would ask nothing.

Leo called to say he'd be late and Stefan wondered if he shouldn't leave tomorrow—wasn't he out of place here?

Leo was very chatty at dinner, asking at one point: "When do we get our tickets?"

"Tickets?"

"For graduation." His mother smiled.

Stefan looked at their waiting faces.

"I'm not going," he said vaguely, because he hadn't *known* until then.

"As a protest?" Leo asked, interested, serious.

"If there's demonstrating—" his mother began anxiously.

"No, not as a protest. I'm just not going."

"It's not important to you?"

Stefan pictured the robes and aisles and hats and little kids and the pop-pop of cameras, the singing. . . .

"I don't want to go." He shrugged.

"When I was a kid in Flatbush," Leo remembered, picking up his wine glass, "high school was a big thing." Leo smiled at Stefan's mother. "Here's to college, though," he toasted. "College is a big thing."

Stefan then announced which college he'd chosen: Fordham at Lincoln Center. "Because it's small," he explained in answer to his mother's glance.

"That's a Catholic school," Leo observed.

"So?"

Leo shrugged. "Just commenting."

Stefan didn't say that he had chosen it precisely for that reason. Columbia and NYU had too many Jews.

They spent the rest of the evening talking about a school Stefan had only chosen to make himself seem more positive and decisive.

But the fog closed in on him again when Leo and his mother went upstairs to bed, leaving him alone in the brightly-lit cool living room. He stretched out on the sofa, lost to anything more specific than the yellow-beige ceiling he stared at, and a vague train of melodies that blurred and twisted each other to make just noise in his head.

"You didn't stay the weekend?" Sasha wondered at the door, taking his bag from him.

"I guess not."

"Something happened?"

"No, nothing." Stefan went to the fridge, pulled it open, let it shut.

"There are letters for you."

"What?"

Sasha had put the bag in the bedroom and now held out two white envelopes. "From your father. From Jenny."

Sasha still had the letters.

"You read his," Stefan brought out, beginning to feel dizzy.

"Are you sure?"

Stefan didn't move as Sasha ripped one of the envelopes.

"It's about the marriage," Stefan said dully, "When, and who she is, and where they'll live."

Sasha nodded as he scanned the single sheet.

"That's all, right?"

"No." Sasha set the letter down on the table. "There's more."

"He wants me to come for the wedding?"

"No—that's next year. He wants you to come for the summer. It says they have a house up in northern Michigan, a big one, that belonged to her family." Sasha met his incredulous stare. "Read it."

But Stefan wouldn't look; how could he go back to Michigan when just two days in Bay Ridge were so awful?

He held out his hand for Jenny's thick letter. He didn't read that one either, not even later when Sasha went to bed and he sat up, turning the unopened envelope over and over in one hand. Sasha said Jenny had called but didn't want the number in Brooklyn. The thick wrinkled letter seemed ominous to Stefan; he was afraid to open it, afraid to set it down or put it away.

Too much made him afraid, Stefan thought, but that wasn't enough to get him to tear open Jenny's envelope.

"Whatever she has to say she can tell me," he thought sullenly, but that was a lie: he didn't want her to tell him anything, he wanted to forget.

There was always something new to forget, something he couldn't bear to think about, at least lately, like when he was a kid, and then after, after the breakup, and coming to live with Sasha and finding out who he really was; forget the time he'd screamed at Leo and thrown a full ashtray at him, missing but covering his own hand and head in ashes, screaming "Get out! Get out!" at the stranger who his mother liked better than anyone; forget how ugly his mother and father had looked at each other the last time he saw them together before his father went away to leave them; forget how he'd hated them all and wanted to rip Scotty apart—poor old Scotty who'd never bothered anyone; forget the time he'd imagined creeping towards the piano with a scissors when Sasha wasn't looking to hurt what was most beautiful to him, to hurt something.

And now Jenny—that night and this letter.

In the morning, he would go to Mrs. Mannion's house. He had to get away. At breakfast Stefan asked: "Do you think I could go to Rockaway this weekend? Did your lease start?"

Sasha frowned, holding a piece of toast in midair as if he suddenly didn't know what to do with it.

"Yes, to both questions." He put the toast down on the break-fast-strewn table. "You'll go alone?"

Stefan nodded.

"I'll call Mrs. Mannion—" Sasha began.

"I can do it."

"Just for the weekend?"

"I guess."

But Sasha eyed him steadily until he said "Well, maybe longer."

"Because she should know."

Mrs. Mannion, in her distant drifting way, seemed pleased.

"So you're not going to graduation?" Sasha guessed when he got off the phone.

"I'm tired of all those people."

"Take linen, remember. Do you need money?"

"Some."

Sasha always gave him money in an envelope with his name on the front, so Stefan never knew right away how much was inside. He never asked for specific amounts; he couldn't, it was Sasha who checked now and then, and Stefan felt off-balance, because the money came from his parents, maybe even from Leo, and he didn't want to have to take it. The only time he'd earned his own money was working at the del Greco's cleaning store, and then last year as a tutor of history and math in a city after-school program at George Washington, but the pay was so low and the people he worked with so unpleasant, he stayed just one semester. The tutors were all much harsher than Jenny's friends, sarcastic and gossipy, always clustering in whispers, disappearing from the large class-room to obscure corners of the empty echoing school to trade secrets. The atmosphere was so mean and stifling he'd had to quit.

On the endless train ride to Rockaway with his repacked bag and an envelope, he almost wished Sasha had asked why he wanted to leave.

Mrs. Mannion was waiting on the porch, rocking and knitting; she smiled as he trudged up the peeling cracked tan stairs, looking at him over the tops of her glasses.

"Would you like some lunch?" she asked. "Something to drink? You're much taller."

Over lunch they talked in a vague disconnected way, merely filling the time until he was done and she could wash up; they had little in common except Sasha, and Mrs. Mannion seemed to hover around his uncle more than actually discuss him.

Stefan went upstairs to unpack. Everything smelled fresh and unused, and the sight of the large bare mattress in Sasha's room depressed him, so he closed that door. It took only a few minutes to hang his towel, store the few toiletries he'd brought and empty his bag. The closet swallowed everything up and once the bed was made he felt displaced, as if the room were someone else's. He plugged in the radio Sasha had reminded him to take, placed it on the blue-painted table, but didn't turn it on. Mrs. Mannion had cleaned the now-buzzing fridge and the cabinets; all he had to do was go down the Boulevard "into town" and buy food.

He put on a windbreaker and went off to the beach.

"It's cool," Mrs. Mannion remarked. "On the beach."

He strode down to the brown-gray weathered boardwalk, stood at the rail for a long time watching the sea. It was all lines here. The endless stretching planks, the shifting line where the sand became mud, the dull senseless waves that foamed and returned, the horizon that was interesting only when it captured a ship. The water was too cool still, and the empty beach looked dirty, so he just ended up sitting on the nearest staircase down to the sand, hands in his pockets, sand occasionally blown up into his hair, and he listened for voices or bird cries or something.

When he got back, someone else was there, Phil, Mrs. Mannion's nephew, who was stopping on the way from Temple University to see a friend in Montauk. Phil shook his hand so strongly Stefan wondered if it was a joke. Phil was very dark and slim; his aunt said, "Phil's on the tennis team. Doesn't he look like Tony Curtis?" And Stefan thought of *Spartacus*, which he had never seen with Louie.

When Stefan said he was just planning on going out for pizza, Mrs. Mannion quietly insisted he eat dinner with them. He felt more relaxed at their second meal, told her about the demonstration and strike at school. Phil seemed very interested, and he kept staring at Stefan as if challenging or daring him.

"And how," Mrs. Mannion began, smile poised to widen, "How is your mother?"

Stefan mumbled something.

197

"Well I hope we see her this summer." She nodded in a mixture of graciousness and solemnity.

They helped her with the dishes and Stefan played a Clementi sonatina for her he knew so well his fingers breathed the music.

"Very lovely music," Mrs. Mannion pronounced. "Delicate."

"Nice," Phil said.

When Mrs. Mannion went out to call on a neighbor Stefan drifted upstairs. He wondered if he wanted Sasha to come here—or anyone. He lay on his bed, eyes closed, trying to relax with what the radio played, but it became too plaintive and melancholy and he had to turn it off before the long sweep of the strings got to him. Sleep was what he wanted, not feeling.

"What's up?" Phil asked, pushing open the door, leaning in the doorway, his shirt unbuttoned on a smooth hairless torso.

"Can't sleep," Stefan blurted, and then was furious for telling that to a stranger.

Phil grinned, showing movie star teeth, amazingly big and white. "You need a massage," he said. "That always works for me."

"Okay."

"I'll look for some oil. Roll over."

Stefan, wearing just his shorts, lay on his stomach, waiting, feeling sad. He was remembering Louie. He had not touched another guy or let anyone touch him since Louie left for college and never came back because Mr. del Greco sold the store and they moved. He made Louie mad the very last time they talked in Louie's room, with almost everything packed and boxed. Stefan had been desperate for Louie to say that this wasn't the end, that Louie would write to him, that he could go out to California and see Louie. When he tried talking about the future, Louie had just cut him off: "Let's just cool it, okay? I don't want to think about this anymore." Louie had then put down his glass of Coke and gone to the bathroom. Knowing he might not see Louie for a long time, Stefan snatched up the glass, gulped the Coke and then kissed the rim of the glass at the place where Louie had been drinking. He'd closed his eyes, holding the glass to his lips. "Get out of here," Louie was suddenly saying, grabbing the glass. They didn't even shake hands.

"I'm back," Phil said. "Ever been massaged?"

Stefan moved his head sideways to say no, not really.

Phil got on the bed behind him, straddled him lightly, weight mostly on his own legs and thighs. "I'm really good at this," he said, and as he squeezed some oil onto Stefan's back, he said, "My aunt's playing cards. We have time."

Stefan started to groan as Phil's strong hands spread the oil across his back, pressing, rubbing, fingers going in circles, or up and down Stefan's spine. It was amazing, as if he'd never been aware of his own body. Phil's hands were like Louie's in a way, commanding, strong, sure.

It seemed to go on forever as he felt himself sinking into the bed. Phil massaged his hands, his legs and feet.

"Wow," Stefan kept saying.

Phil rolled him over, crouched at his side on the bed to grease his chest and stomach. Stefan could now see that Phil was also only wearing shorts, and in the near-dark room, the white slash across the dark length of his body was like a flag of surrender. Phil was as slim as Stefan, but more sharply defined.

"Are you sleepy yet?" Phil asked.

"No."

"Good." And Phil pulled at Stefan's shorts, slipped them off and onto the floor.

"Do you want some more massage?" Phil asked, lightly sliding an oiled hand across Stefan's crotch, which didn't stir. Face up, he was too aware of this as Mrs. Mannion's house, the house Sasha and he came to every summer. To lie there naked with her smiling quiet nephew was like a betrayal. But he didn't ask Phil to stop.

And when Phil slid a finger between Stefan's cheeks, circled, teased, plunged, starting to massage inside, Stefan couldn't believe how hard he was getting. He reached for Phil's shorts, but Phil said, "Wait a little," and bent down. "God, I love sucking cock!"

The words were sharp and shocking to Stefan—not just spoken, but flung out, like a discus powerfully hurtling across a field. He had never heard anyone *say* that. He closed his eyes, his whole body revolving around the finger that played music inside of him. He thought of Tony Curtis, and slipped into *Spartacus*, imagining that it was Louie who stroked and soothed him, as tunic-clad servants waited nearby. . . .

Phil was gone when Stefan got up in the morning and went downstairs. Stefan didn't know how he could ask where Phil was or anything like that without giving himself away. He ate no breakfast, just made coffee and headed for the beach. It was a grim damp-smelling day, enclosing, oppressive, but it hadn't rained yet, so he slipped off his moccasins and went down to walk along the beach. No one was there and the orange wire garbage cans marched off down in each direction out of sight as if they meant something. He ambled to the water line, avoiding the blotches of tar and seaweed, the few bottles and cans of someone's late-night fun, but he didn't look at the sea, or off to where the beach line curved and obscured itself in mist. The steady slow waves spitting and hissing were unpleasant today—he was alone, though, if nothing else.

He felt calmed, simplified—smoothed out like cloth; no wrinkles threatened him, he walked near the water's edge dangling his shoes, not pushing his hair back into order when the breeze blew up, just walked and was only the walking, blissfully nothing more.

But after a while he heard shuffling steps somewhere behind him, and turned.

It was Jenny, her face very pale, her hair all blown and tangled. She held her shoes like a weapon as she came across the rippled sand to where he stood unable to move away. But even when she approached, he felt very far from her.

"You never *called* me."

He hesitated and she nodded.

"I bet you didn't even read the letter, did you? I can't believe it." She followed as he set off down the sand. "What's wrong? It wasn't so bad."

The mindless consolation made him want to strike her so she'd shut up.

"Stefan . . . Stef. . . ."

"Don't call me that!"

"Okay, I'm sorry. I—"

They walked in silence, Stefan unable to escape—there was no such place as "away" he thought, grinding inside with the pain of this.

"I told my folks I was going to visit a friend in Sayville."

"Sayville."

"It wasn't so bad, Stefan. Stefan?" Jenny took his arm and made him stop. He turned, seeing her pale anxious wind-pinched face as if from so great a height it might not have been a face at all.

"Tell me what it is, Stefan. Please?" She paused, and rushed on in her firm public voice saved for large statements of truth: "You don't really like me, do you?"

"That's what it is," he affirmed, staring her down. Without a word Jenny trudged back across to the boardwalk. She would leave him alone; he believed that—it was done between them.

When Jenny was out of sight Stefan let go his shoes and sank onto the sand, sat hunched over, his head down on his knees.

10

Things seemed very false that summer. Stefan couldn't stand talking to anyone for even a moment—the chatty girl in the bakery who was always gabbing about the weather or the onion rolls drove him out onto the street feeling all tight in the throat. Mrs. Mannion bothered him too with her slow, split sentences. He heard her nephew Phil was working on a ranch in Wyoming, but it didn't interest him. He kept away from Sasha as much as he could, went to the beach by himself in the morning and at sunset, at night, just so he wouldn't have to talk about anything. He began to hate conversation. He retreated, drew in, spent hours and hours in the fog, blank. He wondered sometimes if Jenny had really believed him, if she wouldn't walk up the porch steps one day, tentatively, hoping for a smile.

He had torn up her letter without reading it.

Sometimes he pictured Jenny sitting at the back of Dooley's

with friends or another guy, and perhaps his name came up. What would she say? Was he dead for her?

Sasha said one still heat-soaked morning: "You and Jenny aren't—?"

"That's right," Stefan agreed, getting up from the table. Sasha didn't ask any more questions about Jenny.

Stefan thought of her now more than at school, more than even when they'd been side by side in a movie theater idly holding hands, but in a curious unclear way—like a reflection seen in a rippled pond. She seemed blurred, representative, more a figure now than a girl.

But he'd never see her again, unless by accident in their neighborhood which wouldn't be often or important, would just hurt. So it didn't matter what he thought of her, really.

It seemed a terrible thing to him, though, what he'd said to her—this came to him mostly at night, keeping him from even considering sleep and he would walk through the cool sea-scented air to the beach, sit perhaps at the base of the staircase, watching the black and white show of waves. Sometimes there'd be a couple far off, laughing or arguing or silent, or a wild little group round a bonfire that split the night.

He had lied to Jenny to push her away—that was the worst kind of lie, hard and isolating. Even if she doubted him, or wanted to it would always fill the air between them like a clamoring fire alarm at night. How could she forget what he'd said or the way he said it? He had cut her from his life. It was as ugly as how Louie had treated him their last afternoon together.

"And I did that to Jenny," Stefan would murmur, trying to claim the harshness, the lie, understand and own it—but it resisted, and poisoned his mind.

He no longer even had the hope of telling someone about himself, about what his parents had escaped but been imprisoned by nonetheless, and about Louie. He listened to very little music; none of it soothed him enough to stop his thoughts. The only remedy was reading—books he'd always avoided—long graceless

Victorian novels. The words flooded him, bore him down where there was no other reality.

Sasha seemed amused. "No more science fiction? No mysteries?"

"I guess not."

"A good book," Mrs. Mannion contributed from the wicker depths of her rocker, and she paused even longer than usual before finishing: "A good book is a good book."

Stefan, in the shade on the swing at the side of the porch, didn't look up from the largest Mrs. Gaskell novel he'd found on the library's shelves. He liked the faded gilt binding, the yellowed pages and most of all, the book's weight.

"What do you do all day?" Leo asked him a week later, leaning on the boardwalk rail. It was not yet dark and they'd all taken a stroll to the beach. His mother, Sasha, and Mrs. Mannion were barefoot down at the water's edge, their voices high and edged, like children, hands waving shoes at the water, at each other. Leo—in white shorts and polo shirt, smoking his "after dinner cigarette"—seemed very strange and young, as if in disguise. "Looks quiet here."

"I read. I go to the beach."

"Whatever happened to that pretty girl?"

When Stefan didn't answer, but turned to stare at the gleaming light-wild stretch of arcade shops, Leo put a hand on his shoulder.

"It never looks like there's going to be someone else, but let me tell you, there always is, when you're ready. And *you* should have no trouble."

He wanted Leo not to touch him, and he wanted it, wanted Leo to say more things like that about everything being all right. He wanted to hear that simple confidence, wanted to believe it for just one night.

But he was too old to be comforted like that. And Leo wasn't his father.

Then Stefan smiled. Who *was* his father?

Leo caught the smile. "I knew it. Bet you have eyes on someone already."

Stefan heard his mother's laugh; she was leading them across the cool sand to the steps.

Leo grinned at her.

Leo and his mother spent the night, sleeping in Sasha's room. Mrs. Mannion lent Sasha a cot which he silently set up later in Stefan's room. He didn't know which made him more uncomfortable: Leo and his mother next door, or Sasha here in his room. After lying in the breezeless dark for a while, he began to hope the two might cancel each other out. He wore underwear because he wasn't alone and the unfamiliar enclosed feeling was unpleasant. Sasha was still awake, Stefan thought, facing the wall.

"Stefan? Have I done something?" The question was faint, hardly louder than the vague rustle of leaves outside. "Did I do something to make you so quiet?"

"No." Stefan said heavily, to make it sound as if he were almost asleep. "No."

And Sasha soon dozed off, breathing slowly, strangely.

"I should've said something," he thought bitterly, his shoulders going tight. But he never did—he never knew what to say—there was always too much—the time was wrong. How did people have the "long talks" he was always hearing about? How could they stand it and where did the words come from, what drove them out across to someone else? The distances were enormous.

He sat up very quietly so Sasha wouldn't wake, reached to his chair and slipped on his cutoffs, padded around Sasha's cot out to the stairs and down, glad Mrs. Mannion didn't have a dog that would come slobbering and snorting from its sleepy corner ready to play a new game. When he got downstairs, though, the door stopped him—the inner one made no noise, but how could he open the screen without waking someone?

He had to get out, though. So he pushed it just enough to slip onto the porch; the creaking wasn't too bad. Except for the tall dim street lamps, there were no lights on all up and down the street and no noise but a whiff of traffic from the Boulevard and the merged sound of waves, crickets and trees that spread everywhere like the dark.

He sat in one of the rockers, planting his bare feet solidly on the smooth planking of the porch. He'd come down to the hushed dark porch so there would be no pretense of sleep, no struggle to relax. He would just sit there and rock.

What if what he told Jenny wasn't a lie? some voice in him asked. He stopped rocking. What if somehow the truth had forced itself from him on the beach?

Was it the truth? Was it? He demanded an answer from that same voice but it was gone, had thrown its bomb and fled. Had he tried going to bed with her to forget about Louie?

How did you know these things for sure?

From the depths of this whirl came an image of himself years ago waking in the middle of a nightmare and going to Sasha's room, but Sasha didn't wake up so he climbed under the covers and snuggled up feeling very safe.

"I just want someone to hold me," Stefan said through tears now, head thrown back, eyes shut. That was what he wanted— that was what he could understand—that was the truth. What he'd told Jenny was a lie because she scared him.

He wanted her so much she scared him. He wanted *something*.

He should've stayed that night at her house to explain everything. Jenny would've listened and held him and he wouldn't be alone now, wouldn't torment himself with silence and lies, and more lies—they would choke him some day.

"You couldn't sleep either." Leo stepped onto the porch, trying to silence the door. He was barefoot, wrapped in a big green terry cloth robe. "I have trouble sleeping when I'm not home," he said, leaning against one of the honeysuckle-wrapped pillars.

Stefan cleared his throat but said nothing. Leo irked him—his name, his face, the roughness of his manner and voice, his accent. It amazed Stefan that Leo had an accent even though he was American born. A Jewish accent. No wonder his parents and Sasha had worked so hard to make their English sound stripped and pure—it was *this* they wanted to avoid.

"It's pretty here," Leo said. "Quiet, must be good to get away. We're going to France in August. Did your mother tell you? If you'd like to come with us, or if you want to go someplace else, by yourself, I'm sure it'd be okay."

Stefan was still trying to control himself.

"I wish it was easier all around," Leo said, and Stefan suddenly, and for the first time, saw Leo as separate, unconnected, not his mother's husband, not his stepfather, just Leo. He didn't know what to make of this new vision.

"Do you need anything?" Leo queried, hands in his pockets, one hairy long leg crossed in front of the other.

What could he say—what did he need? Too much.

"Are you sure you want to go straight to college? You could travel, work on a kibbutz, do lots of things."

"I'll go," Stefan said; he had to be in school, he didn't know anything else.

"If you change your mind. . . ." Leo shrugged and Stefan warmed to him, found himself far from tears now.

"Thanks," he said.

Leo smiled, nodded as if to a good joke, said nothing more for a while. Going back inside, Leo hesitated with the door open; Stefan saw moths flutter past Leo's shadowed head. Leo only said good night.

Stefan sat very loosely for a while, alive to the night, the sighing wood all around him. Had he and Leo ever shared such quiet relaxed moments, had he ever been able to just be with Leo and not hate or worry? Stefan didn't think so, and at the back of all this was a thought taking on energy, pushing forward: he would tell Leo.

"What would you say?" something in the air seemed to ask, not condemming, not mocking, merely curious.

The glow disappeared and he felt chilled and isolated—there was too much to say.

"I'll go to bed now," he thought, and upstairs, he forced himself to sleep.

Still, in the morning, in the unusual crowding and jostling at breakfast—hardly any remark seemed to get answered or even finished—Stefan thought perhaps there was a chance he could open up to Leo, find peace of mind in that and even reach his mother, not all at once, but gradually. Maybe Stefan could even make Leo what he and his mother shared, since so much else between them had crumbled and most times they were together it was like stirring the ashes of a dead fire.

He realized he was being spoken to.

"What?"

"Will you go out there?" his mother said, eyes expressionless.

"Where?"

"Michigan. For the wedding," Leo said, too casually.

Stefan hated him for butting in. Why were they bringing this up *now?* It was a year away!

"Your father will call if you don't write soon," Sasha reminded him, and Stefan felt harassed on all sides, wanted to hurl the table from him.

"You haven't written?" His mother frowned; Leo's hand slid over hers on the table.

"Yes, just to congratulate them," Sasha lied, and Stefan didn't care—what was the point of tackling the truth of anything?

His mother nodded, relieved.

"It's hard to decide," Leo offered, and Stefan shot him a grateful glance.

"Still, they have to know, eventually." His mother's eyes narrowed, as if picturing the arrangements his father would make.

"Do you want me to go there?" he asked. "For the summer?"

Sasha began clearing up, even though they weren't finished.

"Do as you like," his mother said stiffly.

"I don't want to go," he said, rising, not looking to see if she was relieved or upset. "For the wedding, for anything."

He took up his latest 600-pager and went down to the porch swing.

Sasha, Leo and his mother soon came out chatting, hung about with chairs and towels and bags and baskets and set off with nods and smiles. He had never gotten over disliking the Sunday crowds on the beach.

Mrs. Mannion, back from a little shopping, joined him a while later to read the paper and watch the day grow hotter. She said very little, occasionally murmuring under her breath.

"They're friends," Mrs. Mannion remarked to him at one point, looking up over the tops of her glasses at he couldn't tell what. "Your parents aren't just in love," she continued placidly. "They're friends too."

"Leo's not my father," he shot.

Mrs. Mannion clapped a pink hand to her mouth. "Oh," she said through it, "I'd forgotten."

Now and then he got mail from Fordham at Lincoln Center—announcements and instructions, most of which he couldn't penetrate even on a second reading, so a pile formed on the bureau in his room, one he could ignore because it became so familiar. In August, though, he began to feel pushed; Sasha seemed to be looking at him more and asking questions less, as if waiting for him to bring it all up.

No one Stefan knew was going there; this was a relief, but also a burden: he would have to ride down alone on the bus, wander in search of offices alone, stand in lines and register alone.

But that was only because he'd chosen this college and not the one Jenny was going to, or the others her friends had spread to.

He went back by himself a week before the end of August but he wasn't prepared for the city, even for his block—everything seemed dirty and greased, the air, the streets, cars and faces. The heat came and came with no breeze, no break: one incandescent day after another; how could he stand it when moving was out of the question and thinking impossible? He felt assaulted in the street, glared at and jeered by glass shards and pizza crusts. It was so dirty; just looking out the window made him hotter and riding a bus was like being sealed in a tunnel. He couldn't imagine descending into the vile-smelling subway.

Air conditioning wasn't enough, ice in everything wasn't enough. He couldn't play or read or eat, slept mostly, or just lay exhausted on the couch waiting until he had the strength to lurch into the shower.

209

Orientation in the morning and again in the afternoon was as grim
and as confusing as he'd expected, but the one-building school was
small, and not difficult to get around in. Otherwise it was a dreary
bland tile-and-concrete box that seemed as inviting as a corridor
in a train station. He had bits of conversation with people on lines
or in chairs, mostly agreeing with their mutterings and confusion.
After a while even the blazing air-conditioning was as irritating as
the crowded elevators and proliferating brochures and sheets of
paper. It all took five hours and he escaped, almost relieved to be
blasted by heat, which was simple at least, thought-consuming. In
a sweaty sort of daze he rode home, hardly noticing the green
stretch of Riverside Drive with the gorgeous old brownstones and
serenely ornate apartment buildings, or the turn onto Broadway
later that as a child had always keyed him up because they were
almost home and he'd soon get to pull the cord.

Sasha was back, in his chair, looking very dark and big, looking
very tired.

"It was terrible even at the ocean."

Stefan shrugged, pulling at the damp back of his shirt. He found
a pitcher of ice water in the fridge, poured a glass and went out
to the living room, sank onto the couch clasping the glass to his
face; it was so cold merely holding it, thinking of it made him feel
a bit better.

Sasha nodded. "I'm afraid it doesn't help much," he said, pointing to the air conditioner which whined in defeat. "How was
everything?"

Stefan shrugged, picturing the handful of cards and booklets
he'd dropped on the kitchen table as "everything." He made an
effort to tell Sasha what courses he hoped to take and when he'd
be in school.

"There are cards from France." Stefan glanced at the coffee table,
saw pictures of some castles. "They love it there."

Stefan sipped from the amazing cold glass unwilling to move.

"Water can be so good when you've had none," Sasha brought
out heavily, his face suddenly clouded. Stefan tensed—would

Sasha talk about the War? God, he hoped not, not now, not today. But all Sasha went on to say was: "I'll make something very light for dinner, light and cold."

"Who can eat?"

"Later," Sasha sighed, and closed his eyes.

"You know," Sasha began when they'd washed the dinner dishes and sat with glasses of iced tea in the living room. "I saw Jenny's mother today, just as I got to the corner. Jenny is taking a semester off to stay with cousins in Virginia."

"So?"

Sasha said nothing more, was soon at the piano playing something very stately and baroque.

"Is that Couperin?"

Sasha nodded.

Stefan went to the bathroom and began pouring tepid water; he got right in before there was even an inch of water, the way he did when he was little and had pretended he was an island and the rising water a flood. His body was startling against the white porcelain, very dark, very thin.

"Why did I snap at him?" he wondered aloud—it was so rude and childish, and Sasha seemed more easily hurt these days than ever. Sasha was older, and instead of being kind, Stefan felt edgy with him, annoyed and frustrated. Something had to change, something had to, soon. He stretched out in the tub, head back against the cool tile wall, eyes shut, trying to hear only the water.

Leo and Stefan's mother returned a week later with piles of cards, pamphlets, and books to show them "what it was like." They had spent two weeks in Paris, and two visiting chateaux in the Loire Valley.

"I'm not good with cameras," Leo confessed, smiling, tolerant, it seemed, of anyone who was.

His mother had brought him a beret and a Sulka silk tie, both of which he knew he'd never wear, a Limoges vase, and chocolates. "The chocolate store on Boulevard St. Germain, oh that store!

211

There was a fountain pouring chocolate—incredible! And the aroma. . . ." She sighed. "Everything was exquisite."

"Tell him about the bread," Leo said.

"The bread! My God, the bread has *taste* in France. I forgot what good bread was like."

"Your mother knocked people out—she opens her mouth and starts talking French and they just stare. Every place. The Louvre, restaurants, Chambord—you name it."

She was blushing.

"Tell them," Leo said. "Tell them what people said to you."

"I can't." Then, eyes down, she said softly, *'Mais vous parlez bien, madame.'* "

"You speak well," Stefan translated, impressed. He knew how fussy the French were about accents and how they sneered at Americans.

"In the Loire Valley," Leo raved, "we stayed in this small cha-teau—in a *tower room*—with doves outside. And the restaurant—! I must have gained ten pounds. But it was worth it."

His mother grinned, eyes alight, back very straight, hands clasped like a schoolgirl's.

The rest of the evening was one story after another, a blur of chateaux, meals, conversations with total strangers, avoiding American tourists. Leo and his mother were so happy, teasing each other like children all evening, it made Stefan breathless and when they packed away their show-and-tell and exited, the apartment still seemed full and loud.

"The vase is beautiful." Sasha looked around the living room. "Where—?"

"On my desk," Stefan decided, taking it inside.

The first week at Fordham passed in pantomime because Stefan quickly realized he didn't want to be there; it wasn't college, or even this college he objected to, but being in the same place, in New York still, at Sasha's. He kept thinking of the day his mother had come over to tell him about his father getting engaged, and he'd felt he had to get away. He saw now that he'd actually decided then to go, somewhere. Why couldn't his father just do what his mother and Leo had done—gone off to City Hall and not made any fuss about it?

Staying at this college was just marking time, so he kept himself withdrawn and aloof, became almost a spectator of his presence there. He wanted nothing to claim him, deflect him from his determination to leave.

But where would he go?

Jenny was in Virginia, he remembered, wondering if he couldn't think about her now more easily since she was far away. He dimly imagined calling her, or showing up at night in Arlington, making some small joke about just passing by, but he distrusted those images; somehow Jenny didn't have much to do with them: it was the idea, the drama of appearing that he sensed was strongest. And that was sad, because it meant already that he didn't need her so much, did not feel all he had if Jenny was merely a mental audience.

Where? Getting a job was pointless since he'd still be in the city and he couldn't make enough to live alone.

If his father could get remarried so late, he could do something dramatic too.

He didn't tell anyone what he was planning, or trying to plan, but each successive week of classes, with lectures and readings he only paid surface attention to, made him more sure he had to leave. When Sasha asked him how his classes were going, Stefan felt awkward having to say one thing and mean another—it wasn't exactly lying but close enough to be disturbing, especially since his mother and Leo wanted details, wanted to know what his professors were like, if he'd met anyone "nice."

The answer came quickly, simply. One afternoon in the teeming cafeteria he heard someone at the table behind him talking about transferring to another school. He listened to as many details of the process as he could and spent the next hour checking them in various offices in the building, winding up in front of a bookcase slumped with catalogues which he glanced at state by state, at last poring over the most obvious choice: one of the state university branches far enough from New York to be really away, but still in the state.

That evening, while Sasha was out at a neighbor's, Stefan made a list of what had to be sent when and where, and the next two weeks he lived from one phone call to the next; it was much easier applying upstate now that he actually was in a college—or it felt that way.

He was even more detached than before, picturing himself in a dorm, on the campus that was only a map and some photographs to him. This seemed the first time he'd ever moved so quickly in any direction, and with such excitement.

"Your classes are better?" Sasha asked.

"I feel better," was all Stefan could say and not let it out. The wait to hear about his application counterpointed the featureless days at school where he hardly ever felt present anymore, sat at the back of each class thinking it didn't matter, that he wasn't a part of it. He did his assignments in a sort of haze; the comments on his work began to read: "Too vague" and "Be specific" and "Needs detail."

His letter of acceptance for the Spring semester came a Saturday in December when his mother and Leo had dropped by on the way to visit friends in Connecticut.

"What is it?" Sasha wondered from his chair as Stefan came back upstairs with the open letter. Standing at the steps, Stefan tried to explain, but couldn't; he stepped down to hand the letter, and then stopped. Who should he give it to? Stefan sat at the end of the couch and passed the letter to his mother who held it so Leo could see. Sasha reached for it before Leo finished.

"Are you sure you've given it a chance here?" his mother asked, plucking at the cowl neck of her sweater.

"Why so soon?" Sasha asked.

"He's only going upstate," Leo announced, and they all turned to him. Leo shrugged. "If you don't like a school—and I guess Stefan doesn't—it's good to get out, and early too. No sense in staying someplace when you want to leave."

It was so simple and straightforward Stefan flushed—to be supported and understood by Leo was strange.

His mother said something to Sasha in Russian.

"None of that," Leo joked. "It's not fair to Stefan and me." Leo went on to ask him how far away his new college was, when he had to check in to the dorm, all easily, casually, as if Sasha and Stefan's mother were not sitting stiff and surprised.

"We must go, Leo," his mother interrupted, and they left in a donning of coats and scarves. "I'll call you," Leo promised, and he did later that evening to find out more: "We'll drive you upstate, of course," and to give Stefan some advice: "It's not so much what you tell people as how you do it. If they're too surprised, they always think it's worse than it is. But it's a good idea—you need to be on your own."

Sasha did not seem to think so, nor did his mother.

"I didn't want to talk about going and then it not happen," Stefan began once or twice to his uncle, but he knew this was not completely true and Sasha seemed to sense this, sense Stefan wanted to get away from him.

So planning and packing through December and January were hard on Stefan; he had to try to be less cheerful, try not to laugh when his grades were all B + . He was free, living ahead of himself; he'd never really felt the power of expectation. He counted days, made lists, called his new campus often, listened to upstate weather reports very carefully and even wrote his father.

"It's hard for her," Leo said, leaning back in the tufted leather booth, fiddling with a roll he hadn't sliced open after ten minutes. Stefan had never eaten alone with Leo, and this lunch—Leo's idea—seemed even at the table, even when they ordered, not quite possible. "It's hard for us," Leo corrected himself.

Stefan gulped from his drink, nervous, excited, feeling very young because he felt so grown-up here where everyone wore three-piece suits and the coat racks swelled with camel's hair.

Leo shrugged. "I'd like you to stay, too, but I know you shouldn't."

It was still strange to be championed by a man he hadn't liked until just recently, and made him think he had no right to let Leo say anything in his favor.

"I'm eighteen," Stefan said, not sure why.

Leo nodded. "You'll be fine. Your mother's worried because she worries; I don't think she knows how to stop. Things have been very hard for her."

They were silent for a moment, shadowed by the past. "She's told me some incredible stories," Leo said, rubbing his chin. "It just doesn't seem that was her she was talking about, do you know?"

"It was her."

"And there's nothing I can do but listen."

"That's a lot," Stefan brought out. Could Leo listen because he hadn't been touched by the camps, not his friends, his family, his whole life? Maybe that was something his mother needed—unshared memories—maybe that was helping her?

Their steaks came and for a while they said very little, and then only about the food, which even *tasted* expensive.

"So it's just two weeks," Leo said when they had coffee. Stefan thought to himself, Eleven days, and said: "I hope the roads are good."

"We'll get there," Leo assured him.

Syracuse University was a strange hilly snow-sheeted campus, scattered with awkward-looking concrete and glass buildings mixed in with some elaborate old ones in such different styles that they seemed artificial, like there was nothing inside. His dorm room looked out on a wall and a parking lot so it was almost as if he hadn't come anywhere.

"This is grim," Leo joked when they opened the scratched beige door to his room. "It'll make you study."

His mother inspected the beige wall unit that combined shelves and drawers and closet space.

"It's very clean," she said quietly, as if expecting to be contradicted.

It's mine, was all Stefan could think as they brought up box after box.

His mother sprayed and dusted the unit anyway, put in shelving paper she had insisted on bringing, and hung away his clothes

216

while Leo unpacked the stereo that had been Stefan's "going-away gift." He stopped to watch Leo arrange it on a Parsons table, plug in the speakers, still not believing it was his, this large gleaming machine that gave him music whenever he wanted.

"I wish Sasha could've come." Stefan stacked books on the little desk, pitying Sasha with his flu.

"He will," Leo said, looking for an outlet.

"You can take pictures and send them," his mother suggested, leaning out from the unit.

It didn't take long for the bed to be made, the boxes folded up, everything straightened.

"Not bad," they all said in different ways, looking around. The other side of the room, with its bare bed, seemed comically empty to Stefan.

"Maybe I won't get a roommate."

"No, plan on having one," Leo advised. "Then it won't be a surprise."

They had lunch at a restaurant right at the edge of campus which seemed full of students with their parents. Lunch was very long; Stefan didn't want to go back by himself.

"Let's see Syracuse," Leo said when their check came, and they drove to a lot near the center of what Stefan knew was a city, but compared to New York looked very much like one of those little towns at the side of toy railroads.

"It's so small," he kept thinking, but the thick ranks of bare hedges and trees promised a beautiful spring.

"It will be lovely for you," his mother smiled, stepping to look over a gate at a large stone house with a plaque near its door they couldn't read. "Such a change."

"It's a good thing?" Leo wondered, taking her arm.

She laughed and they walked on ahead. Stefan felt surprisingly proud of them; his mother in her brown boots and thick purple cape and hat, Leo in the heavy salt-and-pepper coat that seemed carved out of warmth. They were old, he supposed, but happy with each other. He saw that so clearly today, away from home, saw it and for the first time didn't feel annoyed or resentful, but

217

hoped he would find someone to make him as complete as they were.

He trailed behind them back to the car.

At the dorm they took a last quick look.

"I'll get some posters at that place in town," Stefan said, noticing how bare the walls were.

Leo shook his hand, clapped him on the shoulder, and his mother held him briefly, the first time in years. He kissed her.

And they were gone. At his window he watched them step through the snow to Leo's Lincoln and drive off.

He sat at his desk with the door open, unwilling to be completely alone; he could hear someone moving in down the hall. Now would be the perfect time to write some long cheerful letters about the ride up and the dorm, but he didn't really have anyone to write to. He'd called Sasha already to say he was in. Jenny wouldn't care to hear from him, and she seemed more distant than ever.

"Gimme a hand," someone ordered in the doorway, staggering under the weight of a large brown box. Stefan leapt up and they brought it over to the empty bed.

"Let it go."

The box dropped with a miscellaneous clatter.

"What's in it?" Stefan wondered.

"All kinds of shit. I'm Gray." A large hand was thrust at him.

"Stefan." They shook; his roommate was very big and broad and flushed.

"It's short for Graham," Gray explained, pulling open the box and digging inside, coming out with a toaster in one hand and a purple water pipe in the other. "Like the cracker," Gray added, beginning to toss the box's contents onto the bed. "Where you from? Noo Yawk? I hear everyone here's from there."

Stefan sat at his desk, warming to this large vague guy who with bowl-cut hair, thick mustache and meaty face looked like a sleepy Viking.

"Where're you from?" Stefan asked, bringing Gray from consideration of a book that'd lost its cover.

218

"What'd I bring this for?" Gray muttered, heaving it over to the desk. "From Northampton. In Massachusetts."

Stefan nodded. "I thought you had an accent."

Gray stared at him blankly. "Accent?" Deadpan, he turned to see if someone else was in the room, glanced back at Stefan. "I got stuff in the car," he threw off and Stefan, grinning, followed him downstairs, not forgetting to lock the door behind them.

On Gray's side of the room the lines of everything seemed blurred; Gray had hung and draped and swathed his bed, the wall, his closet with thin Indian print covers that rustled when the door opened. In this nest Gray sprawled reading with headphones on, sometimes humming—Gray was sometimes very quiet and withdrawn for all his overpowering size.

"Your folks?" Gray asked that first week, picking up the gold-framed portrait photo of Leo and his mother that Stefan had asked for.

Stefan nodded.

"You don't look like your dad." Gray settled back onto his bed to write a letter—he was always writing letters when he wasn't gettting high or considering how much work he had to do. The letters gave him much less pleasure than the grass, which Stefan hadn't liked much in high school and still didn't enjoy.

"I have a big family," Gray explained. "I mean big, like me, and big, like the Senate."

They'd registered together, ate meals together in the noisy dining commons, wandered around campus and into town, talking mostly of what they saw, when they did talk. Stefan felt Gray had also come here to get away.

But Stefan had pushed something between them by saying Leo was his father. Thankfully Gray didn't want to know how he was all the time, and why, but left him to himself. The privacy was reinforced by the floorful of jocks who were always talking about games and "getting it wet," leaving him alone as too "brainy."

Gray was right about the New Yorkers: Stefan found himself talking to people in his classes about the city, what they liked

219

doing there, where they lived. It was almost as if he'd been away for years and not just weeks, but that wasn't so bad. He needed to feel comfortable crossing the wind-torn campus on the way to class or a movie in the campus center and felt stranded, torn from the noise and thrill and weight of New York. Sometimes he wondered if starting here at the end of winter had been a good idea—perhaps the change was too sharp.

But classes were classes, his professors like those in New York, studying and hanging out no different, only the note taking, the hours in the library weren't oppressive because he'd chosen all this: the steamy laundry room downstairs in his dorm, the noisy snack bar a dorm away whose jukebox never seemed to play anything he liked, the lounge on his corridor with its view of a girls' dorm where Gray sat and stared for hours. Stefan came in there one night to ask Gray if he wanted to go to town for a drink.

"It's wicked cold," Gray shook his head as they trudged to a bar in town with a rock night, a Motown night, a free ladies' night and at least six or seven more kinds of nights Stefan couldn't keep track of.

This night was a regular one, so they could settle into a corner booth without waiting or shoving.

"There's a party next Saturday in the main lounge," Stefan said.

"Beer?"

"Of course."

"Huh. . . ." Gray considered that. "You going?"

"Sure."

"Parties bum me out." Gray's eyes went blank, blanker than usual, and he rambled on through three drinks about the ex-girlfriend he'd dated all through high school. "She was part of the family, that was the thing, she liked my folks better than me, liked my brother, my aunts, everybody better than me."

"She was in love with your family?"

Gray nodded solemnly. "But not me. Not really."

"Maybe you'll meet someone at the party."

"That's the thing—I keep meeting 'someone.' " Gray sighed, looked near tears. Back at their room Gray did start crying as soon as he sat on his bed, broad shoulders hunched and shaking. Stefan stood across at his bed, transfixed—he was afraid to move or say anything. But he edged forward.

"Hey—"

Gray gulped and sobbed.

"Hey." Stefan stood looking down at Gray's heavy bent head. "It'll be all right," he tried, sitting next to Gray. He couldn't think of anything weightier to say. Gray kept shaking and wheezing and Stefan suddenly thought of Jenny for some reason—he'd never cried about her. He slipped an arm around Gray's shoulders and went on saying more things to calm him down. Gray soon stopped, lay back on his bed and fell asleep with one foot still on the floor. Stefan took off Gray's shoes, thinking that he'd seen someone do the same in a movie. He was shocked by the warmth of Gray's feet, and suddenly imagined taking down Gray's pants, feeling those large thighs. He went to take a shower and try to forget. But soaping his body made it worse. He had seen Gray nude so often because his roommate seemed very comfortable like that, and never rushed from clothes into a bathrobe or towel or gym shorts, but could stand there humming, scratching his low-hanging balls, as if unaware Stefan was in the room. He was very hairy, and the blond curls on his back, neck, butt both fascinated and repelled Stefan, who imagined stroking them, and shuddered at what they might feel like. Gray was muscular but flabby, with a fat and uncircumcised cock he called Charlie. Showering now, Stefan imagined what it would be like to peel back that wrinkled thick foreskin.

A few days later Gray brought up the usual clutch of mail, but dropped one envelope on his desk.

"For me?"

"Had to happen." Gray lay down for a long read.

It was from his father. Stefan glanced at Gray, who was already lost in his first letter.

It wasn't a letter as much as a check with a note attached; they were well, looking for a new house, hoped he liked where he was, hoped he could use the money for "settling in."

The check was too large—how could he ever spend so much money? It was too serious a sum. He slipped it into his desk drawer face down, and saw a line on the back: "When we get married this summer, come spend as much time as you want."

When he looked up he met Leo's face, his mother's. He took out paper to write letters home, losing his nervousness after a few pages.

"I wish they'd stop seeing her," Gray complained later, sweeping the pile of small sheets away from him.

"Your girlfriend?"

"Ex-girlfriend, except to my folks. They'll probably adopt her and make it legal."

Stefan almost said something then about his family, but it was time to go out for lunch.

Even on the stairs he could hear that the lounge was packed. "They must've put up lots of fliers," he thought, edgy, uncomfortable going downstairs alone, even though he knew lots of guys in the dorm, at least by name. Gray was still deciding whether to get dressed or not.

The lounge burst with people, perhaps because this was the first party in their dorm area, and there were a lot of girls in groups, surrounded by guys. Stefan found a cup of wine and moved to lean against a wall to settle in to the noise and crush. The room boasted two kegs and someone was setting up a tape deck and speakers. A girl from his psych class waved at him and pushed through to the wall, smiling, a little drunk already, he thought, because she kept blinking and smiling no matter what he said about the class. When the first soul song came on he set down his wine and led Gail to dance. She was too blonde, he thought, as she wriggled her hips at him, pouting, but he was glad to be dancing. Jenny and her group had never played good dance music at their parties, just Melanie, Donovan, James Taylor. They hated Motown, Sly and the Family Stone, hated anything you could really dance to.

"That was neat." Gail clapped. "Thanks." And she slipped away.

Stefan found his cup empty when he returned to claim his bit of wall.

"I drank it," a woman said.

He turned.

"You looked okay," she laughed. "I'm Marsha."

"Stefan. You teach here?"

Another laugh. "I'm just a student."

Marsha was a short plump big-eyed gypsyish woman with masses of glossy black hair that made him think how soft it would probably be; she looked under twenty-five, not over, he revised when they stood closer.

"I saw you dancing, you're good. You're from the city? I figured. People up here don't have much energy when they're dancing, it's like they're doing it to be polite. No one dances like a New Yorker. You go out dancing lots? No? Why not?"

He shrugged. Her voice and manner were rich, disarming; she was by no means pretty, but he responded to her slightly bucktoothed smile, small precise hands in a way he found unsettling, dangerous.

"Let's dance." He and Marsha stayed on the floor for a long time, until he felt too loose to be anxious.

"Where'd you learn to dance like that?" she wondered, sipping a beer. "On TV? You must watch it a lot? No?" She shook her head in amused admiration. They found an uncrowded corner, sat on the floor and talked. Marsha lived in town, worked at the largest record store, Phases, had come back to finish school after living with someone—Frank—in Rochester for four years. She talked about that time so casually he didn't find their sudden intimacy at all strange. Stefan knew with a thrill that Marsha was someone he would be able to talk to about himself, someone he'd want to talk to.

"He left you after four years?" Stefan asked, incredulous.

"He said we were too close."

"What did you do?"

She shrugged. "I'm a tough bitch, I said good-bye."

He laughed and they went to dance some more. He noticed Gray at the edge of the dancing looking very glum, but couldn't catch his roommate's eye.

Much later Stefan asked when he'd see her again.

"Right now, if you want," she grinned. "We could go into town for a drink. I'll drive you back."

When he came back down to the lobby with his coat, Marsha took his hand and smiled. He leaned down to kiss her.

"Forget the drink," she said as they stepped outside.

11

"Not bad for a beginner," Marsha said later. "Not too bad."

He lay next to her under a chaos of sheets in a very large bed, a hand stroking her stomach, crossing, recrossing. The street lamp right outside her bedroom window divided the room into sharp shadows, and the steady movement of his hand was the rhythm of the night. He was too tired to be happy, too happy to be tired, lost in the musky-smelling sheets, outside of which he knew it was cold, but he couldn't quite believe in that cold now.

"You smell good," he said, rubbing his face in her hair.

"You got so quiet," she wondered, her words a sort of smile.

"My first time was pretty bad." Stefan felt instantly released of a burden. "I wanted to so much—" He made himself continue: "We never even did it."

"Well I couldn't the first time. Frank and I tried but he just couldn't get through and I bled—there was blood everywhere, on him, on the bed. *God* it hurt."

He pulled Marsha close to feel her against him; she kissed the side of his neck, holding his head tightly. He wondered how this was possible, this miracle of simplicity. The night with Jenny now seemed just a night, no longer a doom he couldn't escape.

He reached down to place her other hand at the back of his neck.

"You like that?" she breathed, sliding a leg over his. Touching her was so different from being with Louie: slower, softer. He reveled in slowly kissing her face and the way she seemed to open up to him, in stroking and kissing her large breasts, discovering them, pushing them together and burying his face in the cleft, licking and nibbling at her nipples until she moaned, and sliding, sinking down into her, then pulling out as she rolled him onto his back and sat astride him, rocking. Time stopped. They didn't have to hurry for fear that someone might find them. They were alone, savoring everything. She smelled so good to him—spicy—and the second time, when she guided his head down between her legs, he was surprised at how good it tasted there and how good he could make her feel with just his lips, his tongue. It excited him to think that he had just been inside her. She called his name, which had never sounded so rich and warm.

It was a long night and even when Marsha finally fell asleep, he couldn't, but held on to her as her body twitched and settled into sleep. He pulled the covers close; his mind was all hazy, but this wasn't the fog that covered pain—it was different, like lying in the sun so long there was only the heat, the smell of it, the feel and sound of it.

He wanted to touch Marsha, learn more of her, but he had to let her sleep. Some time later, perhaps he'd slept, perhaps he hadn't, she woke and moved against him, silently, and this time they said nothing, just held each other tighter and tighter until sleep.

In the morning he felt awkward and out of place sitting up looking around for something to put on—his clothes were every-where.

Marsha appeared at the door in a large blue man-tailored shirt. She stepped over to the bed, leaned down for a kiss.

"What time is it?" he asked when she broke away.

"Seven."

He groaned.

Marsha opened her closet and tossed him a black quilted robe. "It's real big on me," she offered. He slipped it on, pulled the belt tight; it covered enough of him, and he held out his arms. Marsha stood at the bed in his arms for a while, one hand firm at the back of his neck. She slipped a probing finger inside his robe. "We could have breakfast, or we could have this," she drawled.

When he got back to his room a sign stretched across the door: *FIRST* *SCORE*. He ripped it down and opened the door. Gray was absorbed in the *Boston Globe*. Stefan crumpled the sign and shoved it into the wastepaper basket, embarrassed, annoyed, and strangely pleased—perhaps that was the most annoying, to enjoy publicity that made Marsha just "scoring."

"I told them you wouldn't like it," Gray observed.

"It's private."

Gray shrugged. "Not when you leave a room full of people. And don't come back. This is a dorm, people see stuff, talk."

"They shouldn't," Stefan insisted, but he sounded so petulant he had to shrug, and Gray nodded. Stefan wanted to talk about Marsha, and didn't want to; he took part of the paper and sat at his desk trying to read. Somewhere inside, though, he was writing letters to no one in particular, each of which began with "I met—" He marveled at how breakfast had been so liberating, fussing in her small bright kitchen, playing love songs on her stereo. Marsha lived in a small apartment but it was so full of books and pictures and plants and lamps and pillows it seemed large, each small thing opening up to the world of her past. A bit like the del Greco's apartment.

"Frank gave me that," she'd said when he pointed or asked. "That was my mother's," she'd smile and tell a little story about the green alabaster box, the framed Rosetti print, the spider plant; everything, even her large oak desk, had a history.

"I brought all this stuff from Rochester," she explained. "We had a big place."

"You and Frank?"

She nodded.

"Do you think about him?"

Marsha shrugged, played with her hair. They sat after their eggs and bacon on a low brown pillow-rich couch, watching the sun gradually light up different parts of the room.

"It's funny, sometimes I can almost feel him, like he's just down the street, and there's times I can't believe I loved him, like I wonder who that was. It's sure good to get the hell out when you're someplace bad. Lots of people say you should 'Stay and face it' but that's bullshit, it takes a long time before you can slow down running from what happened." She laughed. "Listen to me, I'm *such* an expert."

"What does Frank do?"

"He sells dope, and thinks he's in the peace movement," Marsha frowned.

"Do you have a picture of him?"

Marsha shook her head. "Threw them all out. And the letters too."

"Really?"

"I didn't want them lying around where I could find them. A lamp's different—even if someone gave it to you after a while it stops being theirs, it's got its own reasons."

Stefan thought of the letter Jenny sent him that he never read but just threw away, and that made him angry.

"Do you get mad at Frank ever?"

"For sure. At him, at me, at the whole mess."

Now, in his dorm room, last night and their day together seemed amazing and unreal; he couldn't picture himself with her, so different and changed, open. Maybe it was leaving home, maybe that was the difference, what let him relax.

I won't hide from Marsha, Stefan promised himself, and then felt scared—if he didn't hide he wouldn't be safe, there wouldn't be enough between them to keep them separate. He glanced up to find Gray watching him.

"You look dazed," Gray observed.

He had no classes Monday so he walked into town to see Marsha at work. Phases was a large gleaming-floored hip supermarket, selling records, discreetly worn old clothes, paraphernalia, plants, window shades, art prints, candles, and even panty hose. Marsha worked in the record section at the far end of the store and Stefan dawdled near the door, watching her at the register. She had on a green peasant blouse and large hoop earrings, really looking the gypsy today. She was striking, shaded, with a shifting mobile face that he thought he could look and look at and still be surprised by.

Stefan finally drifted from the scarf display to where she leaned on the high black register. Marsha turned, grinning: "You like the scarves?"

"You saw me?" He reached to squeeze her hand, leaned down for a kiss.

"It wasn't yo' mama I saw."

"When do you get off?" Then he blushed. "I mean—"

"I know. In an hour. I'm going to campus to meet a friend."

"Oh."

"She's in trouble. But I can come to your dorm after."

"Great."

"Now don't think you can chat me up and not buy something," she warned.

They talked through the next hour and only three customers interrupted.

"I need some posters," he remembered before Marsha was ready to go, but inspecting the bins didn't help: Chagall? Bogey? 65 Bridges to New York? He couldn't decide what to put on his walls.

"Hire a decorator," Marsha suggested as they walked to her weathered red Mustang, their words misting in the air around them.

They said nothing on the drive in and the foot of car seat

between them seemed a grave distance. Why did she like him? he suddenly wondered, afraid, afraid she wouldn't be interested in him for long. He was too young; hadn't it gone too well too quickly? Wasn't something awful bound to happen?

When she dropped him off at his dorm he watched her drive away feeling gloomy and cold. It was good so far—how could it stay that way?

Upstairs Stefan lay down in a fog. Gray came in humming; "I'm going to dinner early."

"I'll wait."

On Stefan's desk glaringly open books reminded him he had a paper to start tonight and four chapters of sociology. When Gray left he rolled over and tried to sleep.

There was knocking.

"Stefan?"

He sat up. More knocking. "Come in."

"Were you sleeping?" Marsha clucked.

He rubbed his eyes and face, feeling very dim. "Not really." Marsha took off her down parka and hung it on the back of his desk chair—this annoyed him for some reason. The room seemed very small.

She pointed at his desk. "That your mom and dad?"

"No."

She started at his tone.

"Sorry," he tried.

She frowned. "What's up?"

He hesitated, but then knew he could say it. "Scared, I guess." She nodded quickly. "Me too."

"You?"

"Me. For a long time I didn't want anyone to touch me ever again, just the idea made me pissed. I wanted to be left alone."

He rose and went to her, took her hands; touching Marsha banished the murkiness.

"It's really hard sometimes to enjoy what you can have," she murmured as he hugged her, rested his chin on her head, breathing in the spicy scent of her hair.

"Gray's at dinner," Stefan said, smiling.

"Terrific!" Marsha locked the door, and he pushed her back against it, sliding a hand into her jeans where she was already a little wet. Just the feel of his fingers in her got him hard. She caught her breath, closed her eyes, and he pulled down her jeans, crouched in front of her to bury his face. "Come on," she said, and he unzipped and plunged into her, rocking against the door, not caring that they could probably be seen from the dorm across the courtyard.

A few days later he got a call from Sasha who wanted to see how he was. It embarrassed Stefan, especially since the stereo was playing a sonata Sasha had taught him, but he had only listened to the pure lines of it without thinking of his uncle. They talked for a while and Stefan promised to write that week.

He hadn't called or written to Brooklyn either, or thanked his father for the check. Marsha had come between him and his parents—all four of them. Stefan hurried some notes, sealed and stamped them to take downstairs, but they said almost nothing because he kept thinking of Marsha's hungriest smile.

He liked walking across campus or in town with an arm around her, or holding hands. He liked kissing her whenever he wanted, wherever they were. It was a freedom he hadn't known he was missing. He liked waiting on campus for Marsha, in the Hall of Languages, or one of the corkboard-lined coffee shops; the waiting relaxed him and he could read or go over notes with concentration that was unlike him.

A lot since he'd met Marsha was unlike him; sometimes he wondered who he was, what he'd become in just a month of being with her. He knew he wasn't the same, but what did that mean? He couldn't tell—what he did know was that waiting for Marsha filled and quieted him.

"Hi." She placed some books on the corner table, sat and leaned to him for a kiss, stroking the back of his neck.

"Why do you like that?" she wondered, eyes glowing curious.

"Well why do you like it when I—?"

Marsha clapped a hand over his mouth. "Let's not put *all* my business in the street."

He kissed her palm and they decided to see a new French movie in town after dinner at her place.

"How was your friend?" he asked, closing the campus paper. Marsha had been seeing her troubled ex-roommate a lot lately.

"Candy? Bad."

Candy and she had lived in a house at the edge of town last year with four other people from the university but the whole arrangement collapsed because Candy was in love with Tom who lived in the room next to hers; she'd slept with him, disastrously, since it obviously hadn't meant more than a few nights of not being alone to Tom, and Candy, a year later, was still trying to recover.

"I keep telling her to go somewhere, get out of this dump so she can forget Tom, not ever run into him."

"What's he like?"

She grimaced. "One of those beautiful hunky men who makes everyone miserable, especially themselves. He just oozes sex—it's horrible, and it's not really his fault."

Marsha told Stefan that there'd been fights at the house, late-night reconciliations, side-choosing, sneaking around, tension—lots of tension—and an explosion at a party when Candy tried to push Tom off the porch.

"It's like a soap opera." Stefan wondered at the brutality of love.

"Except there weren't any commercials—we could've used a station break."

Later, in bed, Stefan asked: "Why do people get involved like that? I mean your roommate."

"It's exciting," Marsha breathed, at the edge of sleep. She fell asleep and he turned that over and over. Was she right? Marsha rolled onto her back and began snoring in tiny gasps; he nudged her and she stopped. She knew so much about people, had done so much more than he had; it was frustrating to think he knew almost nothing, had been so separate and closed off, held back from everyone around him. Was being with Marsha a real change or would he slip back into the fog without her, lose this new tenuous hold on—what?—life? Stefan turned to her, lay very close stretching an arm across her waist, reassured at least until she woke.

In the morning he was up before her and after he made himself coffee he wandered out to the living room to look for a book. He hadn't paid much attention to her books before, and now he noticed that most of the ones on the bottom shelf of her bookcase were on Jewish subjects. He sat down on the green rug and pulled at the nearest books to take a look. He knew Marsha's last name was Gold, but hadn't asked if she was Jewish, hadn't even wondered. She had a handful of books on the concentration camps.

"I have a Jewish girlfriend," he thought. It seemed ridiculous and strange that he had picked *her*.

"Good morning," Marsha said coming to join him on the floor. She kissed him and plucked at her robe.

"I didn't know you were Jewish."

She peered at him. "It never came up. Is that a problem?"

What should he say? "I'm Jewish too."

"*You* are? With a name like Stefan Borowski?"

He nodded, and could feel Marsha curious, alert, though he didn't look at her.

"I hate being Jewish," he said.

"Oh God, I know," she said. "I can't figure it out myself."

"What do you mean?"

"I could never do anything as a girl. We were Conservative, so I couldn't participate in services like the men could, I wasn't as good as them! So I hated it. I stopped going as soon as I left home."

He didn't exactly follow, but he said, "What about now?"

She smiled. "I have no idea. But wait, why do *you* hate it?"

He breathed in very slowly, and started to tell her about his parents and Sasha, the No-Jew Club, the divorce, finding out from his father how they had all lied to him, being Jewish and too ashamed and betrayed to do anything about it. Every time he was in a library or bookstore he wanted to find the religion section, but couldn't make himself do it.

The eager, open look on her face pulled him along. Marsha held his hands, sitting opposite him, smoothed his hair, listening, listening, shaking her head, sometimes looking like she might cry.

"What a mess," she kept muttering.

"And then in New York, if I see one of those guys with the beards and black hats and the curls? I feel like I have to throw up. It's like, that's me! They look so gross, and then I think how Jews are pushy and loud, they love money, I wonder if my nose is too Jewish. All this stuff I've heard all my life without even knowing it, and it's inside of me!"

"What do your parents say about it?"

"We don't talk about anything like that."

She led him to the kitchen. "Sit down. I'm going to make you a fried egg sandwich, and fresh coffee." The clatter and mixing smells brought back Sundays as a child. He felt open suddenly to the whole of his past, unable to push any of it away, unable to pretend he lived now, felt now and knew nothing else, nothing deeper.

He ate two sandwiches, and the coffee was a dream. Marsha ate more slowly, chatting about people she worked with, about annoying customers, guys who came on to her, even one girl who had.

"At least I thought so," Marsha said.

"How can you handle all those customers?"

She shrugged.

"It'd make me nervous." Stefan imagined himself behind a register, exposed, on trial, not fast enough at the keys.

"Well, I could never be a waitress," Marsha said, clearing the table, filling the deep sink with hot water. "Keeping all that stuff straight?" She whistled. "Once in Rochester at this little place I asked the girl to bring me another knife 'cause mine was dirty and she burst into tears." Marsha shrugged.

They went to sit in the living room, where Marsha had reshelved the books. She turned on the radio very low.

"You know—" He sat with Marsha leaning back against him. "My roommate got all down about his girlfriend. Ex-girlfriend. We were out drinking and back at the dorm he started crying. It was embarrassing to watch."

"You just watched?" she asked in an undertone.

"No, I tried to help." He locked his arms around her, feeling much more solid and in control of himself—but it wasn't rigidity, not anymore.

"Once, when it was really bad with Frank, and I walked out on him, when I came back I slept on the couch the first night and the next morning I woke up crying and I didn't even care. I was lying with the pillow over my head, crying, it was just so damn hopeless between us and I guess that was when I finally knew it was hopeless. But you know something? Frank was there all the time, standing in the doorway, watching. Watching me cry. He told me later. It amazed me he could watch and not do anything."

"I like when you talk about him."

"Why?"

"Because you love him."

"I don't anymore," she murmured. "At least not the way that hurts."

Now he was ready to go back to himself. "That picture on my desk at the dorm?—the man and woman?"

She nodded.

"That's not my dad, not really. He's my stepfather, Leo. The guy in the other picture is my mother's brother, Sasha." Spoken this way the facts seemed harmless, ordinary.

And Marsha seemed prepared to help him. "When was the divorce?"

"I was eight when things got bad, eleven when it was final."

They said nothing for a while and sat comfortably together; his thoughts shifted, waiting.

"But I told everyone he was my father. I let them think it. Everyone thought so."

"Your stepfather?"

"My uncle. Sasha."

Marsha twisted around to look at him. "Wait, I don't get it. What about your real father?"

"It's a mess, just like you said."

"And you really never talk about any of it? Like the camps?

"Head down, he murmured, "I can't."

"How do you get work done?" Gray asked one afternoon, lying in a pool of letters. "You're over there all the time."

Stefan grinned. "Inspiration."

"I need some of that."

Sasha wrote him briefly reminding him it would soon be his mother's fifth anniversary—a stiff little note that hardly bore a trace of his uncle. Stefan read and reread the note, wondering at how he'd grown past Sasha somehow, though he wasn't even sure what that meant. When he put the letter away he decided he would go down to New York to help them celebrate this one.

He called Marsha, asking her to meet him at the snack bar near his dorm.

"What's up?" she asked, joining him at the table where he sat with an untouched cup of coffee. She was wary, amused by his withholding silence.

"My parents'—my *mom's* anniversary is in two weeks."

"And?" Marsha unbuttoned her coat, struggled out of it.

"I'm going to New York."

"Oh. How long?" Her voice was flat.

"Why don't you come too?"

"What?"

He told her in great detail what they could see, talking at length through her strange silence until he noticed her eyes were wet.

Marsha had never been to New York. "It's just so great," she sniffed, rubbing at her eyes, and that was pretty much all she said for the next days while he made their plans; her quiet astonishment and pleasure was something new to him.

"What is that?" Marsha asked one day, leaning over him to inspect a piece of paper. "You've got the times down for every-thing?" She read at random: "Saturday morning: breakfast, leave Bay Ridge 10:30 to Museum of Modern Art. . . ." She peered down her nose at him. "This is a *weekend*, not a forced march."

236

He disengaged the timetable from her hand and said with dignity: "I want to be sure you have a good time."

"With you? In New York? Impossible," she laughed, ruffling his hair.

Stefan phoned Leo. "I want to bring someone down."

"That's fine. Your roommate?"

He hesitated. "I've been dating someone. Marsha." And then he added, "She's Jewish."

There was a silence. "Tell her we'll be glad to meet her."

"What should I wear?" Marsha began asking more and more as the Friday they were leaving crept up.

"You always look nice."

"But I've never been to New York, I want them to ask me back."

"My mother and Leo?"

"The mayor, *everybody*. What do you wear to an opera?"

The bus ride was very long and grim, with rain sheeting the windows most of the way down. Marsha slept, waking once to mumble, "Are we under water?" The closer New York came, the more peculiar Stefan felt; it was nervousness of a kind he hadn't known. Back at school the distinctions were clearer—he had his classes, his schedule, his talks with Gray, and there was all the time with Marsha that defined his life there. But he was going home, bringing her with him, a symbol and proof of his independence: it was almost too important a weekend.

Marsha held his hand tightly all the way off the bus to the subway. "I'm glad we didn't bring much," she said in the crowded train.

"What a beautiful house," Marsha said when they turned the corner in Bay Ridge.

The door opened before she could say anything else. Stefan impulsively hugged his mother and Leo, making a mess of the introductions. Everybody smiled.

"Are you hungry?" Leo asked, hanging away their coats. They were.

"But I'd love some coffee first," Marsha said, and Stefan's mother led her into the kitchen.

"You'll sleep in the study?" Leo asked him. "And Marsha in the guest room?"

"Sure."

Dinner was long and noisy. Marsha talked about where she worked and even told Stefan's stories about Gray and his letters. Stefan noticed that Marsha was as relaxed as a member of the family, and across the table from her it was like meeting her all over again. Her face shone with comfort; she could've been warming herself at a fire. And while that was beautiful, he felt uncomfortable that she was having so much fun with people he didn't trust. He was proud of her, and jealous. Why was it so easy for her?

"She's some girl." Leo smiled when they were stacking dishes into the dryer. Stefan nodded, but that didn't seem enough.

"She's great." But that wasn't right either, and he knew he wasn't enthusiastic enough.

"Maybe next time, we can have a Shabbat dinner," Leo said softly, as if waiting for Stefan to get angry.

He shrugged. "Maybe." He didn't even know what a Shabbat dinner was, exactly, and he was too embarrassed to admit it.

When they were all done shelving and straightening, Marsha asked if he'd play something.

They had Benedictine in the living room, where Stefan was suddenly focusing on the menorah that he knew his mother and Leo lit, though he had never come to their house for Hanukkah, which had quietly replaced Christmas in his mother's life. That left only a blank for him and Sasha.

They talked idly about the news while Stefan went through the pile of music at the piano.

"But some of this is mine," he wondered, turning to them.

"Sasha brought over a few things you might like."

"Should I call him now?"

"He's not home." His mother smiled.

"Where is he?" Marsha asked, echoing the playful tone.

"At Mrs. Mannion's. He's been there often."

"In the winter? It must be freezing."

"Sasha's finally teaching her to play," Leo said, eyes wide. "He said she's not a very good student and will need a lot of lessons."

Stefan pictured Sasha and pink Mrs. Mannion at the piano in her bedroom. After the disaster in Michigan, he had asked Sasha why he never got married in America, and Sasha had told him about being forced into a ghetto when the Nazis took over Poland, the starvation and the terror, and seeing Rushka, the girl he was in love with, clubbed to death by an SS officer because she didn't get out of his way quickly enough. "After that," Sasha said, "Who could care about someone?" And Stefan couldn't ask Sasha anything else, like why there was always tension between him and Stefan's father; the reason would surely be something that would leave an ugly, indelible scene inside of him.

"Your uncle's dating someone?" Marsha asked.

Stefan shrugged, turned to the keyboard to play a jubilant Haydn sonata he'd almost forgotten he knew, but his fingers never faltered and knowing they were listening, and that Sasha had made some sort of decision, filled him enough for the music to come naturally, with ease. Maybe it was his leaving for school that gave Sasha permission to change his own life. He felt a little guilty. Maybe taking care of *him* all these years had kept Sasha single.

He played two more pieces, but without that first excitement, and his hands were tired.

"Your rooms are both ready," Stefan's mother said, standing. "I'm glad you came down." She stepped across to kiss Stefan good night and take Marsha's hand. "Tomorrow it's museums and the opera? I hope you'll have dinner with us before." She went upstairs.

"I'll get these," Leo said, collecting the liqueur glasses and taking them into the kitchen. "Good night," he called to them from the stairs.

"They're neat. Your mom's so classy and your father's a beautiful man." She swore. "Stepfather, sorry."

"He is my father, I guess—more than anyone else just now." Marsha came to sit on the floor by his chair, head back against his knees; she reached for his hand.

"You know what I was thinking?" Marsha asked after a while.

"I was looking at this room, and your mom, and I couldn't believe anything terrible ever happened to her. I mean, in the war."

"It did," Stefan said vaguely. And now, instead of feeling resentful, as he had before, he thought that maybe Marsha could help him find a way to talk to his mother without feeling so much bitterness smothering each possibility. He was surrounded by mine fields—he needed help to pick his way through to freedom, or at least safety.

"Remember I told you my dad was getting married again?"

"In the summer, right? What about it?"

"I've been wondering. I might go. And if I do, I want you to come with me."

She frowned. "Why? To throw rocks?"

"I'm serious. I think I could do it if you were there." He imagined a beautiful outdoor wedding amid lush flowering shrubs, a gazebo, dancing with Marsha in his arms, feeling he *belonged*, feeling his father was proud of him. But it would probably be a Jewish wedding with one of those canopies, and Jewish prayers. He wouldn't know what to do, he didn't know anything about being Jewish. How was he supposed to learn, where could he start?

"What's wrong?" Marsha asked him.

"I just feel so stupid sometimes."

"Join the club! Tell me, how come you don't play the piano in the dorm? Isn't the sound good? You look so cute when you play."

"We should get to sleep."

"I forgot your schedule. We have to be up at five o'clock? Don't you dare tickle me!"

They kissed good night, and going off to sleep by himself wasn't as strange or lonely as he'd thought it might be.

He found his mother and Marsha deep in conversation the next morning, wrapped in their robes and the odor of rich morning coffee. He poured a cup and stood at the counter listening to his mother tell a story he'd never heard before about her first days back at school and how nervous she'd been. Marsha leaned forward, face bright with attention; she really was someone you told things to. Even his mother felt that and responded—something in Marsha's eyes or tone or movements was soothing and encouraging. He'd never be afraid of her.

Watching his mother, with her short gray hair flattened by sleep and her face still a bit heavy, he thought she looked different. Maybe he was just seeing her as a person, like the night on the porch in Rockaway when Leo had looked different.

From the stairs he heard Leo humming louder than he thought anyone could hum, and then Leo burst in on them, growling, "Where's my coffee?"

"So you'll be back at four-thirty?" his mother checked again when breakfast was over, and once more as he rushed Marsha out onto the street.

"If I don't collapse!" Marsha called.

All day—hovering in front of *Guernica*, gawking at the Plaza Hotel and strolling up Fifth Avenue—he saw nothing so clearly as Marsha and her pleasure. She kept beginning sentences of adulation that faded into helpless smiles, pointed and stared and nudged and stopped like a busload of tourists. At the Frick Museum, he let her wander while he sat on a bench opposite the Ingres wondering if this blue-satined Countess didn't look just a bit like Marsha, there at the neck, or maybe the eyes, it was probably the eyes, yes they definitely had similar eyes, somewhat. . . .

"We could do the Guggenheim, it's just up Fifth from here," he offered when Marsha at last joined him on the bench.

"Oh honey, I'm arted out. Let's eat."

But before they left, Marsha bought a small print of the Ingres for his parents. They went down to O'Neal's near Fordham, and across Lincoln Center, where he had sometimes hung out, but being there didn't mean much. When he had first seen pictures of Lincoln Center in the newspaper, they were of a model, and even all these years later, he saw that same vision of anonymous, bland concrete, a shell.

They ate hamburgers, and Marsha spotted a few famous dancers that Stefan only knew by name. She was ecstatic, though. On the way home, an arm around her shoulders, he wondered at how

241

quickly the day was passing, but he seemed to stand at the center of it, motionless, close to Marsha.

They were back in Bay Ridge after five and had to rush dressing. Marsha came upstairs to show off her black boots, plain-lined black dress and cameo. She'd pulled her hair back at the temples.

"You are gorgeous," he said.

She eyed his dark double-breasted suit, shaking her head. "If you let anyone near you tonight, I slap."

"Me or her?"

"Both—I told you I'm tough." She brushed his lips with a kiss. Downstairs when they slipped into their coats, his mother put on a mink he had never seen before. She looked stunning and serene. Leo drove a bit unsteadily to the small Czech restaurant on the East Side he and Stefan's mother had gone to a lot when they were "at school together."

"When you were dating?" Marsha asked.

"I suppose it was dating," his mother agreed, murmuring something to Leo, and for the rest of the ride there were two separate conversations. Stefan kept squeezing Marsha's hand, playing with her fingers, nervous, excited.

"Here," Stefan said as soon as they'd ordered dinner, and he placed two small boxes on the table. "The green one's for Leo."

Leo and his mother unwrapped their gifts. "Stefan." His mother held the silver chain from which hung a small blue glass drop shaped like a tear, put it against her white blouse. "It's so beautiful," she marvelled.

"There's a crafts store in town and everything's handmade." He'd used his father's check.

Leo's gift was a silver tie bar with a similar glass tear. "Beautiful," he echoed, putting it on after slipping off the plainer one he had been wearing.

"Marsha helped me pick."

"I didn't, not really." She handed across the flat brown bag and Leo and his wife grinned when they saw the print.

"How did you know?" Stefan's mother asked.

"She's our favorite. We'll have to frame this."

Dinner was soon over and in the car riding downtown to the theater he hardly remembered what they'd eaten.

"Here." Leo slipped him a bill when they stopped down the block from Lincoln Center. "Take a cab home, okay?"

"Enjoy the opera." His mother smiled her thanks.

He followed Marsha through the crowd to the red plush and gold and glare inside, dazed by the Chagalls, the enormous staircase, the crowds, and a little drunk despite the coffee, and for hours he was more aware of Marsha's intense appreciation and applause, when she shifted in her seat, when she smiled at him, than *Faust* itself or anyone around them.

He fell asleep in the cab and couldn't really tell who it was helping him to bed.

It was cold in Rockaway—gray and windy and they walked from the train station the next afternoon close together. Without sunshine Mrs. Mannion's house looked very lonely and old. They had to knock hard to be heard over the wind pulling at trees and tormenting a garbage can down the street. Marsha had seemed intrigued when he told her he wanted to show her where he'd spent so many summers, and have her meet Sasha. Now she was almost jumpy.

"Hello. I'm Mrs. Mannion." She beckoned them in. "You two must be cold." She sat them down in the living room, poured two brandies and called out: "Sasha? Sasha!"

Stefan gratefully sipped from his glass, surprised that Mrs. Mannion could raise her voice. Sasha walked in fiddling with the buttons of a large blue cardigan Stefan felt sure Mrs. Mannion had knitted. He shook their hands and poured himself a drink; they eased into conversation about yesterday's museums and the opera.

"New York," Mrs. Mannion said now and then, adding nothing more. Sasha seemed embarrassed, Stefan thought, and during dinner he tried not to notice; it worked because Sasha played for them later: waltzes, light music.

"I love this," Marsha practically squealed, hugging herself. "We

243

always take a walk," Mrs. Mannion said when Sasha finished, "Before retiring."

"With that wind?" Marsha wondered, while Stefan was thinking how easily Sasha and Mrs. Mannion could use a word like "always"—it pleased him.

Mrs. Mannion sailed out to prepare herself and Sasha took him aside: "Both bedrooms upstairs are ready, you can use either." When Marsha was in the bathroom, Sasha said, "I'm glad you brought her here."

Stefan wondered if this was some kind of oblique reference to Louie.

But Sasha went on: "She's quite charming. Shall we play a duet for the ladies tomorrow morning?"

Stefan grinned. "Great idea!"

"You choose," Sasha said, giving him a quick hug. Then he went off after Mrs. Mannion.

Stefan and Marsha sat up cuddling in the living room.

"I wish we could stay all week," she said more than once.

"Wouldn't you get tired?"

"With you? In New York? Impossible." After some minutes she said, "Will you wait up for your uncle? I mean maybe you want to talk?"

"Tomorrow," he said, feeling that there was lots of time.

They turned off all the lights except in the hall and took their bags upstairs to what had been Stefan's room. They were both uneasy about making love in a strange place, and Marsha quickly fell asleep with one arm entwined in his.

Nothing had gone wrong, Stefan kept coming back to that; everyone seemed to like everyone else and nothing went wrong— it was a wonderful rich time. But there was something else that kept him from falling asleep and it wasn't the house or the wind or the sounds of Mrs. Mannion and Sasha coming back from their walk and stirring around downstairs.

Marsha woke up, yawned and stroked his face in the dark. "What's wrong? You don't feel well?"

He couldn't really see her face, which made it easier to say,

"There was this guy, Louie, when I was in junior high." He waited for a question that would keep him talking, but was surprised by the one she asked: "You were in love with him?"

"Maybe." And then he sighed and said, "Probably. We had sex. I liked it. I liked it a lot."

Marsha chuckled. "Well why not? Sex is great. I've slept with women. That's one reason why Frank and I argued. I tried bringing it up with you before, when I mentioned that girl coming on to me. But you didn't say anything, so I thought I should wait a little—"

"What's it like for you?"

"It's just different than men." She hesitated. "It's so strange, touching a woman like this," she put Stefan's hands on her breasts, and then between her legs, "And there—somehow it makes me feel that I'm more of a woman. I can't explain it well."

There was a dreamy softness in Marsha's voice, as if she were a very old woman sitting on a back porch with her children, rocking, knitting, enjoying the sunshine, taking herself back to a time when she had been happy, whole, content.

"What do you think it means? Are we homosexuals?" He had never said the word before.

"I don't have any idea, babe. Does it matter? And do we have to figure it out *tonight?*"

She lay back against him.

He was thinking of his one night here with Mrs. Mannion's nephew Phil, and how letting Phil inside of him had felt just as overwhelming and right as entering Marsha the first time. Perhaps somewhere between those two experiences was complete truth. And maybe he didn't have to tell all this to Sasha or Leo or his parents, not yet. Maybe it would be enough to start with Marsha, which, in a way, would be starting with himself.

"Let's take a walk," he said.

"What? Where?"

"Let's go walk on the beach."

"Now?" Marsha was sitting up, and he could see that she was smiling.

"I want to know what it *feels* like," Stefan said.

245